A Web of Vengeance

by

Cheyenne Meadows

A Web of Vengeance

Cover Art by *Debbie Taylor*

The Wild Rose Press, Inc.
PO Box 708
Adams Basin, NY 14410-0708
Visit us at www.thewildrosepress.com

Publishing History
First Fantasy Rose Edition, 2019
Print ISBN 978-1-5092-2830-0
Digital ISBN 978-1-5092-2831-7

Published in the United States of America

"Karate. I studied the other martial arts, too, but leaned toward karate."

"You're a champion at target shooting and at paintball, too." He lifted his glass but didn't move it toward his lips. "Interesting choices of hobbies. Did you study those things for a reason? A future career in the military? A spy? Or perhaps an assassin?"

Taryn looked away from his intense stare. Uncomfortable, she forced herself to not wiggle under his scrutiny. Instead, she pulled on her sassy nature for a response. "Well, I could tell you, but then I'd have to kill you." She met his eyes with purpose.

He remained expressionless for a few seconds before a slow upward curl appeared on his lips followed by a chuckle.

The sound strummed her heartstrings and her sense of humor. She knew she would easily become addicted to it.

Too bad men are off my to-do list.

"Taryn, you're one of a kind." His smile held on.

"Is that good or bad?"

He stabbed a chunk of potato. "Let's just say there's no being bored around you."

She took that as a compliment.

Other Books by Cheyenne Meadows

A previous release with Wild Rose Press is
ONCE UPON A SNOWY MOON
released in December 2018.

Dedication

For all those who continue to battle
in order to achieve their dreams.
This is for you.

Chapter 1

Taryn stared through the scope, easily finding her target as he inched his head over the barrier. He fired in her direction, but the shots went wide. *Too rushed, bucko.* Slowing her heart rate, Taryn blew out a breath, then gently squeezed the trigger. The minimal kickback she readily absorbed from her crouched position behind a large, round pipe.

Red coloring splashed across the man's previously clear visor.

He jerked, wiped at the substance, then glared at her through the bright smeared paint staining his head gear.

She grinned back as the judge tagged the player as out, then blew his whistle to indicate the game was over. Lowering her rifle, she soaked up the moment of satisfaction. *About damn time, buster.*

Brandon, her adoptive brother, rushed over and enveloped her in a hug, then lifted her high enough to swing her around. Her rifle fell to the ground in the process.

"You did it! We won!" Brandon set her back on her feet only for Dalton, the third member of their team, to come rushing over and scoop her into another whirlwind embrace. He was Brandon's first cousin.

"I'm getting dizzy." She laughed, noting the big grins on the guys' faces as soon as Dalton returned her to her feet.

"I can't believe that last shot. It was incredible." Dalton shook his head. "You're an ace. The best that ever played the game."

"Now, I know that's far from the truth. There's many better than I'd ever be." She never felt comfortable with high praise. Sure, the shot was a challenging one, but she'd made more than her fair share of those. Call it a talent, but she always excelled when it came to hitting her mark, whether it be a paintball gun or a real rifle.

"I doubt it. You're the best, and everyone knows it," Brandon reaffirmed.

Taryn shrugged, then bent over and picked up her paintball gun. "The opportunity came about. I just took advantage of it is all." She glanced across the course to see Eric and his team huddling with much less enthusiasm. They grasped their guns at their sides and shot scowls her direction now and again.

"It's time for the award ceremony. If both teams will come to the announcer's table," the voice boomed through the public announcement system.

Brandon nudged Taryn ahead of him. As a unit, they walked the short distance.

Taryn stopped in front of their opposition and held out her hand. "Good game." Two of the guys shook it. Eric sneered and ignored the gesture, keeping his hands at his sides. His jaw ticked, and fire flashed in his blue eyes. Anger, certainly. Eric had an ego the size of an ocean. Anyone that beat him took a chunk out and felt his resulting wrath.

Taryn arched an eyebrow at his audacity, wondered how she ever could have ever been blind enough to date the creep, and stepped to the side.

She didn't fear him in the least. Pity, maybe. In truth, he was a spoiled brat and didn't cope well with being on the short end of the stick. He might yell and grumble, even snub the guilty party in public. At least he never raised his hand toward her. That would have landed him somewhere he never wanted to go— namely, under Taryn's foot. She could hold her own against any person, man or woman, with martial arts or weaponry. Her entire life had been spent learning the skills necessary and perfecting each one. Eric might be a good-sized man, but he didn't have the ability to defend himself or his balls from her when it came down to it—and he knew it.

"He's a sore loser," Brandon said as he took the spot next to Taryn.

"Tell me something I don't know." Eric was one of those men whose outside was so much better than the inside. She'd learned that particular lesson the hard way. Now, she avoided him, tried to be civil when their paths crossed, and vowed never to let another sexy bad boy under her skin.

Bad boys were her Achilles heel. She found something compelling and irresistible in them. Like a moth to a flame, they drew her in only to end up breaking her heart. She should have learned after the first one, Dominic. He stole her heart, but he couldn't keep it in his pants to save his life. The bastard had cheated on her right and left. When she found out and confronted him, he shrugged it off as nothing, claiming to be in the process of "sowing his wild oats." As if that was an excuse. *Come to think of it, it probably was.* A couple more men out of the same mold followed,

3

though she didn't hop into the sack with either. Eric came along last year. He seemed like a good guy, a health nut she met at the gym she worked at. One flash of those dimples and bright smile landed him a first date with her. That turned into a second. A third. Then, the highly polished exterior began to chip off, showing signs of tarnish underneath.

She called it off, felt the lash of Eric's tongue, heard the rumors he'd started at the gym, and worked really hard to ignore the hurt thrown her way. While her social life withered away, she focused more on her life's mission—to discover the men who killed her grandfather.

Years had passed, but she'd never forgotten. Research led to hundreds of dead ends, but she hadn't given up hope. No way. She would persist until she found those responsible. Nothing else mattered more.

"What the hell did you ever see in him?" Dalton asked.

"Muscles. Eye candy," she admitted without shame.

"Blind as a bat, I swear." Brandon shook his head.

Taryn eyed him critically. "Don't go there. Or did you two so quickly forget how you both go gaga over boobs?"

"Touché." Brandon gave her a slow nod just as the announcer for the games stepped over to them, mic in hand.

"Congratulations, Taryn. You've been voted MVP for the tournament. How do you feel?"

The middle-aged announcer with perfectly styled brown hair and straight, bright white teeth, shoved a microphone in her face. The deep blue vest he wore sported the name of the television station on the pocket. She offered up a plastered-on smile, not comfortable with the attention. "It's been wonderful. All the teams are amazing, talented, and skilled. We just caught some lucky breaks along the way to make it to the top."

"I'd say it's more than lucky breaks. Some of those sniper shots you made were nothing short of amazing. Tell me about that last one. Eric Marshall hadn't taken a hit in the entire tournament until you got him." He pushed the mic at her again.

"My teammates worked hard and neutralized the front pair. I settled in and just waited for my chance. Eric missed. I didn't." She peeked over at Eric, who shuffled on the other side of the reporter, obviously more than ready for his turn to speak or for her to shut up, whichever came first.

"I wanted to thank everyone who came together to put this on. Everyone from the news crew to the refs to the concession workers. Without all of you guys, this paintball tournament wouldn't have happened." She waved to the crowd when they cheered.

"Well said." The reporter turned back to the camera. "So that's it from the Minnesota State Paintball Tournament in Minneapolis, Minnesota. I'm Stan McClean signing off until next time."

A young girl in pigtails trotted over and handed out medals. Taryn thanked her sweetly, gave one more wave, then started for the sideline and their vehicles. She had a few hours reprieve before having to return to work early the next morning. That time, she intended to use to her advantage.

"Hey, sis. Where are you going in such a hurry?" Brandon jogged to catch up.

"I've got things to do, Bran. I'm a working girl, and there's more than enough chores to fill in the free hours."

"Can't they wait?" He pulled abreast of her.

She slowed her steps. "Why do you ask?"

"Well"—his expression turned sheepish—"I was hoping you might help me with something."

Her attention snared, she stopped moving. "Such as?"

"I left my keys at the office." He dragged his toe through the grass, then met her gaze. "Please? If my boss finds out that I left them again, I'll be in deep shit."

Taryn blew out a frustrated sigh. "What is this? The second time in a month?"

"I've been distracted lately."

"Uh, huh. What? You're so busy picturing yourself in the sack with Jennifer that you can't focus on your job?"

Brandon bobbed his head slowly. "I'm afraid that's it. She has me so worked up that I can't focus. Can't wait to get to her place and…"

Taryn waved her hand. "Spare me the details of your sex life." She took a few more steps. "I should let you suffer the consequences. Maybe that will help you get your head out of your ass."

"Taryn. Please?" He sounded on the verge of begging. "I have to open the west office early Monday morning. I can't do that without the keys, and the home office won't open until later that morning."

"Why don't you attach them to your car key ring like everyone else does?"

"Because we're not allowed to. The boss is afraid

we're likely to lose them or have them stolen. You know how careful he is about these things. We have to check them out each and every time. I signed my name down as borrowing the key for the west office but forgot to bring it with me." He rolled his shoulders as if trying to ease the tension from them. "The race car industry is big money. Any tiny advancement could be worth millions. He's always working on something new. If that leaked out, he'd be in a world of hurt. So, yeah, the guy has a reason to be paranoid when it comes to his company."

She sighed, unable to deny him this boon. "Fine. Let's go already. I *do* have important things to get done."

"Thanks, Taryn. I really appreciate this."

"Yeah, yeah." She quickly loaded her equipment, then followed Brandon back to his work about an hour and fifteen minutes away.

Taryn recalled those first few days at the Gold house. She was in shock, scared, too traumatized to do more than stare at the strangers around her. Meredith, the mother, tried everything to get through to her. Coaxed her to eat. Helped her clean up. Even bought her new clothes to wear. Ben, the father, gazed at her often in curiosity, as if trying to figure out a particularly complex puzzle. Taryn knew he grappled with the reason she was there. Hell, she did the very same thing.

Only Brandon, their son, seemed unbothered by her presence. He saw her, asked if she was staying, then offered to let her play with his toys. He might have been a few months older but seemed much more mature than his seven years, opening his small world for her. It was Brandon and his kindness that finally pulled her out of her shell. That and Meredith's habit of reading to him.

Taryn's heart broke the first time Meredith read to them. She'd cried that night, sobbing herself to sleep. The next morning, she'd turned a corner, determined to make the best of things. After all, she had a promise to keep to her Poppy.

She closed her eyes as an all too familiar memory flared to life.

Things began to get fuzzy, but not before she noticed a tattoo on the man's lower inner forearm, just above his wrist. The sleeve pulled up enough to show off the artwork. It was unusual, a delicately patterned web with a black shiny spider sitting on one side. A bright red spot on the arachnid's back drew her attention, as did the animal's eyes, which stared back at her. Scary, it added to the terror of the moment. Stoically, she focused on that mark, memorizing it. The spot became smaller as darkness began to invade her vision.

I'll find them and make them pay, Poppy. I will.

She opened her eyes and took a deep breath, willing away the anxiety and fear that always came with that particular recollection—the sight of her beloved grandfather dead on the floor and being carted away by his killers. The worst night of her young life at six years old. And the day she made the solid promise that drove her still.

Those days haunted her, yet seemed such a distant past. The more time marched by, the fuzzier things became. Often, she wondered if her endless search for those culprits was a mere futility. It had been so long. Hundreds of hours on the computer netted her nothing.

Perhaps it never would. She always came to a dead end. Frustration built even as her once newfound hope began to falter.

But then what?

She took her vow seriously. Yet, her hands seemed to be tied.

Is it worth it? Am I wasting all my time on a mystery that will forever remain unsolved?

How many times had she asked herself that question? Just about as many as there were drops of rain in a storm. Still, she stayed the course. She simply didn't know what else to do.

Lately, she'd been restless. Needing something more. Her life was all right. Not grand or wonderful. Just okay. Status quo ruled, and she'd begun to find it lacking. But change was hard, especially when she had no trail to follow or arrow to point the way.

No use crying over spilled milk or the fact that life is hard. She was in the boat along with everyone else she knew. There didn't seem to be any favors or free passes, even for a previous orphan.

She sighed, turned on the radio, and focused on the road again.

A couple of hours after they left the event, Brandon remained with the cars, standing as a lookout, as she tiptoed around to the backside of the business and waited. Brandon told her the security guards switched out at seven a.m. and seven p.m. All she had to do was wait for the replacement to show up, then sneak in behind him. Until then, she stayed well out of range of those security cameras and behind a large, metal, green trash receptacle.

She'd pointed out that he could just walk up to the

building, rap on the door, and tell the security officer the situation. Brandon vetoed that option, citing that he was already treading the line and one more incident might cost him his job. He was supposed to keep those keys sealed up tight, not hanging out in his desk where anyone walking by could get ahold of them. He had higher level security keys but not a free pass to the whole place. Since the security officer would document the situation and he'd be caught on camera, there was no getting around his boss not hearing of his latest forgetfulness.

Taryn shook her head, barely refrained from scolding Brandon, and went to her station to wait for the change of shift.

Right on time, a uniformed man walked over to the back door, dug out his keys, and opened the lock.

Taryn quickly concentrated until she felt the familiar tingle. She reached out with a hand, broke the plane of the security camera's focus, and waited a beat. When no alarms sounded or lights blinked, she knew her invisibility talent camouflaged her completely. A second later, she hurried to stand directly behind the man, careful not to bump into him. As soon as he pushed the door open, she turned sideways and slid in. Not wasting a single moment, she made a beeline for Brandon's office, carefully opened the middle drawer of his desk, then pulled out the only keys she found. She wrapped her fingers around them, able to disguise them with her powers as long as they were covered. With the target in hand, she made her way back toward the back door, watchful to avoid knocking into anything. Despite being the invisible woman, she could still screw up.

The talent appeared just before puberty, scaring her half to death when she woke up only to find her lower half gone. A scream brought her adoptive mother, the only one home at the time. To her credit, Meredith didn't panic. Instead, she sat on the bed, took Taryn into her arms, and used both of their hands to pat Taryn's invisible legs. After all, Meredith had seen it before, while Taryn slept over the years. The first time rattled her, but she was able to feel the limbs, so realized that while it might be unusual, it wasn't lethal. Reassured, Taryn started asking questions. Some, Meredith could answer. Some she couldn't.

That's when Taryn really stepped into the detective role. Too many unanswered queries weighed on her shoulders. She still had plenty left to answer, but this one she'd long since figured out. With a thought and a whole bunch of mental energy, she could disappear from sight. A skill she didn't think really useful except for helping her forgetful brother out of a jam now and again.

Her shooting abilities proved only marginally more useful. She refused to hunt, not having the heart to kill animals, even for food. So, she destroyed targets, won a few competitions, and helped her paintball team attain the pinnacle of success. None of those things paid the bills, thus her full-time job at the gym.

And helped Brandon out when he was in a pinch, like now.

She used to think that was enough. Now, she wasn't so sure.

Her attention back on the task at hand, she eased a little closer to the exit, keeping her eyes on the men at all times.

The security men greeted one another, shook hands, then began to talk.

Oh, hell. She tiptoed near the back door and waited, praying they would hurry. She could only hold the state for a few minutes. Just like holding one's breath, there was a limit before the body would take over. She knew hers, and it didn't allow for idle chit chat.

A sheen of sweat formed on her skin and trickled down her neck. She maintained her state through sheer determination and will. To appear now would land her in jail, something that would pretty much end her career at the gym and throw a really large monkey wrench in her life, however dull it might be.

Come on. Come on.

Finally, the men parted ways, with one moving toward the door, his thermos in hand.

Taryn bit her lip, sidled up close, and darted out the second he opened the door. Picking up the pace, she didn't stop until she was well out of sight behind a couple of large trees. Only then did she release the tight hold on her power. Relief came instantly, along with a healthy dose of fatigue.

Bone tired from the mental drain after a busy day at the paintball tournament, she walked over to Brandon, who leaned back against the passenger door of his truck with his arms crossed and a concerned expression on his face. "I was beginning to worry about you. That took too long."

"Not my fault that the guards decided to get chatty." She held out the keys and dropped them into Brandon's open hand. "Here. Pay more attention next time, will ya?"

"Yeah." He appraised her. "You okay?"

"Yep. Just worn out. It's been a day."

He nodded slightly. "That it has." He lowered his gaze to the ground, then met hers again. "Well, thanks again. See you soon." With that said, he jumped back into his truck and drove off.

Taryn made her way to her car, slipped into the driver's seat, clicked her belt, then headed for home. A desktop computer waited as did several pages of growing notes. Each time she hoped to gain a tiny bit of ground and closer to her goal—finding Poppy's killer.

For years, she'd been stymied. The spider tattoo on the one killer and kidnapper's wrist haunted her day and night. She drew pictures of the unusual artwork, showed it around, and searched the internet. Nothing came to light. Then, one evening, a word locked in the recesses of her mind resurfaced. A memory took hold and replayed, netting her the elusive clue that set her on a whole new course. A single word—Dalliance.

Since then, she'd been hammering on that word, valiantly seeking any tidbit of information she could find in her free time.

Just like today.

The first thing she did when she returned home from the event was to turn on the computer, go online, type in that word, and begin searching. She'd done it a hundred times, yet she was missing something. She just knew it.

So, page after page she scrutinized. Occasionally, she clicked on a link, only to close it back. Minutes turned into hours before she caught a small blip of interest. An old newspaper article mentioned the word in an obituary. Taryn carefully read through, picked out the location, and added it to the keyword list.

Another link came up, one she'd never seen before. Intrigued and hopeful, she clicked on it, only to be denied entrance. Her gut told her this was the place, if only she could see what the protective blocks hid.

I'll find a way to get past it. One way or another, I'm getting in.

With that vow, she marked the site as a favorite, shut down the desktop computer, and headed to the shower.

Chapter 2

Quint Warren paused at the threshold of his father's office inside the main wing of the large Dalliance complex. The walnut-stained door stood open, but he didn't enter. Manners and respect demanded he wait until invited. He noticed Reginald sitting in his large leather chair, poring over some papers, oblivious to Quint's arrival. That, in itself, seemed odd. His father claimed to have eyes in the back of his head, and Quint didn't doubt it for a second.

He rapped lightly. "You wanted to see me?"

Reginald glanced up from his work and waved his hand. "Shut the door behind you, and have a seat."

Quint did as bidden and sat in the old plush chair opposite his father.

The large wooden desk separated them. Files and papers cluttered the area. Piles sat to one side. A laptop computer, presently closed down, occupied the center area. How anyone could keep all that mess straight amazed Quint. Yet, his father managed just fine. If there was an inherited skill for organization and memory, his father sure possessed it.

Quint stretched out his long legs and folded his fingers together as he noticed the crags in his father's worn face, the dullness in his eyes. A twinge of unease rushed through Quint. The old man carried a lot on his shoulders as CEO of Dalliance, but this particular burden, whatever it was, seemed to be the heaviest yet.

"Good job on the last case. Tracked him down fast. Captured without a scratch. I'm impressed."

Quint accepted the praise with a half shrug. "He was pretty far gone mentally. Wasn't much to collect him and drop him off in the hospital wing." He thought back on yesterday's mission. "Honestly, I think he was relieved to see me."

"That always helps." Reginald rested his hands on the desk. "How are you holding up? You've been constantly on the road. Little down time. Been after rogues endlessly for the past several months." He studied Quint with a knowing eye.

"Fine. No worries on that front." Quint answered honestly. While fatigue was pretty much a daily issue, he didn't fail in his job or resent the lack of a social life. He controlled his work hours. If he needed a day off, he took it. No biggie. Except his Type A personality demanded he press onward, capturing another rogue before they could do further harm. However, now that he thought of it, a long vacation was in order. Somewhere peaceful. Quiet. Without the pressures of the rat race whipping him into a frenzied pace. A place where he could download all his stress and revitalize himself into a human again.

Soon. I'll make it happen. Very soon. After I capture Davis.

"How's it going with Davis?"

Quint didn't even blink at the question. Reginald had been reading his mind from day one, so the fact he pulled Davis's name out of Quint's head didn't come close to qualifying as a surprise. "Not as good. The bastard disappeared again. Just vanished into thin air."

Quint had been after Davis for a few months. Ever since the guy, a former Dalliance agent and fellow paranormal, turned rogue. At some point, Davis had flipped from a strong employee to a psychotic maniac with a hobby of murder. Since Davis possessed the unusual and frightening ability to get inside another person's mind and unleash a psionic blast, leaving the victim in a vegetative state or dead, the whole paranormal community worried about the havoc and damage he could do.

Davis had been Quint's number one priority for the past six months. Not that it had done any good. No matter where Quint went or what he did, he always seemed to be one step behind. *At least I haven't ended up swimming with the fish like the last agent did.*

No one had the ability to keep up with Davis, not even the best trackers at Dalliance. Computer models failed to predict the man's next location and victim, leaving everyone concerned pretty much up in the air when it came to finding the serial killer. If only Quint got close enough, he knew he could corral the guy. He had that much faith in himself and his powers. Too bad that Davis didn't glue himself to one spot for long. Or, better yet, if they could predict his next target. With such a weapon of knowledge, Quint could beat him there and take down the number one man on the wanted list. He had no doubt he was up to the task. No doubt in the least. Davis might be strong, but Quint knew the score. Preparation made all the difference in the world. And Quint had prepared in many ways.

During puberty, Quint's talent emerged. As both his parents had special abilities, the fact that he possessed them wasn't a revelation—the variety, however, was. He could steal another paranormal's power—borrow it, or even shut it down cold. Practice over time perfected the gift, giving him a huge advantage. Because of that skill, he'd been recruited right after high school to work for Dalliance, the security company headed by his father, Reginald. He'd gladly accepted, though insisted on juggling college for a while until he graduated with a degree in psychology of all things. Now, he worked full time for Dalliance, home away from home to him.

He possessed another, less flashy ability, which allowed him to follow trails to link steps together to form a strong line. He called it intuition; others declared it more than that. Whatever the term, Quint could solve puzzles and do it well. That wasn't the gift Dalliance focused on with him. Not when he was the only one employed with the ability to mentally match up with the criminals and come out ahead. There might be an assassin or two on the payroll, but they performed their job in the old-fashioned way, killing with a weapon. Messy, but effective. Quint possessed a much cleaner version.

Dalliance cornered the market on the paranormal population. Pretty much all the staff held some sort of superior mental strength over the rest of society. Fine and dandy, except every once in a while, someone would go off the deep end. That's where Quint came in. He tracked down the individual and brought them back to Dalliance for medical attention or detention, sometimes both. At times, the criminal chose another route. He took care of that as well. Elimination just came with the territory, though it wasn't his favorite part.

Overall, not a bad job all in all. He traveled the world free of charge, garnered a good salary, and enjoyed full acceptance of who and what he was from both his family and the other employees of Dalliance. Even if some gave him a wide berth.

"Last report, he was hanging out in the Great Lakes area, right?" Reginald asked.

"Yeah. Thankfully, it's summer there, but he's been in that neck of the woods for the past few weeks. Normally he doesn't stay that long anywhere. Something must have caught his interest this time." From everything Quint knew from pursuing Davis, the man was like a tumbleweed, always on the go. His travels took him around the globe and back. So, for him to hang out in one area told of a goal—most likely nefarious in content.

Reginald met his eyes. "He's looking for Taryn."

The admission shocked Quint. He'd never heard of anyone by that name. And if Davis was interested in that person, why was his father only now telling him? "Taryn?"

Reginald picked up a file from his desk and handed it over. "Taryn Brisk."

Quint accepted it, opened the cover, and scanned the contents. He smirked as he picked up some interesting details. "Black belt in karate. Target shooting winner and a paintball champion." He glanced up at his father. "A Rambo wannabe?"

Reginald sighed. "More like a practicing assassin."

"What the hell?" Quint frowned as he noted his father seemed to age twenty years in the past few minutes. Deep valleys appeared on his face. Worry lines. Now that Quint looked closer, he saw the dark circles under Reginald's eyes as well. Both were signals that something bothered his father and interrupted his sleep more than a single night. "An assassin?"

"A good possibility, considering her vow of revenge."

"Revenge? On who?"

Reginald scrubbed his face. "I've never told anyone this story before."

Quint's gut clenched. His father was the strongest person he'd ever known, powerful in his abilities to read minds and detect lies. But also a good soul and a great father. To see him in obvious distress jacked up Quint's unease.

"It's not my crowning moment, by any means." Reginald grinned slightly without humor. He rested one hand on his desk and idly fumbled with a paperclip. "Davis and I were paired up to confront a mob boss, Ruford Dyal. The guy had been implicated in at least a dozen murders—everything from political figures to local authorities. Anyone that crossed him met a pretty rotten fate." Reginald's attention dropped to his desk. "The plan was to sneak past his security that night, to confront him, and arrest him." He grew quiet.

"Can a person like that, with money and ties, ever be contained and unable to exert influence from prison?" Quint highly doubted it. He understood where the story was going.

"Probably not. Which is why Dalliance was after him instead of the feds. He didn't fall under our usual jurisdiction, but someone needed to stop him. Anyway, we didn't have a chance to find out how far his influence extended. He was incensed when we showed up, threatening us with all kinds of promises. We'd taken out his security guards with tranquilizers or we would've found ourselves in the middle of a war zone. As it was, the old man was livid, promising to pull some mighty high strings. Next thing I know, the guy grabbed his head, then fell to the floor. Dead." Reginald lifted his gaze to meet Quint's.

"Davis's first kill."

"Yes. I should have stopped him. If I had known then what I know now…" He sighed. "The man was as bad as they come. I didn't think his demise would be anything but a blessing." He paused. "We didn't understand back then what Davis had become. Looking back, his sanity had started to slip at that time. Too bad it took six more deaths and two years for us to realize the monster we were truly dealing with."

"He hid it well."

"Yes, he did. Then Moben reported that Davis had been killed in a plane crash. All evidence pointed that he was on that plane and now deceased. Yet, last year, a trail of suspicious deaths started again."

Quint nodded. He'd thoroughly investigated the background on his nemesis. "And this woman? Where does she fit in?"

Reginald lowered his gaze once again to his desk. "Davis had just disposed of Ruford when we heard a sound. A cry. A frightened yelp." He paused. "We tracked it to a bedroom closet and found a little girl. Six years old."

Quint's breath caught.

"No one knew she was there. We had our faces covered with masks, but knew she could identify us by other means—our voices, our body build. Davis wanted to kill her."

"The bastard." Fury raced through Quint. *How could any guy who called himself a man even consider harming a child?* The fact that Davis wanted to only added fuel to Quint's motivation to eradicate the rogue, and fast.

Reginald stared at Quint. "I refused, put my foot down. She was an innocent. So I promised to take her far away to stay with another family. Ordered the official documents drawn up. Figured she'd grow up and forget the whole thing or at least not become an issue for us."

"And that's not the case?"

"No." He released the paperclip, letting it fall to the desk. "Davis carried her through the house while I went to get the chloroform. He took her through the living area and the kitchen where her grandfather lay dead. She saw him."

"Oh, shit." Quint couldn't imagine what that must be like for such a young person to see such a ghastly scene. Not only was her family member dead on the floor, but to be kidnapped by the men that killed him. She had to have been terrified.

Curious, Quint had to know the rest of the story. "Then what happened?"

"I dropped her off at an old friend's house in the boonies to get her away from Davis, to protect her and keep her out of the sometimes traumatic and risky foster system. They agreed to take her in and raise her. Davis never knew her name. As far as I know, no one did, with the exception of me and her foster family. She told us that much when she arrived at their home. The rest took some string pulling but was accomplished in record time. Like I said, I had the official documents drawn up to give them guardianship and adoption. As far as the rest of the world knew, she didn't exist and Ruford Dyal was dead. An unsolved mystery, for sure, as Dalliance certainly didn't want to show its hand and lose our invisible, behind-the-scenes status. And the last thing she needed was the mob searching for her or for Davis returning to finish what he started."

"What about her parents?"

"After I transported her to Minnesota, I managed a quick search, finding only a couple of notes on the situation. Her parents were deceased, and Ruford was her guardian. That was it. I didn't pursue it further as nothing would change anything that I had to do."

"Tough life for a child." Quint rubbed his forehead, trying to imagine how such losses could affect such a young kid.

Reginald paused with a breath. "That was eighteen years ago. She's grown up and can't forget that night."

"Do you blame her?" Quint knew that sort of horror would never vanish from a child's mind. Hell, adults wouldn't be able to forget it either, no matter how hard they tried. Mentally, a person could only handle so much. Such violence passed the limits by leaps and bounds.

"Not at all. I would prefer she stop spending all her free time researching and trying to backtrack those responsible. She's taken a vow of vengeance and is determined not to stop until she's found us."

"You know this how?" Quint asked.

"Her father sends me regular updates. She's not been quiet about her intentions."

Quint gave a short nod. "Understandable. If he was her sole relative, especially. I'd do the same thing."

"She's been knocking on the door of Dalliance's web presence. Not made it in yet or found out anything, but she's got the right idea. In the last two days, she's hit the barrier and been shuttled to the alternative location three times."

"Are you sure it's her?" Anyone, including Davis, could be hammering at the software shield.

"Absolutely. The IT team traced it back to her. There's no doubt. She's persistent." Reginald's voice carried respect. His eyebrows furrowed as if a particularly complex maze puzzled him.

"The virtual protective walls will hold up. Our IT guys are the best." Quint respected the team who kept their information well protected. He'd worked with them through high school and college while spending free time away from school developing his powers, fine tuning them, learning to sap another's talent to use for himself or suffocate it down to nothing. His particular abilities along with a dedicated practice of self-defense and weaponry made him the ideal candidate for tracking down rogues who threatened society. In short, he was born and bred to be a hunter. And a damn good one at that.

"That's not what I'm worried about."

"Afraid she'll find you one day? Enact her revenge?" Quint couldn't imagine his father scared of anything, especially a young woman. Even if she happened to be highly trained for a career as an assassin. He glanced down at the picture again. Something in her face told him the truth. She wasn't a killer. But she would defend those important to her. That made for a toss-up when it came to her intent toward Reginald.

"No. I'm afraid Davis will find her."

The puzzle pieces started to fill in. "Let me guess. She lives somewhere in the Great Lakes area."

"Minnesota."

"Well, hell." Quint sat up straight in the chair and blew out a breath. A man like Davis would see her presence as an affront to his power and ability. He'd be on a mission to take her out, to keep his record intact. "So that's why he's been in the same area for so long. But why now after all this time?"

"I think he's finally stumbled across some information that allows him to close in on her. He discovered something about her and is on the hunt. My guess, and it's only a guess, is that he remembered her. Maybe something sparked that memory. Who knows? Regardless, he must have thought of her and decided it was time to tie up loose ends."

"So he's got a scent and is nose to the ground to find her."

"Yes. That's what I think anyway. It's only a matter of time before he comes across her." Reginald grimaced. "Taryn is tough. She had to be to get through what she did. That trauma she suffered—that's on me. I placed her there, and now she's in danger because of it."

Quint could see the burden pushing his father's shoulders down. The toll could easily be seen in his father's brown eyes, so like his own. "Cruel, rabid monsters have to be eradicated. You did the world a favor." It all fell under the category of saving lives and getting justice for those who'd been wrongly done. "You're the greatest lie detector around. You saw what he was doing—heard it in his words, read it in his mind.

Knew what he would have done to her if you hadn't stopped him. Dad, you did what had to be done. Nothing more, nothing less. Even if that wasn't the plan from the get go." Quint willed his father to see reality, to ease the burden presently shoving his shoulders down. "Who knew Davis had the ability or the want to murder at that time? Even for a good cause. You can't blame yourself for that."

"I was there and in charge of the mission. That puts the responsibility back on me." Reginald drew in a deep breath. "Killing the old man isn't my biggest regret. Putting Taryn in this position is."

Quint read the remorse in Reginald's eyes. "You did what you could for her. Saved her life. It's not your fault Davis turned into a serial killer." He was proud of his father for stepping up. Even though he saw the toll the decision took now, he knew it would have been one hundred times worse if Reginald hadn't intervened for the girl. Still was, if the truth were known. Reginald had done his best to hide and protect the girl, give her a semblance of a normal life. The protection would only last so long though, especially if she persisted on uncovering the past and tracing the men who took out her grandfather. By digging deeper, she made herself known to not only Dalliance, but possibly to Davis as well. As a former agent, Davis had many resources. Hell, maybe he could still tap into the Dalliance website despite the tight security. While that information might not give him information on Taryn, it could still provide tantalizing clues. Nothing was secret these days with the open book policy on lives in the world of technology.

A smile devoid of humor appeared on Reginald's

face. "She's spent her life preparing to confront me, to make those that took her beloved grandfather away pay."

"No telling what he would have done to her. Sounds like the mean old bastard deserved what he got. She was better off being raised by others, well away from the violence of mob life." Quint appraised the file once more, noting Taryn's hometown listed as Lone, Texas. Reginald had relocated her to Rushing River, Minnesota, presumably well away from the nightmarish memories.

He studied a picture of her. Lithe, pretty, with long brunette hair. Though straight, it was thick. A tiny smile played on her lips, giving an indication of a mischievous nature. A short-sleeved shirt showed off toned arms while beautiful green eyes, with a hint of a tilt, gave an impression of sharp intelligence along with confidence. She looked the part of a woman well versed in not only protecting herself but in taking down any threat. A will of steel coated by a beautiful body.

A note about an incident drew his attention. Seemed a burglar broke into her apartment and threatened her with a baseball bat. She surprised him with a martial arts move, took the bat away, and beat the shit out of him before cops showed up.

Quint grinned in amusement. "Damn. Gotta give the girl credit for putting the hurt on the guy with the bat."

Reginald's lips twitched. "I found that pretty entertaining, myself. She's spunky and fearless."

"A real barracuda."

Reginald chuckled. "That she can be. Regularly bests the boys in shooting and paintball. Works at a gym. She knows her stuff, I'm told. Able to handle the biggest jerk with a glare and a lash of her tongue."

"Wonderful. Icy much?" Quint snorted.

Reginald sobered and sat forward, resting his forearms on the desk. "She's not really like that at all. You're dealing with a girl who basically watched her only living relative die right in front of her eyes, someone she loved. Then she was kidnapped by the killers, dropped off in the middle of nowhere with strangers. She vowed to get justice for her grandfather and spent her entire life so far preparing to do just that."

Quint tried to put himself in her shoes. A six-year-old child present and witnessing one of the most horrific situations possible. He didn't blame her for the path she had chosen. He'd sure as hell do the same thing for his family. "You think there's something soft inside her still? Or has she gone cold with vengeance?" He ran his fingers across the picture, trying to decipher what Taryn must be made of. Strength and determination for sure. But could there be more to her than meets the eye?

"She's a woman molded by circumstance, but more than that, she's a phoenix that has risen out of the ashes. Like any other wild animal, a gentle hand and kind soul can tame the most ferocious beast.

"Uh, huh. Not the qualities I excel in." Sarcasm dripped from his words.

"Nothing worth having is easy."

Quint didn't miss the telltale twitch of his father's lips. It didn't take a rocket scientist or a man gifted with the ability to weave his way through complex puzzles with ease to figure out what his father was thinking. "Let's just focus on the task at hand—keeping Taryn, the barracuda, alive."

If Davis had been trolling the area and asking about her, he would likely come across someone that knew her, she stood out that much. "Does he know her by name?"

"Not that I'm aware of. I made sure to keep all of that highly secret," Reginald affirmed. "However, it doesn't take a genius to go back through newspaper articles and public documents to discover a name. I had a head start already knowing her name, but that doesn't mean Davis couldn't have followed the same path to Dyal's heir. " He sighed heavily. "I knew better than to let her keep her name, but that was all she had left. I couldn't steal that away from her, too."

Quint's heart ached at his father's confession. "How well do you trust the family you deposited her with?" He needed to know the score. When it came to Davis, there was no gray area. People took sides. Anyone helping him out would be considered an accomplice, no matter what.

"I worked with Ben Gold growing up around here. We were best friends until he moved away. We kept in touch over the years. He briefly worked for Dalliance before getting married and moving to Minnesota to be near his wife's family."

Quint nodded once. "So you'd bet Taryn's life on this guy?"

Reginald met his eyes. "Absolutely. I did once and still do."

"Good enough for me. What about the rest of the family?"

"I suspect Ben only told his wife, Meredith, about Taryn and the circumstances. They have a son that is about her age. Since they were so young, I'm sure they spared him the details. I highly doubt they ever told him the story. Doing so would only hurt her. And they do care for her. Love her like their own child." Absolute faith conveyed through Reginald's words.

Quint sighed. "I have a feeling using her as bait is going to royally piss her off."

Reginald shrugged. "Davis is already hot on her tail. Technically, she's not bait. You're there to protect her and capture Davis in the process."

Yeah, right. He had a feeling if Taryn found out the true reason he was about to drop into her life, she'd take the baseball bat to him. Or worse, castrate him with a spoon.

Reginald grinned. "Yeah, I'd be worried about my balls, too."

Damn his ability to read minds. Quint narrowed his eyes at his father in annoyance. Sometimes his father's ability sucked. Hell, most of the time it sucked. Never once had he gotten by with anything. As a teenager, Quint resented the fact his father knew all his secrets and intents, everything from the time he ditched the library to meet a girl for some good old-fashioned necking in the back seat of his car to the small stash of dirty magazines stowed away in a shoebox under his bed.

He still couldn't claim to be thrilled with his father's talent when aimed his direction, but he didn't mind so much lately. *It is what it is.* At least his old man was a good guy, unlike the scouting report on Taryn in his hands. She carried a chip on her shoulder, raised her head high, and didn't take shit from anyone. He had no reason to doubt those findings. "She's a barracuda all right. How do you propose I get close enough to watch her back?"

"You're a smart kid. You'll figure it out." Amusement flashed in Reginald's eyes.

Well, crap. Sometimes Reginald's sense of humor proved lacking. This was one of those times. *Look at the bright side. I get to hang out with a pretty woman. One who just happens to be able to hit the center of a shooting target from a mile away. Wonderful. Talk about being between a rock and a hard place.*

Still, he couldn't deny the sense of excitement at meeting such an unusual lady. Of course, it was mixed with a bad premonition.

"Watch over her." The order came through loud and clear, as did the deep responsibility Reginald felt for the woman.

File in hand, Quint stood up and walked to the door. He rested his hand on the knob and turned back to his father. "You owe me one."

"Make it happen." Reginald met Quint's gaze firmly.

"Will do." Quint left the office, headed to his smaller one, and turned on the computer. He never entered a mission without some research first. Get the lay of the land, so to speak. After that, he could formulate a plan. If that didn't work, he could wing it.

His gut told him that watching over Taryn would pretty much be a wing it kind of mission. *Not a good omen at all.*

Chapter 3

Three days later

Quint stepped into the gym, taking a moment to let his eyes adjust to the lower light compared to the brightness of the summer day outside. He'd arrived at the apartment he'd rented yesterday, just two doors down the hall from where Taryn lived. The owner had been all too happy to let him have the room, which made Quint a little edgy. Either the place was a dump or the census of Rushing River was too little to support the apartment business. It worked in his favor, at least.

And being so close to Taryn would be perfect. He could keep track of her comings and goings easily. He'd packed a listening device or two to strategically place in her home but hadn't decided to use them yet. His conscience pinged at the invasion of privacy he'd be committing. So, for right now, he was just going with a close proximity to Taryn. That surprise he'd save for later, though. *First things first.* He took long enough to get changed, grab some lunch, and drive the rental car he'd picked up at the airport to the gym. GPS helped greatly, although the smaller town didn't prove to be too complicated. Nothing like he was used to in Portland, Oregon, anyway.

He'd noticed the open, rural set of the area surrounding the town. The population listed on the city sign boasted of one thousand citizens. Personally, he believed that number to be a little optimistic, judging by the lack of foot traffic, cars, and the mere score of businesses in the entire place. No skyscrapers, no taxis. Just Main Street with a few shoppers, Mom and Pop stores, and neighborhoods surrounding them, enough to cover a few blocks. Plenty of farmland radiated around the so-called business district, adding to a decidedly lazy atmosphere that encouraged him to sit back and take a load off.

As much as he'd love to do just that, he had work to do—in the form of finding and making contact with Taryn Brisk.

"Hey there."

Quint blinked to find a pretty blonde standing right in front of him. She wore a cut-off top and shorts that barely covered the essentials. Her long hair hung past her shoulders, lighter at the ends and much darker at the roots. He'd bet his next check that she dyed her hair. She was young, maybe barely legal. Not the woman he was seeking at all. "Hello."

She shifted her weight and played with a lock of her hair. "You must be new here."

"Yep." He glanced over her head and scanned the large room. To his right were free weights. A handful of men occupied that space. The center area appeared dedicated to the cardio equipment with four televisions mounted from the ceiling and in front so people could watch their favorite shows while exercising. The left side sported a large climbing wall and a handful of brightly colored drapes attached to the ceiling and hanging down to the floor. He lifted his gaze, stopped when he locked on a lithe brunette beauty dressed in black tights, bright green socks, and a loose gray t-shirt. Gracefully, she performed a turn, ending up in a split position, the two pieces of fabric wrapped around her legs and arms, supporting her weight. She bent one leg, pulled it close to her chest, then returned to the former position. A ponytail held her long hair in check, the strands bobbing with every movement.

The grace and power she possessed awed him. Sure, he'd seen advertisements for circus performers who took to the rafters in such a manner. Yet, he'd never expected to see such a thing from Taryn.

As he watched, she pulled herself up, arched her back, and extended her legs. That position lasted a few seconds before she tumbled downward, the silks unrolling as she went. Just as he thought she'd take a hard fall, the knots held, stopping her progress and leaving her in yet another split. She bobbled, then flipped over, finally stilling upside down with her feet about as far apart as they could get.

"Excuse me." He brushed past the blonde, making a beeline for the tangled woman. For a fierce barracuda, she seemed a little stuck and helpless.

Marching right up to her, he stopped just a few inches away. "Umm. Do you need some help?"

Her t-shirt had fallen over her face, leaving only a pretty white sports bra covering her cleavage. He took note of the decadent sight of a toned trunk topped off with modest, but perky breasts. The view sent an electrical zing through his whole body. *Damn. The last thing I need is to get all hot and bothered by her.*

She pulled the errant t-shirt back down to its original spot, held it there, and stared straight ahead, which put her eye level with his crotch. His body sat up and took notice, especially of her extraordinary level of fitness and flexibility.

The longer she checked out his shorts, the more he thought about the possibilities of such athletic abilities in bed.

On a mission. Remember, Barracuda here bites.

Slowly her gaze traveled up his body until it met his eyes. "I'm fine. Thanks for asking."

Independent, too. Was there ever a doubt?

He put on his best friendly expression. "Are you sure?"

Indecisiveness flared as she tried to kick loose with one foot. "Well…"

Chivalry to the rescue.

Quint didn't wait for her to ask. Instead, he grabbed her around the waist as she levered herself upwards. A quick couple of steps back and she was free of the material tangling around her body.

He enjoyed the feel of her against his chest. Curvy yet solid. Even her hair tickling his neck added to the pleasant sensation.

Reluctantly, he deposited her on her feet and dropped his hands.

She smiled up at him. The expression lit up her face, brought brilliant sparks to her already beautiful green eyes, and showed off straight white teeth. "Thanks for the assist."

He inclined his head in acknowledgement. "Nice moves up there." He couldn't get the image of her performance out of his mind. Definitely impressed, he hoped to see her climb the fabric once again to showcase her power and exquisite grace. A natural, she'd draw everyone's attention as she went through a series of elegant and nimble maneuvers high above the ground.

"Oh, no. Not another one." She rolled her eyes, huffed, and spun on her heel.

What the hell? Confused, Quint hurried past her only to stop in her path. "Not another one?"

She paused in her trek. "You know. Horny guy sees girl on silks, imagines her pole dancing in his bedroom, doing a private strip tease, then commence wham, bam, thank you ma'am." She waved her hand. "Not my cup of tea."

Wham, bam, thank you ma'am? Where did she come up with this crap? Obviously, she'd been dating the wrong men. "And you automatically assume that I'm one of those?"

She pursed her lips, scanned him, then shrugged with one shoulder. "Well, yeah."

"That's a little shortsighted of you, isn't it?" He hated the fact that she goaded him so quickly. Why he cared if she thought he'd suck in the sack shouldn't matter. Yet, for some reason it did. In a major way.

"Maybe."

"Seems you should give a guy a chance before calling him a selfish bastard," he scolded.

She seemed to consider his suggestion for a couple of beats. "Sorry, not interested. Bad boy complex here." She started to walk away again. "Been there, done that. Learned my lesson the hard way."

What in the hell did that mean exactly?

He cut her off, blocking her path. No way would he let her just march off, not with that kind of attitude toward him. She was beautiful, quick, fit. Her emerald eyes flashed with intelligence and fire. Her demeanor could only be called one thing—prickly. Pretty as a lark, but prickly as a cactus.

Oddly enough, the combination intrigued him, compelled him, instead of turning him off the way it should.

Arrogantly, she crossed her arms over her chest and arched an eyebrow.

Time to soothe the savage beast. And make up for my less than tactful words. "Look. I think we might have gotten off on the wrong foot." He blew out a breath and held out his hand. "I'm Quint. Quint Warren."

Taryn only hesitated a couple of seconds before shaking it firmly. "Taryn."

"Nice to meet you." He glanced around before turning his attention back to her. "I just moved here, yesterday in fact. Came across this gym and thought to check it out. Maybe make a few friends, too." He offered up a smile of truce. "It's not always easy being the new guy on the block."

"True." The tension left her body. Even her expression turned from a mask of stone to one of cautious friendliness.

Quint hesitated to congratulate himself on the small progress, fearing he'd step into it again and soon. Arguing with her right off the bat would only prove a detriment to his mission. Staying close meant being nice, not bickering and flexing his masculine muscle in the form of proving her insights wrong. *At least for now.* "I take it you work here?"

"Yep. I'm the manager."

Quint nodded and scanned the room once again. "Nice facilities. To be honest, I was a little surprised to find this place considering the size of the town. This is really upscale, even for the big city."

Taryn tilted her head. "I take it you're from one of those?"

"Yeah. Portland, Oregon, to be exact." He saw no reason to lie to her about the basics. The chances of her rushing home to her computer and looking him up hovered around zero. Besides, she wouldn't find much on him at all. Dalliance made sure to keep the identities and details on their employees absolutely secret.

She studied him for a few seconds. "What brings you to our neck of the woods?"

"Tired of the rat race, I guess." He added a smile, hoping to sell the fib.

"Uh-huh."

The flash of intelligence and skepticism in her eyes told him she wasn't buying his story. She was too damn sharp for her own good.

"Well, I have to get back to work. Feel free to try out anything you'd like. Macy, our membership specialist, can get you set up if you decide you'd like to sign up." Taryn started to walk off, paused, then turned around. "Welcome to Rushing River." She added a grin, then changed course and headed for the front desk.

Quint watched her go with avid interest. Her steps were graceful, confident. She seemed to float over the ground. Not only that, she greeted people as she went, smiling at them, speaking to them. A small laugh from her sent a rush of warmth over him. That particular sound he could easily learn to crave.

She came across as sweet and welcoming. He had a sudden wish to explore that side of her. He'd glimpsed the sour part. Now he so wanted a taste of the sugary attitude she showed to others.

Whatever happens, this mission should prove interesting.

With that thought, Quint rolled his shoulders, eyed the weight machines, and decided to take advantage of the situation. He kept in shape out of both habit and necessity. Now he had the luxury of combining work with pleasure.

His gaze found Taryn once more.

She might possess a thick outer shell, but he vowed to delve deeper, to slide through the cracks and discover what she was truly made of. Something told him he wouldn't be disappointed. Not at all.

She's bait, remember? I can't protect her if I'm too distracted with getting her into bed.

The sharp bite of reality doused his thoughts and forced him to focus on the reason for his appearance. Besides, if he didn't keep his eyes peeled, Davis could easily sneak in. The healthy dose of anger and responsibility cleared his head. He had a job to do. Taryn's life depended on it.

****

Holy macaroni, he's hot. Taryn couldn't get her fill of his fine body no matter how long she looked. He reminded her of a running back or perhaps a tight end. Certainly, his end was tight, as evidenced by the shorts molding over his backside when he bent over. She licked her lips.

Standing a handful of inches taller than she, Quint could be considered average height for a talented athlete at around six foot and a little extra. He had dark brown hair and matching chocolate eyes. Those made her stomach flip as much or more so than his toned body. A square jaw promised stubbornness even as his gaze reflected intelligence. Yet something was missing. Warmth, perhaps? They seemed a little chilly. Preoccupied, maybe. She couldn't hold it against him. After all, she knew nothing about him or his past.

The slight ruggedness of his face spoke of adventures in life, not a man who spent his free time planted in front of a television set. Graceful movements told of familiarity with his body and with motion. He appeared to glide from one piece of equipment to the next. No clomping of his shoes. No rushing. Just a continuous flow that came with ease.

She could imagine he excelled at dancing, giving the sheer grace that she saw in action.

His frame carried powerful mass, roped, thick muscles promising strength and stamina. Large biceps drew her attention as he pressed the weights upward, causing the muscles to snap and flex. The motion emphasized his wide shoulders and chest, flowing into a narrower waist. He wore a black t-shirt that complemented his shorts and shoes. Too bad. She would have loved to watch what had to be a grand six-pack in action. Powerful thighs carried definition, just as the rest of his body did, at least what parts she could see. Quint knew his way around a gym. One glance at the guy told the story. Not only that, but he'd been put together just right. No denying the facts.

He wasn't pretty and would never grace the cover of a fashion magazine—fitness ones, though, definitely. A rugged and regal bearing came across exceedingly well. She imagined he could have been a caveman in another life. A mountain man. Even a gladiator. He had that kind of physique and demeanor.

He exuded confidence and something more. A vitality she'd never seen before. Purpose. And a fortitude of steel. She'd never seen the likes in her lifetime, which only added to her curiosity about the man who showed up out of nowhere, rescued her from a near fall, then went on the defensive to her off-putting intentions. It was a rollercoaster first impression, definitely. Whether it held true down the road, she couldn't say.

But one thing rang true. When it came down to male specimens, other men paled in comparison to him. If he were a horse, he'd be the herd stallion. Any mare in her right mind would recognize prime quality when she saw it. While less motivated by the need for protection and great genes to pass on to offspring, Taryn couldn't suppress the basic instinct of lust.

Her heart picked up speed and her breath whooshed out as she appraised him with interest.

So this is what it feels like to have your socks knocked off.

Realization struck. She'd been playing around with the boys. Now, she'd finally met a real man. The knowledge both excited and concerned her. As much as she'd love to jump on his wagon for a ride, her pride refused. After all, they'd just met, and she had morals. Maybe not as strong as others', but they were there just the same. Which meant she could admire from afar. Anything more, no matter how much she longed to strip him out of that shirt and shorts and nibble, would just have to go unfulfilled.

Perfect. Now, the hormones go rampant. Just what I need. Not.

She'd given up hope on finding someone suitable.

While not opposed to a casual affair, she had other priorities right now. Sex-on-a-stick Quint might be a delicious distraction, but that's all he could be—a distraction. She wasn't naïve enough to believe in undying love. One just had to look at the divorce rates to prove those kinds of facts. Her own experiences tended toward short term and unsatisfactory.

Besides, she wasn't even sure she liked him. They'd butted heads. He'd snapped back. They called a tentative truce and went to their separate corners. An iffy beginning, for sure.

So, which is it, Taryn? You like him or you despise him? She snorted to herself as he bent over once again, showing that shapely rear.

He's gorgeous and I'm horny. Relationships have been based on less. She appraised him once again, noticing her stomach flip flop with enthusiasm.

Self-criticism and pride reined her in. *Since when did I turn into a cat in heat?*

Argh!

Annoyed with her line of thoughts, Taryn forced her attention elsewhere. No matter how sexy the guy, she had principles. One of them happened to be she didn't pick up strangers and take them back to her apartment. She'd meant what she'd said before. Bad boys were off her list. And Quint was definitely a bad boy.

Although a damn sexy one.

In an effort to put distance between herself and the temptation Quint presented, Taryn stepped into her small office and plopped down in her seat. A couple of papers littered her desk. Numbers. And flimsy ones at that.

She sighed heavily, spun around in her chair, and stared at the back wall. In the past few weeks, the bottom line had sunk, now hanging just barely in the black. In truth, the gym was on the verge of entering the red. If that happened, the owner, Trent Dyson, would most likely shut the doors. He'd alluded to it more than once in their recent meetings.

The numbers didn't lie. Nor did the real-life facts. Rushing River wasn't large enough to support a massive gym. While interest peaked highly at the first opening, it now had leveled off. Many of the members were die-hard exercise enthusiasts. They supported the business. It was the others, who made an effort then soon tired of stopping by, that hurt. With each canceled or expired membership, the bank account grew thinner.

Trent had cut back staff, leaving just her and Macy to handle the daily business. He owned three other gyms in the region and rarely drove to their little neck of the woods. When he did, it usually meant another anxiety-ridden meeting with discussions about why the place wasn't thriving. Taryn told him the way things were in the small town. Times were tough. People worked hard, but many drove long distances to those jobs. They were tired when they arrived home, not wanting to stop by for a workout before getting to their downtime. Others simply fell on difficult times and could no longer afford the fees. Finally, more just lost interest. She'd tried all sorts of ways to draw in new members, but nothing seemed to make a lasting difference.

We're breaking even. That's what counts. Taryn boosted her spirits for the moment. She pushed a stray lock of hair aside and spun back around to peer into the gym. The silks dangling from the ceiling caught her eye. *As soon as I can perfect those, I can offer another class.* She snorted to herself. Perfection was a long way off.

Quint walked through her line of vision.

Then again, maybe it's not.

Chapter 4

"Surprise seeing you here."

Taryn blinked up at Quint. "It is. A big one. You live here?"

He gave a quick nod. "Yep. Apartment 3-A to be exact."

"I'm in 1-A." Rushing River didn't sport many apartment buildings, only two that she knew of, anyway. Both were fairly small, with around a half-dozen rooms each. Even with such low numbers, the manager of her building had a hard time keeping them rented. Most people that grew up locally couldn't wait to head to the big city, or at least something with more excitement than a small town. They might move away from home, land in the apartments for a few months, then decide to spread their wings farther. Others came from surrounding areas, seeking different scenery. Neither seemed to stay long. In essence, the Cherry Tree Apartments ended up being a stepping stone for most, with seemingly a constant turnover of patrons.

Not that she minded. The place offered a quiet place to stay, very little crime, and a landlord that was as kind as he was gray-headed. His wife, one of the sweetest ladies around, baked for special occasions, sharing her fare with the residents. She'd even remembered Taryn's birthday and brought her a small cake to celebrate. For the special attention, she'd continue to pay her monthly rent without a single complaint.

Sure, she could have moved back in with her parents after college but couldn't bring herself to do so. Her independent nature demanded she step out into the world, even a baby step, and make it on her own. Her brother, Brandon, had moved about an hour and a half away, to the suburbs of Minneapolis. He loved the fast pace of city life and all it had to offer. The company he worked for had a very large office in the city, which afforded Brandon a short drive each weekday. To hear Brandon talk, he adored the job. As he'd always been a nut about cars, taking a position for one of the leading race-car specialty businesses was right up his alley. Always on the go, Brandon did make time for their paintball team and for Sunday lunch with their parents. Otherwise, it was work and his latest girlfriend, Jennifer.

Taryn had her own busy schedule with plenty of activities to keep her busy. Boredom was never an issue. Paintball and target shooting occupied her weekends, while her week was filled with work. In between, she researched, studied, and read everything she could find on her grandfather's death. The scant information she'd discovered thus far only whetted her appetite for more. Officially, the police called the event a burglary and a resulting heart attack. She wasn't buying it. Yes, her grandfather was well off, but he had security guards. She'd seen them on a daily basis. For someone to get past those men took a grand feat and plan. It wasn't random in the least. The heart attack didn't pan out, either. She recalled a few words from that terrifying night which told her that her grandfather was targeted.

"It's still early. Did you want to get something to eat?" Quint offered.

Taryn studied his face, trying to determine if he possessed ulterior motives. When she found nothing but a friendly suggestion, she gave in. *Maybe I'm being way too cynical. Eric is a jackass, but that doesn't mean every other man under the sun is too.* Since he'd just moved in, Quint probably knew no one. Obviously, he'd be a little lonely and happy to have some company. She'd feel the same way if she were in his shoes. "Sure. My treat."

He frowned. "I asked. I can foot the bill."

"Nope. Consider it a welcome gift." She fit her key into the lock. "Let me just change really quick."

"Sure." He closed his door behind him, turning the knob to verify that it did lock.

Taryn paused in the doorway, then stepped inside. "Come on in. No sense in standing out in the hallway waiting for me."

Quint came inside, stopped, and looked around. "Nicely done."

Taryn smiled at his observation. She shut the door behind him, then made her way into the middle of the living area, dropping her purse on the kitchen counter along the way. The light blue faux suede couch occupied one wall. A glass coffee table sat in front of it, the legs painted in a similar hue to the sofa. An extra fluffy recliner angled next to them. All faced an average-sized television sitting on a wooden stand. Inlaid rocks of pastel colors added an upscale whimsical atmosphere, especially in relation to the pine hardwood floor. To the left, a large window overlooked part of the park. Each piece and placement, she'd chosen carefully. Settling in had been easy once she found the right furniture to turn it into a true home.

She ran her hand over the top of the couch. "Thanks. I wanted to present a homey, but light feel. Uplifting, I guess."

Quint checked out the area and gave a quick nod. "I'd say you nailed it. Very nice." He took a couple more steps, stopping at the window. "You've got a flair for interior design. With that sort of talent, I'm surprised you're living here and working at the gym."

Taryn shrugged. "I'm a small-town girl, I guess. Didn't have much motivation to pull up roots, head to the big city, and find my way. I like the gym. Get to work out for free, too. That's a definite bonus."

Quint smiled softly. "I'd say. You've got some great moves on those drapes. Never seen such a thing in my life."

She peered over at him. "Aerial silks or ribbons. Drapes makes me sound like an overactive kitten climbing up the window sheers."

Quint's eyes lit up with humor. "A kitten, huh?"

Taryn groaned dramatically. "Flattery will get you nowhere." She found herself enjoying the conversation. Quint's laid-back nature put her at ease, something the other men in her life hadn't come close to accomplishing. They'd added a sense of adventure and the promise of an electrifying tryst with a couple of hot men who knew their way around a bedroom. Taryn took a dip and found the waters too cold for her liking. Quint exuded strength. Ability. And a certain need for companionship. Friendship. Definitely, a nice change. His handsomeness and wit didn't hurt, either.

Before she could make a fool of herself, she strode to the bedroom and shut the door behind her. While a shower would have been best to wash the sweat off, she knew there wasn't enough time. Instead, she went with a quick change and wipe down. She stripped down completely, dressed again, and spent a few minutes in the bathroom freshening up. Quint wore jeans and a t-shirt. She opted to match him. Butterflies danced in her stomach, though she reminded herself half a dozen times that it wasn't a date. *Just casual dinner with a new friend. That's it. Nothing more, nothing less.* The lecture didn't quell her excitement in the least. Odd. Since she'd broken up with Eric not too long ago, she'd sworn off men. She hadn't had an issue with avoiding a social life until Quint arrived. Now, she couldn't seem to recall why men were off limits entirely.

Satisfied with her appearance, she walked back out into the living area, finding Quint staring out the window as if deep in thought.

"What do you like to eat?"

He turned to face her. "Anything is fine. I'm not picky."

She gave a short nod. "Bobbie's it is, then."

"Bobbie's?" Quint asked as he followed her to the door.

"Best place to eat around here. Home cooked meals. All kinds of entrees. Nothing fancy, really, but it's good." Taryn picked up her purse, ushered Quint out the door, and shut and locked it behind her. After dropping her keys into the purse, she led the way out the front door of the apartment building.

"I'll drive." Taryn made her way to her car, clicked open the doors, then slid into the driver's seat. Quint wedged himself into the passenger's seat, seemingly a little squashed with the smaller car's dimensions. His knees bent up high. Still, he managed to fasten his seat belt and shut the door.

"Kind of snug, huh?"

"It's okay."

Taryn grinned at his nonchalant attitude. "The bar is under the front of your seat."

He found it, pulled, and his seat scooted back several inches. "Much better."

"Ready?"

"Yeah." He sat quietly for a couple of minutes before rubbing his chin. "Tell me about yourself."

Taryn placed the keys in the ignition, cranked the engine, and backed out of her parking space. Only when she entered the road did she answer. "Not much to tell."

"Have you always lived here?"

Taryn kept her attention focused on the road. Not that traffic was an issue. It never was. She just didn't care for the distraction Quint presented, nor his innocent questions. "No."

"So you and your family moved here?"

She spared him a glance. "Maybe we should backtrack to why you landed here. It's not like there's a major river crossing or fort here. The wagon trains don't stop by. Heck, I can't tell you the last time a plane flew overhead."

His full lips softened. "Like I said, I was looking for a place off the beaten path."

Taryn snorted. "Well you found it. I don't know how, but you did." She slowed the car for a stop sign. "Have you purchased a parka yet?"

"Nope. Do I need one?"

"If you're going to be around for winter, yeah." She hit the gas again.

"I'll look into it. You can probably point me to a local store. If not, I guess I can get one online." His mouth thinned out a bit. "Surely it doesn't get that horribly cold. Snow, yeah. But the frozen tundra seems a little overkill."

"Don't believe that for a second. It gets plenty cold enough that frostbite is the least of your worries." *How odd. He moved here without really researching first.* The fact only added to the mystery that surrounded Quint.

"If you tell me that we have to build an igloo, I'm going to call your bluff." He arched an eyebrow.

She shook her head and chuckled as she pulled into the parking lot at Bobbie's Restaurant. "You're in luck. I'm a crappy igloo builder myself." She found a spot near the door, cut the engine, climbed out of the car, waited for Quint to shut his door, then hit the fob to lock the doors. Rushing River didn't have much crime. Still, there was no excuse to give potential miscreants an opportunity.

Quint reached the entrance first and held the door open for her to enter.

"Thank you." Taryn pushed the strap of her purse over her shoulder as she neared Caitlin, the hostess. They'd gone to high school together. Caitlin followed in her family's footsteps with the restaurant.

Unlike me, who happens to be plotting an assassination.

She pasted on a smile. "Hi, Caitlin."

"Good to see you, Taryn." She smiled up at Quint.

"Where did you find him?"

"He just showed up on my doorstep." Taryn waved her hand and chuckled.

"Aren't you the lucky one?" Caitlin licked her lips.

Quint inclined his head. "Quint. Nice to meet you." He scanned the room. "Where would you like us? I'm hungry."

Caitlin gave a quick nod. "Booth or table?"

"Booth," Taryn answered. The best seats lined the wall, and those were all booths.

"Follow me." Caitlin grabbed two glasses of water, a couple of straws, and two menus before leading the way through the mostly empty dining area to a corner booth. "Here you go." She deposited everything on one side, then the other. "Becky will get your order in a sec." She turned on her heel and returned to her post after a slow, long look back at Quint.

Taryn plopped down with the knowledge that the whole town would know about her meal with Quint by morning. Caitlin was a decent enough person, but she couldn't keep a secret to save her life.

"Would you mind if we traded seats?" Quint asked.

She blinked at him. "No, not at all." She scooted out of the booth, side-stepped around Quint, then sat back down. Curious, she waited for him to settle in before asking, "Why didn't you like this one?"

He glanced to the door, then back to meet her eyes. "I have a thing about having my back to a door."

"Oh." She pondered that for a second. "Military?"

"Why do you ask?" His eyebrows furrowed.

She shrugged. "Just trying to figure out where you would learn such survival behaviors that would follow you around for life." Taryn studied him for another second. "Either cop or military," she stated with firm conviction.

Quint didn't react in any way to her statement. "Think you can pick those kind of men out easily?"

"Yep." She lowered her gaze to his left side. "I'll wager you're packing, too."

"If I was, would it bother you?" Quint eyed her steadily.

"No. I'm a decent shot, myself. Though I use a rifle, not a handgun."

"A woman who shoots rifles? Not many of those around."

Taryn sat up a little straighter. "Nope. I can hold my own, though."

"Darn tooting, she can." A middle-aged woman with short, dark hair stepped up to the table. "Taryn isn't one to brag, but she can hit the center of a target from a mile away." Becky, the waitress, smiled wide.

Taryn's cheeks heated. "Not that far, Becky."

Becky waved her hand. "Far enough. Bested the boys in all the turkey shoots this spring."

Quint's eyebrows shot up. "All of them?"

Taryn opened her mouth but Becky beat her to it. "Yep. Every single one of them. The men were moping around for a week after the last one." Becky grinned. " 'Bout time they realize that shooting isn't just for men."

Taryn cleared her throat. "Becky, this is Quint. He just moved here. Lives a couple doors down from me. Quint, this is Becky. She owns this place."

Quint tilted his head. "I thought this place was called Bobbie's?"

Becky chuckled. "That was my grandmother. She

started the place. Been gone a while now, but we weren't about to take her name off it. No way. She'd haunt us from the grave if we did anything to her baby."

"Understandable. Nice to meet you, Becky."

"Same here. Have you two decided what you'd like?"

"Umm. Not yet." Quint grabbed the menu, opened it, and scanned the listings. "How's the roast beef?"

"Best roast beef you've ever tasted," Becky answered.

Quint grinned. "Why do I get a feeling she'll say that about everything?"

Taryn smiled. "Probably because she will, but it's true. The roast beef is very good, not fatty like some places."

"That'll work. Roast beef with a side of mashed potatoes, no gravy, and iced tea. Unsweetened." Quint closed the menu and handed it over.

"I'll take the grilled chicken salad. Ranch dressing, please."

"And your usual sweet tea?"

"You know me well." Sweet tea was her downfall. She craved the stuff, especially during the summer. While it might be loaded with sugar, she simply looked the other way. An extra few minutes on the treadmill would make up for her splurging.

"Yep, I do." Becky took both menus in hand. "It'll be just a few minutes." She walked off, deposited the menus in the stack, and disappeared through a doorway, presumably to the kitchen.

Taryn took a sip of her water. "No gravy, huh?"

"Nope. Never cared for it." Quint slid his straw into the glass and took a long drink.

"Sweet tea?"

She smiled. "My addiction." She recalled his order. "You don't like sugar?"

"It's not something I have to have."

"Interesting." Taryn found the small details about Quint intriguing.

"No, what's interesting is that you're a crack shot." Quint set the glass down and met Taryn's eyes. "I've never met a woman who cared for guns."

She glanced down at the table then back up at him. "A lot of men would find my marksmanship skills off-putting."

"I'm not most men." Confidence and truth carried heavily in his tone.

The sound reassured her to open up to him, at least a little. "My family grew up living off the land, for the most part. Gardens. Hunting." She shuddered. "I hated the hunting part. Never participated in it. Couldn't bring myself to eat the meat."

"It's not for everyone," Quint softly replied.

Taryn appreciated his kindness in the comment. "I practiced enough to be good. Entered the first turkey shoot at sixteen. Won, too. After that, I decided that could be a way to give back to my family. Not only the money, which they insisted I keep, but the frozen turkey that came as the top prize." She smiled at the memories. "Kept us in so many turkeys, everyone grew sick of eating it."

Quint smiled. "I bet." His rubbed his thumb down the side of his glass. "You said 'my family,' not we."

He's sharp. Too sharp. "Caught that, huh?"

"I'm really good at details."

Unsure what that meant in this context, Taryn took

her time removing the cover from her straw. All the locals knew her story. Well, the part about the Golds taking her in and keeping her. As far as she discerned, no one had a single clue about her life before that. No one but her. And the bastards that killed her grandfather in cold blood. She mentally shook aside the bitter thoughts and returned to the conversation at hand. "I'm adopted."

"Nothing wrong with that."

"Nope. Nothing at all." Taryn dropped the straw into her glass and took another drink of her ice water. "What kind of job do you do that you can relocate here?" She thought for a second. "And you never answered my question, military or police?"

Quint peered up at the exit, then across the room as if taking a second look at the other diners. "I'm an IT consultant. Can work from anywhere. And neither."

Chatty, he's not. "Software guru, I take it?"

Quint's shoulders visible relaxed as did the tension in his face. She hadn't noticed its presence until it eased. "Guru? No. I just know my way around a computer is all." He took another swallow. "And before you ask, I'm not running from a nasty divorce or dramatic breakup." He offered up a lopsided grin, one that invited her to join in the fun.

"Not that I was going to ask..." She smiled back.

"It was on the tip of your tongue," he reaffirmed with a rueful grin.

Damn, he's good. She cautioned herself to tread carefully around Quint. It was like he could read minds. Not a good trait to have in her book. "So why Rushing River? It's not like we're a busy metropolis. It's hard to find, truth be told."

"It's quaint. I wanted somewhere out of the way."

"That doesn't explain how you got here," Taryn insisted.

"I have the ability to work from anywhere. Once I get bored with a location, I throw a dart at a board, do a little research, then pick up and move. Get to see the country that way. Live the culture, not just stay for a week and leave again."

"Must be a nice life."

"I'm not complaining." He unfolded the napkin around his silverware. "Looks like dinner is served."

Sure enough, Becky headed their way with two plates in hand. She set the meal down in front of them, then made a second trip for their glasses of tea. "Anything else for you two?"

"No, thanks." Taryn switched her straw from her water glass to the tea before dribbling the dressing over her salad.

"I'm good. Thank you." Quint smiled up at Becky, grasped his fork, and dug in. One bite and he closed his eyes. "This is amazing."

"Told you so." Taryn dipped a chunk of meat in the ranch dressing before taking her first taste. "It's always delicious."

"Remind me to make this my nightly dinner stop."

"Okay." Taryn watched the way he cut up his food, then took generous bites. Poor guy was hungry. Idly, she wondered how long since he'd had a decent meal. Judging by the way he shoveled the roast beef in, it had been a while.

Something about that bothered her. Certainly, he wasn't starving, but still. The mystery around Quint deepened as she considered his vague answers about his work. In her experience, men loved to brag about themselves. Quint seemed to be the polar opposite. He steered her away from the topic with abrupt answers.

He was hiding something. That puzzle piece seemed to fit. What, she didn't have a clue.

Although she already had more than enough on her plate, she found room for a little detective work concerning Quint. As much as he compelled her, tempted her, and intrigued her, she needed to make sure he was on the straight and narrow.

If he turned out to be an ax murderer, she'd be very disappointed.

Okay. Maybe not an ax murderer. That would be creepy. More like an international jewel thief. That would be still be disappointing. She peeked over at him. *Very disappointing, indeed.*

"Want to play paintball with me Saturday?" The words tumbled out before she could bite them back.

Quint's eyes widened. "As a date?"

She gulped. "Well…" *I'm such an idiot.*

He smiled mischievously. "No backing out now. You asked. I accepted. We'll toss a coin as to who gets to wash off whom afterwards."

She frowned. "That's not exactly how it works."

He shrugged. "So you teach me a few things."

A little voice nagged at her. She took a drink of sweet tea. "I feel I should warn you that I'm not good dating material."

He pinned her with those gorgeous, all-seeing eyes. "Why is that?"

"I meant it when I said I have a bad-boy complex. Problem is, I don't look before I leap, and they all end up being toads."

Quint's lips turned up in a quirky grin. "I happen to be free of warts."

She blinked.

"You can check for yourself."

"Umm. No, thanks." She blew out a breath and picked at her food. Barely, she resisted the urge to squirm in her seat. Self-preservation and a still-wounded heart reminded her of the last time she took a chance on a bad boy, and the reason she vowed never again. "Can't we just go as friends? No pressure. Nothing except for a good time."

"Deal."

She peered up at him from under her lashes. He didn't appear angry or upset. Instead, he carried an air of confidence, ability, and competence she'd never seen in another man.

Leave it to me to be turned on by competence. Not quite romantic, if I do say so myself.

Mentally, she rolled her eyes and resumed eating.

"Becky said you were an ace," Quint said.

"If you're worried about fairness, I'll give you a handicap."

He snorted. "Don't need one."

"Male pride or do I detect you've had some experience with firearms?"

For a few seconds, Quint worked on his meal. "I can hold my own."

The low timbre of his voice and the spark in his eyes sent a tiny shiver down her back. He'd said nothing, but again, everything.

"You're safe with me, Taryn."

She met his eyes, stared back for a long moment, then gave a brief nod. "I'll hold you to that."

Chapter 5

The next early afternoon, Quint sat down on the lumpy, old couch in his apartment, placed his plate and a glass of water on the coffee table, and picked up his cell phone. After typing in the memorized number, he waited for it to be answered.

"Hey, son. How's it going?" Reginald's voice came in loud and clear.

"Okay. Not much to report. Any news on Davis?"

"Nothing new. As far as we know, he's still in the Greater Lakes area. But no recent kills, either."

"That's something." Quint plucked his sandwich from the plate and took a large bite.

"How's Taryn?"

The open-ended question amused Quint. "Interesting."

"Yeah, I got that much."

Quint frowned. "You can't read my mind through a phone conversation, can you?"

Reginald chuckled. "You never know."

Ugh. Quint took a drink of water before setting the glass back down. "She's fiery, as you predicted. Cautious, though. Very careful and close-lipped. When I asked about certain things, she changed the subject."

"Yeah, I didn't figure it would be easy with her. She has an agenda and seems to like her privacy."

"For sure." Quint leaned back against the cushions

of the couch. "I don't think she's going to confide in me any time soon, not that it matters. That's not what worries me. Davis does." He wondered again how close Davis would have to be in order to use his psychic powers to kill.

"We don't know his range. Certainly, the closer he is, the easier it would be."

Damn his paranormal abilities. Still, Quint didn't protest. He'd had a lifetime of his father busting in on his thoughts to become accustomed to it. "He's too slippery."

Reginald sighed. "Tell me something I don't already know."

"Wish I could." Quint sat forward, picked up the sandwich, and took another mouthful. "I might be here for a while."

"This is your only task right now, so whatever time you need, take it."

"Will do." Quint swallowed. "I'll check back in when I know something more."

"Do that. And I'll keep you posted if any of the trackers come up with anything on Davis."

"Thanks, Dad."

Quint disconnected the call, finished his sandwich, then washed it down with the rest of the water. His meal finished, he carried the dishes to the sink and laid them down.

He returned to the living area and stood at the window overlooking the front of the building. Ordinarily, the rustic scenery and rural area would offer him peace. Not this time. He'd begun to doubt if anything could.

The years of trailing after villains and disposing of

them had taken their toll. He was a hunter, yes—a trained killer with the unusual ability to squash the life spark out of a man in a matter of seconds. Sure, he only went after the worst of the worst. That used to salve his soul. Now, he saw it as a job. Locate and offer an out. If they refused, then destroy. The same process repeated over and over again, taking his ability to care with it. Emotions had leached over time, as did his sense of compassion and goodness. He fought a new battle that no one, not even his father, knew about. The battle for his humanity.

Without an anchor, someone or something that fed the light back into his darkness, he found himself floundering. Deep down, he worried he'd lose the war and end up becoming one of those criminal rogues who tore society apart. The same kind of men that he sought and destroyed right now.

After this, I'll take a break. A long one. Just to get away and find myself.

He'd promised himself that for the past two years. Assignments came up, one after another. No one else had his abilities, leaving him to shoulder the burden. Alone.

A subtle knocking on a door caught his attention. Since he seemed to be the only tenant home during the day, the situation prickled his sense of wrongness. The sound of a knob being jimmied, then a door opening solidified that feeling.

Quint poked his head out into the hallway, finding it empty. He stepped out, quietly walked a couple of steps, then stopped at Taryn's door. Closing his eyes, he simply listened. The sound of a piece of furniture scooting and a muffled curse set up red alarm flags.

For a second, he considered who might be breaking into her room. Davis came to mind, though the sounds from inside spoke of an amateur burglar rather than a professional. Davis wouldn't be tripping over things or whispering in anger if he did. The facts pointed to a lesser threat and one that Quint could easily quell.

Quint gripped the door knob and slowly turned. He managed to open the door, slip inside, and close it behind him without the least amount of sound. The sight of a brown-haired man he'd never met standing in Taryn's apartment, holding a trophy in his hands, both surprised and angered Quint.

"What in the hell are you doing?"

The guy swung around, juggling the trophy, and nearly dropping it in the process. He glared at Quint, not seemingly afraid, nervous, or ashamed at being caught. Aggression broadcast from his body posture, and anger flashed in his blue eyes. Dressed in jeans and a t-shirt, he appeared more of a passerby rather than an experienced thief.

"Get your ass out of here, and mind your own business," the man snarled.

Quint hooked his fingers in his front pockets. "Since I can't do that, maybe you should tell me what you're doing in Taryn's apartment and why you're taking her stuff."

The guy's eyes narrowed on him. "Like I said. None of your fucking business." He clutched the trophy and marched toward Quint.

Big and strong, the guy's sheer size would make many men step aside.

Quint didn't budge. Instead, he held his ground. "Actually, it is. So put the trophy down, and we'll have a little chat."

"Go fuck yourself."

Quint *tsked*. "I guess we're doing this the hard way." In a sliding motion, he closed the distance between them, stomped the intruder's foot, smacked him hard in the upper nose, yanked the trophy away, and placed it in a nearby chair. The entire time, he kept his attention on the man. "Now, you ready to talk?"

"Get out of my way." The man tried to brush past him, paused, and slammed a fist into Quint's stomach.

Quint jumped back enough to receive only a fleeting brush. The punch aimed at his head missed entirely. Reaching out, Quint grabbed the guy's arm and, using it for leverage, flipped him over and onto his back.

The guy yelped as he hit the floor hard.

Quint rested his foot on the man's throat, preventing him from getting back up. "Talk. Now. Before I really get mad."

Fear lit in the man's eyes. "Okay. Okay." He squirmed until Quint put more pressure on his windpipe. "That trophy belongs to me."

"How so?"

"It was my win. I bested everyone until that bitch came along. She cheated."

Quint easily read the man. The jealousy, the humiliation of losing to a woman. He reeked of it. "How did she cheat?"

"I don't have a fucking clue. She was in my sights, then gone. Disappeared. The next thing I knew, she'd tagged me."

"I see." Quint nodded slightly. "Who are you?"

"Eric."

"Well, Eric. I think you have one hell of a chip on your shoulder and are a bad loser to boot."

"What do you know about it? Are you dating the bitch?"

Quint eased more pressure on the man's throat. "First of all, her name is Taryn, not bitch. Secondly, we're friends."

Eric drew in a breath and stilled. "She's a lousy date. The only thing she's got going for her is that body."

Quint tilted his head. "Don't tell me. You and her?"

"Stupidest thing I ever did."

"What the hell did she see in you?" Quint didn't realize he'd spoken the question out loud until Eric answered.

"I'm the best stud around."

Quint snorted. For some reason, Quint couldn't see the two of them as a couple. Eric was too shallow and Taryn too strong a personality for his kind. His insight pinged on a strong point. "She dumped you."

Eric's expression went from irritation to rage. "No woman dumps me."

Oh, yeah, that hit a big nerve. "Wrong. Taryn did." Quint released the pressure, grabbed Eric by the wrist, and hauled him to his feet. "Now, you're coming with me to the gym to confess to Taryn what you did. Then you're going to promise to stay out of her life. *Capisce?*"

"Bullshit. You and what army is going to make me?"

Quint pinched the junction of the man's shoulder and neck hard enough for Eric to flinch while wrenching his arm behind his body. "What were you saying?"

"You're a jackass."

"Better than being a thief." He motored Eric forward, out of the apartment, and all the way into his car.

"What are you, some kind of cop?" Eric eyed him from the passenger's seat.

"Just a concerned friend."

"Uh, huh. You've got the hots for her and think dragging me in is going to win you brownie points."

Quint glanced over at Eric and pulsed his psychic powers, just enough to put fear into the idiot. Because, as it was, Eric's ego and bravado were more than enough to outweigh any common sense he possessed.

Eric's eyes widened, his mouth opened. A second later, he blinked, faced forward, and kept his mouth blessedly shut. Quint didn't use his skills without conscience, but determined a moment of mental pressure would be much better in the long run than beating the shit out of the guy.

Thankfully, a few minutes later, they were standing in Taryn's office at the gym. She stood against the back wall, her arms crossed over her chest, and green eyes filled with fury as Eric confessed his actions. Every now and again, her gaze lifted to land on Quint before returning to Eric.

"You're such a jackass, Eric." Her tone and words scathed hot enough to draw blood. "Can't stand to lose, can't stand up to be a real man." She scowled at him. "And to think I was stupid enough to go out with you."

"That trophy belongs to me. You know it." He stared her down.

Taryn didn't cow. Not in the least. Instead, she strode over to Eric, stopped a couple of feet from him, and lowered her voice to a whisper. "Do you really want to go there?"

He lifted his head. "Try me."

Quint, who had been leaning against the side wall, stood up straight, ready to intervene.

Taryn shook her head at him. "You want to take this to the mat? I'll kick your ass in front of everyone, and you know it."

Eric flinched slightly. "Fine. Keep your fucking trophy. It's a stupid piece of tin anyway." He spun on his heel and marched out of the office with angry steps, slamming the door behind him, or would have, if Quint didn't catch it just before it flew shut with a loud bang.

Taryn blew out a breath. "Stooping to burglary. That's a new low for him." She scrubbed her forehead and plopped down in her chair. "Thank you for intervening. I really appreciate it."

Quint took the seat opposite, watching her face. Where fire existed before, now exhaustion and worry trod, as if a huge weight had been added to her burden. His heart tugged. "He won't bother you again."

She peered over at him. "I'm not so sure about that." A second of silence passed as if he were considering her words. "But even if he does, he knows he can't win. I can take care of myself."

Quint had no question about that. "What did you mean about taking it to the mat?"

A ghost of a smile tickled her lips. "Once before, he wanted to go all caveman. I challenged him to a sparring match. Ended up kicking his ass."

Quint grinned. "Yeah, I can see how a guy with his

ego wouldn't live that down."

"I thought he'd relegated himself to snarling and hateful digs. Guess not."

Worry darkened her pretty eyes and pressed her shoulders down. A flood of protective instincts flared inside Quint. "Still, I don't think he'll be much of a bother."

She tilted her head. "What did you do to him? He's all about pushing his weight around. Yet you managed to drag him in here for a confession."

Quint shrugged. "We had a little talk."

"Uh, huh." Her expression turned curious. "Military or cop?"

He smiled a little. "We've been through this before."

"Yep, and you never answered the question." Her lips curled up a smidgen at the corners.

"Well, it's not good to blab my whole life story on the first date, is it?"

"Hmmm." Taryn rested her elbows on the desk and tapped her lips with her steepled fingers. "Maybe we should try again?"

"Dinner. On me. At Bobbie's."

"Deal."

****

Taryn peered over at Quint, noting the way he handled his fork with efficiency—no extra actions, no tight grip, just a firm hold and motions filled with finesse. She'd noticed he moved in the very same way. Nothing hurried or jerky. Just fluid confidence with a cat-like grace. No one came by that kind of ability completely by nature. While some were born less klutzy than others, she'd never seen anyone with as much polish as Quint before. A trait, perhaps inherited, but certainly honed with years of practice.

Then, there was the shock when Quint showed up at the gym with Eric in tow. A couple of looks and gestures followed before Eric spilled the beans. Shocked, she could only listen to the confession, disbelieving in what Eric said. Not because he tried to steal the trophy from her. No, that pretty much lined up with the snake that he was. What stunned her was that Quint had persuaded Eric to not only show up to tell his tale, but also to apologize and promise to leave her be. Never in her life would she have expected anyone to hold power over Eric. Yet Quint did. Someway and somehow.

"What did you do to Eric to get him to confess?" She posed the question again, knowing Quint would likely dodge the answer like before. He seemed to hold onto secrets amazingly well. Most men would be boasting how they took the mighty Eric down. Not Quint.

Quint met her eyes. "We had a chat. That was all."

"Why do I think it's more involved than that?" She took a bite of her meatloaf and chewed.

"He's not entirely stupid." Quint sipped his water. "What I don't understand is what you ever saw in him."

Sheepishly, Taryn shook her head. "Blinded by muscles. That's the only excuse that I have."

Quint's lips twitched. "Hormones and throwback instincts, huh?"

She sighed heavily. "Unfortunately, some of us aren't as highly evolved as others. It causes some moments of stupidity."

Quint grinned. "It happens."

"To you?" She paused with her fork halfway in the air, eager to hear his answer.

"Sure." He took two more mouthfuls without saying another word.

"Such as?" she prompted.

He shrugged. "Oh, the usual teenage stuff, I suppose. Showing off for girls. Staying out later than curfew. That kind of stuff. Nothing big."

"Drooling like a puppy at the sight of a fine female rear?"

"Maybe." A tiny grin followed, indicating probable guilt. He wrapped his fingers around his glass, drawing her attention to a tiny cut.

"What happened there?"

"Where?"

She gestured with her hand. "The cut on your finger."

He lifted his hand up, glanced at it, then shrugged as he reached for his glass again. "Just a little scratch. Nothing big. No clue what caused it."

She pursed her lips in frustration. Trying to get the truth out of Quint was a challenge and probably a task of futility. Oddly enough, that fact gave her a bit of comfort. If anyone could handle her invisibility trait, they had to be able to keep a giant secret from the rest of the world. Her life hung in the balance.

"I'm still impressed you wiped the mat with Eric. He's a good-sized dude."

A smile filled with pride came along with the memory. "He was so full of himself. Thought since I was a woman that he'd knock me down in two seconds." She shook her head. "Never underestimate a woman. A woman who just happened to study martial arts for as long as she can remember."

Quint studied her. "Unusual undertaking, especially in these rural areas, I'm sure."

Taryn shrugged. "I liked learning."

"What degree did you earn?"

"Black belt, of course." She grinned at him. "Seventh degree." She forked another bite. "I would have pursued even higher, but that's the limit my instructor could do. In order to advance, I'd have to go to the big cities, and that's a heck of a long drive."

"Wow. That's incredible." Respect and admiration reflected from Quint's gaze. "No wonder you kicked his butt."

She shrugged. "The bigger they are, the harder they fall."

He smiled. "I suppose that's right."

"Oh, yeah. It is." She took a drink of her sweet tea and returned to eating.

"So, you're a seventh-degree black belt in…?"

"Karate. I studied the other martial arts, too, but leaned toward karate."

"You're a champion at target shooting and at paintball, too." He lifted his glass but didn't move it toward his lips. "Interesting choices of hobbies. Did you study those things for a reason? A future career in the military? A spy? Or perhaps an assassin?"

Taryn looked away from his intense stare. Uncomfortable, she forced herself to not wiggle under his scrutiny. Instead, she pulled on her sassy nature for a response. "Well, I could tell you, but then I'd have to kill you." She met his eyes with purpose.

He remained expressionless for a few seconds before a slow upward curl appeared on his lips followed by a chuckle.

The sound strummed her heartstrings and her sense of humor. She knew she would easily become addicted to it.

Too bad men are off my to-do list.

"Taryn, you're one of a kind." His smile held on.

"Is that good or bad?"

He stabbed a chunk of potato. "Let's just say there's no being bored around you."

She took that as a compliment.

Chapter 6

Taryn tapped her pen on the desk and sighed. Despite the big open house and a discount on memberships, the numbers didn't bounce up. No matter how many times she did the math, it fell short.

"Dang it."

"Dang what?"

Taryn glanced up to find Quint standing on the threshold, dressed in dark shorts and a white t-shirt. As always, he appeared impeccable, unlike her, with her hair escaping her ponytail after another lackluster practice session on the silks. "Oh, nothing. Come in for another workout?"

"Yep." He offered up a small smile. "I had fun last night."

"Me, too." She bit her lip slightly. While she spoke the truth, she hesitated to put too much emphasis on sharing a meal with Quint. It smacked of dating, and she'd pretty much tanked on that before. *Friendship, remember. Just aim for friendship.*

Quint opened his mouth, then closed it again, as if he changed his mind. "Let me know when you want to get together again. I'm always up for a nice dinner with great conversation." He offered up a slight wave and headed to the cardio equipment.

She watched him go with a sinking feeling. *It's best to deter him.* Her mind agreed the thought was rational but fell short of her true wishes.

Quint climbed on the EFX, set the program, and started. His arm muscles flexed and extended as did his legs. Large, rolling muscles which spoke of power, stamina, and rock hardness. Muscles that could last. And last. And last.

"Taryn. Earth to Taryn."

Taryn blinked and lifted her gaze. Meredith stood in the doorway. "Oh, hi, Mom."

Meredith frowned. "What in the world are you daydreaming about?" She stepped into the office.

"Nothing much."

Meredith glanced out over the gym. "Uh, huh. Wouldn't happen to be because of the hunk out there, would it?"

Taryn sighed again. She really didn't want to have this conversation with her adoptive mother. "Okay. I can't tell a lie. I was checking him out."

"Ah, I see." She smiled and looked once more. "He cuts a fine figure, for sure."

Taryn rolled her eyes. "Yeah, so did the others. They were all jerks in the end."

Meredith took the seat opposite Taryn. "Live and learn, dear. The rules of the dating game."

"Yeah, well, I stink at the dating game."

Meredith pursed her lips. "I think it's because you have such a tiny pond to fish in. Find a bigger pond, and you'll catch better fish."

She'd heard the same advice before. It hadn't stuck then, either. "So, what brings you by?"

"Lunch."

"Lunch?"

Meredith nodded. "I was in town shopping and

decided to pick us up some food so we could have a meal together."

Taryn smiled. "That's kind of you."

"Let's go to your apartment. It's only a few blocks away. That way we don't have to eat in here or in the hot car."

"Sure."

Meredith stood and waved her hand. "Besides, if I don't feed you now and again, I'm afraid you'll wither away."

"I'm not that bad." Taryn snorted.

"Living on sweet tea isn't the same as eating."

"Maybe. Maybe not." Taryn shut her office door behind her and followed her mother to her car. Without hesitation, she took the passenger's seat. The scent of fried chicken made her stomach growl.

A few minutes later, they sat at her small kitchen table, busily eating the fare Meredith provided.

Taryn appraised her adoptive mother. "So, what did you want to talk to me about?"

Meredith sat up straight and wiped her hands on a napkin. "Picked up on that, huh?"

"Yep. So, what is it?" Taryn waited impatiently for Meredith to spill the beans.

"Nothing really. I just wanted to touch base with you. See how things are going."

"The same." Things rarely changed in Rushing River. Everyone and everything worked on a routine schedule.

Meredith took a drink, her attention on the table. "Susan Redmon said the gym is really slow, that there's rumors of it closing."

Wonderful. Just what I didn't need—scuttlebutt

about the gym closing. If there was anyone thinking about joining, they'd change their mind and quickly. Taryn finished chewing her mouthful and swallowed. "Not that I want such bad publicity to get around, but yes, it's true. We're struggling. Hanging in there, but struggling. I'm pulling out all the stops to prevent it from happening."

Meredith's face pinched. "What are you going to do?"

"Go down with the ship, I guess." Taryn shrugged.

A true frown followed. "You can move back home. Your room is just like it was."

"No." Taryn paused. "No, thank you. I'll figure something out."

Meredith eyed her for a long moment. "What's keeping you here? You have so much talent, so pretty. You should be out exploring the world, not pinching pennies in this backwoods place."

A little exasperated, Taryn wiped her hands and rested her elbows on the table. "I've got everything that I need."

Meredith narrowed her eyes. "Family is a great thing, don't get me wrong, but sometimes you have to spread your wings to achieve greatness."

Taryn's shoulders fell. "I'm doing just fine."

"Really? Your car is ten years old."

"It runs just fine, too," Taryn defended.

"You have what? Three pairs of shoes?"

"I've never been a fashionista. You know that. Shoes and clothes aren't an obsession. They're just necessary items to get me through each day." She put a lid on her building temper. "The number of shoes or dresses don't equate to being a success."

Meredith folded her hands on the table and met Taryn's gaze steadily. "The case of your grandfather's death has been closed for years. Why can't you let it go?"

Taryn sucked in air. "You know why."

"Taryn. You can't change the past. You can only move forward. I hate to see you wasting all your time searching for something that doesn't exist."

Her appetite lost, Taryn took a large drink of water and chose her words carefully. "I appreciate your concern. I really do. I'll figure something out. Always did before and will do it again."

Meredith waited a few seconds before slowly nodding. "You've always been independent, maybe too independent for your own good."

"I've made it just fine." She rolled her shoulders to ease the tension. "I know you care for me—"

"Love you."

"And love me just like I love you. It's just that…" She struggled for the right words. "I need to make my own way. If the gym closes, I'll figure something out." She offered up a small grin. "Life is what happens when you're making other plans, right?"

Meredith shook her head. "That's how the saying goes. Unfortunately, I don't think that applies to everything."

Taryn took another sip. "I'm keeping my eyes open for options. Always do. I just don't know what the best path is. Right now, I'm staying the course. If things change, then I guess I'll change, too."

"The joys of youth." Meredith blew out a breath. "Got the world by the tail and not afraid to get bitten."

"Something like that," Taryn agreed.

"Well, if you need any help, you know your father and I will be more than happy to do whatever it takes."

"I know. And I really appreciate it." Taryn started picking up the trash from their meal. "And thank you for lunch. It was a great treat."

"You're welcome." Meredith stood. "You are coming for lunch on Sunday?"

"Yep. I'll be there."

"Gonna bring that fine young man with you?" Meredith's eyes lit up in curiosity.

"Nope. I gave up on men."

"You're too young to say that. Just wait."

"I know. I know. You want grandchildren one day."

"I do." Meredith hugged Taryn. "But I want you to be happy most of all. Don't give up on love. One day it will find you."

Unwilling to beleaguer the point, Taryn gave in. Marginally. "We'll see, Mom. We'll see. Thanks again." She shut the door behind her mother and finished clearing the table. After checking her watch, she walked back to her bedroom and peered into her closet. All her clothes fit inside easily. One pair of flats sat on the floor along with a spare pair of sneakers. Two dresses ended the line of workout clothes, t-shirts, and sweaters. She couldn't remember the last time she'd dressed up.

Maybe Mom's right. I'm withering away here in Rushing River.

And maybe those answers to Poppy's death aren't to be found either.

She walked back to the living room, sat on the sofa, and rested her head in her hands.

The light driving her seemed to be flickering and fast on the way to burned out.

If only a beacon would appear, one that could be relied on to show her the way.

Yeah, right, Taryn. Might as well wish for Prince Charming to rush to my rescue, sweep me off my feet, and carry me to his great castle where we'd love one another immensely for the rest of our lives.

Too bad fairy tales weren't true.

She snorted to herself. "This is modern times. I don't need a man to save me. Not when I can save myself and probably him, too."

She lifted her head and wiped at a tear. "Pull yourself up by the bootstraps, Taryn." The sound of her own voice cheered her only a little. "One day at a time. One crisis at a time. It'll work out."

If only deep down she believed it.

Chapter 7

Four days later

An instinctual feeling woke Quint from his bed. For a second, he remained absolutely still, trying to determine what nagged at him. Finally, he heard it—the sound of a shower turning on.

He glanced at the clock and groaned. Six a.m. *Of course, she'd be an early riser. Every single day of the week.*

That first afternoon, he'd decided to respect her privacy. Then, her crazy ex, Eric, broke in to steal her trophy. The very next day, he changed his mind. The girl never slept. He noticed her trend of staying up late, working on the computer—trying to track down Dalliance. He didn't even have to guess as she'd cursed at the computer often about being blocked and dead ends. Then, she'd be up at the crack of dawn, get around, and on the go. Sometimes she headed to the gym. Other days she took a jog around the nearby park. Fine and dandy, except she made an easy target gallivanting around by herself. She might have excellent self-defense skills, but they couldn't save her from Davis's bullets or the psionic blast from his mind.

"She's too damn hard to protect." Not to mention she was wearing him out.

He was already fatigued. Worn down. Hunting was

a wearing marathon. More than that, he feared repercussions of his job. Not pissed-off relatives or friends tracking him down. No, he worried about his slow but consistent loss of compassion and emotions. He'd become more stoic. More serious. More on task. Each kill stole a little more of his precious soul. As much as he wanted to halt the progression, he didn't know how. No one else at Dalliance possessed his particular talent. He was a natural for the job. A necessary one for the benefit of others, but one that was slowly sucking the humanity from him.

The distinct sound of counter doors opening and closing drew his attention back to Taryn.

He'd taken advantage of her absence from home during work hours a couple of days ago, slipped into her apartment, and placed a single listening device in the living room. Like a baby monitor, the system conveyed each noise straight to him. He warred with the guilt of invading her privacy versus keeping her safe should Davis appear. Unless Quint was by her side every minute of the day, he couldn't protect her. Two doors down didn't count. Safety won out in the end.

He'd learned a lot about her in that short period of time. Her dedication and relentless pursuit of information earned his respect while her sharp wit and short temper with the computer amused him.

He stretched and yawned.

Too bad she wasn't cozy in his bed. If she wanted to rise with the roosters, he could put her early morning energy to good use.

Just the idea lit a fire in his groin.

Not what I need this morning.

Taryn compelled him, intrigued him, and kept his

libido firmly on simmer. She was attractive, bright, and witty—a great combination, if it wasn't for the situation. He feared she'd deduce something was up with him always being around. When that happened, he didn't have a clue what he'd say. Lying wasn't a strong suit. Nor was defending himself against a baseball bat raised in anger.

The lady had spirit, a quality he found more than attractive. It was alluring. Tempting. And maddening just the same.

He climbed out of bed, scrubbed his face, and started getting ready. After all, it was Saturday, and paintball awaited.

In truth, he'd been looking forward to this since she'd invited him to play. The days since, he spent time at the gym, careful not to appear a stalker. Afterward, he researched, checked for updates from Dalliance, and tried to figure out Davis's location and where he might possibly make his move. Trouble was, no one had any information, and Rushing River was an open land, filled with ample hiding places. The residents would easily pick up on a stranger, but he sincerely doubted Davis would bother to show himself in town. No. He'd reconnoiter, keep a low profile, then spring when the opportunity presented itself. Unfortunately, he had more than a few of those opportunities.

A cringe of regret washed over him. He hated using Taryn as bait, but like his father pointed out, she was in the crosshairs one way or another. His only shot at protecting her and nabbing Davis in the process was to stick to her like a burr in a donkey's tail.

He grinned at the analogy and hurried to the bathroom.

Two hours later, Quint scanned the paintball course with a keen eye. "This is it?"

"Yep." Taryn stopped about four feet from him. "Unless you've changed your mind?" She arched an eyebrow at him in obvious challenge.

He snorted and shifted his weight from one foot to the other. "Are you sure you're up for this? I might be an IT guy, but I'm not a slacker." Quint rested his paintball gun on his shoulder as he peered down at Taryn. She'd tossed out the invite; he'd jumped on the offer. After all, he'd been salivating to see Taryn in action since before he'd arrived. No matter how much she squirmed to try to get off the hook, he wasn't about to let her go. Not when they were in a dense wooded area known locally as the paintball forest. No fanciness with courses and obstacles. Only Mother Nature greeted them. Trees, brush, and a canopy of branches threw shadows upon the land. Hiding places galore existed.

He'd have put his foot down, except there had been no signs of Davis. As it was, his argument to start with a more open course was met with a scowl. Without a way to change her mind, he opted to stick to her six instead. Whether she liked it or not.

She smirked at him. "Absolutely."

"You think you're going to kick my ass, don't you?" Quint grinned with amusement at Taryn's inflated self-confidence, even though he enjoyed her playful spunkiness. No doubt she'd give him a run for his money. *Would she win? Probably. Was he going to make it easy? No way in hell.*

"Uh, huh." Her eyes twinkled with playful excitement.

He loved the sight. Eagerly, he accepted the

challenge. "What spoils go to the winner?

She sucked on her bottom lip. "I don't know. What do you suggest?"

A couple of ideas ran through his mind. Quickly, he discarded them both as too much too soon. "A kiss?"

Her face clouded up in confusion. "A kiss?"

He offered up a soft grin. "Yeah, why not? You know how, right?"

She scoffed. "What's your point?"

He leaned in closer. "My point is I'm wondering if your lips taste as delicious as they look."

Her gaze fell to the ground. "I…" She sighed.

Her obvious discomfort with his suggestion chided him with scathing accuracy. *Leery little vixen.* "Or…whoever loses treats the other to dinner?"

She peered up at him from under her eyelashes. A flicker of relief crossed her face. "That's a deal."

"Good." He looked around. "Where do you want to start, and what are the rules?"

"We'll count to ten, then commence shooting. That gives us both a chance to take cover. Whomever gets hit first loses. That's the extent of the rules." She hefted her rifle off her shoulder and into her hands.

"Got it." Quint mirrored her actions. "So, who's going to count?"

"One, two, three, five, ten." She was off like a doe, flying through the woods.

Well, hell. He hurried to the side, narrowly avoiding her first shot as he ducked behind a tree. Pinned down, he wracked his brain for a foolproof plan. After all, he was good at details.

****

"IT consultant, my left foot. You're military." She

studied him with a keen eye.

"I can honestly say I've never been in the military." He skirted the topic as best he could. His gut pushed him to tell her the truth. Good thing his more rational mind kept his mouth shut.

"Then what? People aren't just born with that kind of skill."

I'm a hunter. The words remained unsaid out loud. "I still wasn't up to beating you."

A small grin tickled her lips. "True, but you came dang close, so don't get down on yourself. That's more than most teams at the paintball tournaments have been able to do."

He offered up a small smile. "Either way, my loss. I'm footing the bill for dinner. Just tell me when and where."

Crack. Splat.

The telltale sounds put Quint into defensive mode. He launched himself at Taryn, took her to the ground, and covered her with his body.

"What?"

"Shh. Be still." He buried his face in her shoulder, protecting her in the only way he could.

When no other gunshots rang through, Quint slowly raised off Taryn, keeping one hand on her back. "Stay down. I'm going to look around."

She tensed under his hand. "I'm more than capable—"

"—of listening and doing what I tell you." He added command to his voice, hoping she'd obey.

Who would be shooting at them—with live ammo, no less—leaped to priority in the line of a dozen questions. He doubted Eric had the balls to go after them, not after his confrontation with Quint. That left a couple of options—Davis or some other lunatic hunting humans. Neither bode well.

Quint opened up his mind and put out feelers, trying to locate any hint of paranormal powers. Nothing reflected back. Not unusual, as he could only pick up on the residual energy when it was in use. If Davis tried to kill them the old-fashioned way, with a lethal gunshot, he didn't have to use his powers in the least.

Yet, the more he thought about it, the less likely it was Davis. He'd boast of his strength and unstoppable powers. To shoot them was simply too easy. That didn't mean he wasn't above terrifying them beforehand.

Quint maintained his crouched position, moving quietly and quickly to another area of brush. Lifting up, he peered through the cover, trying to locate the culprit. A quick shot put him right back down.

Shit. He crept a few feet farther to the side, slunk behind a tree, before edging forward in the shooter's direction.

Another shot rent the air.

Quint glanced back, found Taryn gone, and cursed to himself. The need to find her and keep her safe outweighed just about everything else.

A thud and grunt followed.

Quint peered around a bush just in time to watch a red pickup tear out of there, skidding on the gravel as it went.

That didn't shock him near so much as Taryn reappearing before his eyes. At the same time, he picked up on traces of paranormal power and knew, just knew, she carried a special ability—one that he'd never personally ran into before.

Standing, he hurried out of the brush and to her side. "Are you okay?"

She studied him for a moment before crossing her arms over her chest, a defensive mechanism he was beginning to recognize. "Yep. And you?"

"Fine." He tried to slow his speeding heart and catch his breath at the same time. Not from the exertion but from the knowledge that Taryn used her skills to protect him, and that could have easily cost her life.

Turning his attention to the cloud of dust still wafting in the air, he forced himself to think. "Any idea who that truck belongs to?"

"Nope. No plates, either. He was wearing one of those pull-over Halloween masks, so I didn't get to see his face." Frustration and annoyance laced her statement.

He appraised her, finding nothing out of the ordinary that couldn't be explained by a game of hide and seek in the woods. She wasn't tense or crying, not even uptight. If he was judging her right, she was in her zone, which really said something. Anyone else that had been shot at would be jittery from adrenaline. Taryn appeared calm and steady, though a bit tired. If he hadn't already known better, he'd have pegged her for that assassin label. Or an experienced beat cop. One of the two.

"How did you get up here so quickly?"

She glanced away. "He was focused on you, leaving me free to approach. Typical paintball strategy."

He couldn't say she was lying, but she definitely was leaving something important out, namely her ability to evade being seen. How she did it, he didn't have a clue. Whether she could jump large spaces like with teleportation or simply disappear from sight, he didn't know.

Something else tweaked his memory. He didn't recall anything being mentioned about her grandfather carrying any paranormal abilities. Certainly, Reginald would have known if that was the case. The trait might have come from the other side of the family or just skipped generations. That stood to reason. However, his gut told him something didn't quite fit. He made a mental note to pursue that lead later. Right now, he had other issues more pressing.

"Who would shoot at us? Eric?" He wondered out loud.

"If he grew a pair of balls that huge in the past couple of days, I'd be greatly impressed." She scowled. "He wouldn't dip down to murder. Paybacks, sure. But using real ammo isn't his style."

Quint considered her input. "Maybe he paid someone?"

"Could be." She rolled her shoulders. "Either way, I guess we've had our fun for the day."

"When I find out who's responsible, I'm going to take it out of their hide." He stepped close to her and cupped her chin with his hand. "Because nothing is going to happen to you on my watch."

She frowned. "Since when did you become my keeper?"

"Since now."

She pulled away from his touch. "Forget it, Quint. I can take care of myself." Turning, she tromped back through the woods, presumably to retrieve her rifle.

He chafed at her rebuff and independent nature, but

knew that was one of her strongest, most compelling features. Releasing a slow breath, he regained his composure before catching up to her. Gently grabbing her arm, he stalled her progress until he could step in front of her. "If there's a person on this earth that I believe can take care of themselves, it's you. However, we're still mortal, and those bullets are a reminder of that."

Taryn peered up at him. "Thank you, I think." She worried her lip for a second, the only sign of nervousness in the whole ordeal. "Why do I have a feeling you're going to have another 'chat' with Eric?" She did the quotation marks in the air.

He managed a tiny smile. "Are you a mind reader?"

"Nope. It's written on your face, along with that feral smile that tells me you're going to enjoy every minute of the encounter."

"There's that." He released her in order to gather his supplies.

"I don't need you to defend me." The words came out as a firm order.

He glanced back at her. "Hey, they were aiming at me, too. That means we're in this together." The words sounded right to his ears.

She spared him a look as she pulled the strap of her paintball rifle over her shoulder.

After latching onto his gun and bag, he led her back to the car. "I had a good time. Well, until someone took pot shots at us."

She smiled over at him. "Me, too. Never a dull moment around you."

You can say that again.

Too bad she was putting off vibes of independence. He'd gladly take her home, wrap her up in his arms, and chase the lingering adrenaline away.

One look at her face crushed that particular plan.

She exuded confidence and determination, like she'd embraced the battle of life and death and won.

Technically, she had. So far.

He intended to see that trend continue.

****

Taryn returned home, cleaned and stored her paintball gun, grabbed a bottle of tea out of the fridge, and sat at the table. *Okay. Now you can have a nervous breakdown.*

Oddly enough, only a few jitters happened. Someone tried to kill her and Quint, and yet she handled the stress like a seasoned pro. *What the heck?*

As soon as Quint separated himself to draw the fire, she used her talent to become invisible. Without hesitation, she made a beeline for the shooter, caught him with a kick and a right hook. The widening of his eyes in obvious surprise only lasted for a moment before he raced back to the truck, climbed in, and sped off.

Even then, she wasn't uptight or shaky. Just angry. So very angry.

"I guess that's better than falling apart." She looked to the bright side. Her timely interference might have saved their lives. On the other hand, she was pretty sure Quint noticed her disappear and reappear once more. *Not good. Not good at all.*

She glanced around the room, finding it somehow lacking. The peace she once claimed hanging out at home seemed to have fled, being replaced by restlessness.

Too much happening at once.

The excuse sounded solid. Yet she wondered if things would ever settle down again.

A quiet knock interrupted her thoughts.

With a weary sigh, she answered the summons, finding Quint standing in the hallway. "Hi."

He offered up a small smile as he studied her face. "I wanted to check on you. Make sure you were okay."

A protective hunk. She could do worse. *Heck, I have done worse.* "Yeah. I'm fine. Just getting ready to hit the shower."

"Okay." He didn't step inside, just waited in the hallway. "Want to go out to lunch? My treat. All spoils of the paintball loss, too."

Taryn hesitated. Sure, she could hang around her apartment and clean. Or go to the gym for a workout. Or even a run in the park. Watching television didn't excite her, especially as she only had the basic three channels. Extra money didn't exist for anything more. There was always endless research on the computer or grocery shopping. None of them appealed. Spending time with Quint made her a little leery after this morning and what he presumably saw. Yet she'd have to face the choir at some time. Besides, she was hungry. "Okay."

A true smile brightened his face, making him all the more handsome. "Great. Where did you want to eat? Bobbie's?"

"I don't care, but if we keep showing up at Bobbie's together, people will start talking."

"So?"

"So, you'll be the subject of town gossip."

He shrugged. "Doesn't bother me. Does it bother you?"

"No. It's not the first time I've attracted their attention. Probably won't be the last." Not that the community turned mean. Not at all. Taryn just considered them bored. With nothing much to occupy their time, they turned to tidbits of gossip for entertainment. "There's a little burger place near the lake. They have good food. Great waffle fries. And the view is excellent overlooking the water." Soothing. Relaxing. Away from it all. *Yeah, that place will do nicely today.*

"Perfect. I'll drive. You point the way."

About an hour later, Taryn chomped down on a waffle fry and stared across the blue waters from the covered balcony of the restaurant. The slight breeze cooled the air, making the day much more temperate. All the other customers chose to hang out inside, leaving Quint and Taryn enjoying their meals to themselves.

"These are great." Quint held up another fry.

"Told you so. As far as junk food, this is the place to go." She offered up a smile. "Can't beat the view."

"It's perfect. Something about the water is so relaxing. Reminds me of home."

"Where is home?"

"Portland, Oregon."

"Aha. Pacific Ocean."

Quint nodded before taking a bite of his burger. "Yep."

"Yet you're here." She tilted her head and grasped her plastic cup of tea.

"I travel around. Remember? Seeing the sights as I

go."

She took a drink. "Find a place you want to call home?"

He shrugged. "The wanderlust still pushes me, if that's what you're asking."

If the gym closed, most likely Quint would pull up stakes and head off to greener pastures. The thought pushed Taryn's shoulders downward, adding to the already hefty burden she carried.

"Where do you practice your target shooting?"

The change of subject momentarily stifled Taryn. She paused with the burger partway to her mouth. "There's a shooting range not too far. I sign up for times." *Until I no longer have a job.* When the money dried up, so did her practice sessions. Local law enforcement and residents frowned upon individuals tromping through the woods and shooting at random targets. Without practice time, her skills would grow rusty, eliminating one potential source of income. Certainly not steady income, but picking up a winner's paycheck now and again bolstered her bank account. "Thinking about giving it a try?"

"Yeah. I'm not a stranger to shooting. It's been a while, though. Might want to try my hand again."

She smiled and placed her food back on her plate. "I'll call, see if we can reserve the range for after lunch." Pulling her cell phone out of her purse, she punched the contact number. Two minutes later, she returned her phone and met Quint's waiting expression. "Two o'clock. They've blocked off the west range for us."

He blinked. "Wow. A whole range for us?"

"I'm there a lot, and they know that I need space

and long range." She picked up her burger and took another bite.

"What made you want to be a sharp shooter in the first place?"

The pertinent question made Taryn think. She hated to fib, but telling him the absolute truth would be a leap of faith. Trust wasn't her strong suit. "It's a challenge. And I enjoy besting the men. They hate it, but I like showing that women can do anything a man can."

"You're a barracuda." He stared at her with an expression of amazement and respect.

She laughed. "Not sure about that, but I'll take it."

Taryn ate a little more, enjoying the day, the outing, and the company.

"You never really said what drew you to being an ace shot in the first place."

Taryn stalled by taking another drink, deciding on her answer. "Did you ever have a dream, a grand ambition as a kid? Something you just knew you could do and wanted to do above anything else?"

"Yeah."

"What was it?" she prodded.

"I wanted to be the starting catcher for the Cardinals."

She grinned at the revelation. "A huge baseball fan, I take it."

"Yep. I watched it all the time. My parents enrolled me in Little League. I practiced and practiced, even attended a couple of camps."

"So, what happened to that dream?"

"I discovered I was pretty damn average by the time I hit junior high. Sure, I could have worked harder, but the bubble had been burst. I guess that I grew up and my goals changed."

She nodded, finding the glimpse into Quint's childhood enlightening. "I guess it's like that sometimes. I grew up knowing I wanted to be an ace. To be better than anyone else. To fulfill a...dream." She faltered for just a split second but recovered quickly.

"Like the Olympics?"

"Sort of." *A good enough and safe reason. Too bad it wasn't the truth.*

"Are you still after that dream? Or have you decided on a new one?"

His insightful question made her pause. "I really don't know." At least, that was an honest answer. "Lately, I've been asking myself that same thing."

He picked up another fry. "Which way are you leaning?"

She shook her head. "Steady as she goes unless life throws in a monkey wrench, I guess."

"Life does have a way of doing that." He offered up a half smile. "Are we going to have a prize for the winner of our little marksmanship competition?"

Curious, she leaned toward him. "What are you thinking?"

He rested his arms on the table, placing himself just a few inches from her. "That kiss."

Her stomach flipped over at his softly spoken words and the unmistakable hint of sensual hunger in his eyes. "One kiss?"

"One kiss. Unless you want more."

She thought for only a second. "One kiss. More is optional. But I'm going to win."

He studied her for a long moment. "Probably so. That just means I get to kiss you."

She should protest or at least balk. Those soft lips and his presence tipped the scales easily in his favor. "So, if I win, you kiss me. If you win, I kiss you?"

"Yep." His eyes held a hint of satisfied challenge.

"You're on."

Two hours later, she grinned like a banshee as her final shot nailed the target in the exact center, sealing her victory. "Bullseye."

"Damn." Quint stared at the target that had traveled all the way up a long line for them to see. "Dead center."

"Yep." She lowered her rifle and pointed it to the ground. "Don't discount yourself, though. From that range, most people can't even hit the target, let alone within a few inches."

Quint shrugged as he laid his rifle on the ground. "You're amazing." The spark in his eyes spoke of truth and something else.

She tilted her head and eyed him warily. "Uh, huh. Why are you looking at me like I'm a strawberry sundae with a cherry on top?"

He chuckled. "The wager. Remember?"

A kiss. She wanted to kick herself to agreeing to such a silly reward. "How could I forget?" She shifted her weight from one foot to the other in delay. It wasn't that she didn't want to give him a test run. Nope. It was the almost certain knowledge that he'd become as addictive as her sweet tea that had her a bit leery.

Before she could think of a way out of the dilemma, he cupped her cheeks, leaned in, and ever so lightly brushed his lips over hers.

Soft. Full. Delicious. She savored the moment their lips clung before he lifted his head.

His eyes danced as he read her face.

She offered up a tentative grin. "To the winner goes the spoils." With that said, she wrapped her arms around his neck and swooped in. Tender and hesitant fell to the wayside as she let her reservations free.

Quint met her with equal enthusiasm, pressing and just as demanding. Then, he opened his mouth and traced her lips with his tongue.

A tremor raced through her at the small, intimate caress.

Startled out of her momentary loss of control, she staggered back a step, her gaze locking on Quint's face. Her heart raced, and her breath hitched. Butterflies took flight in her stomach despite the quickness of the affection.

He smiled wickedly at her. "I'm up for more."

She composed herself with a sarcastic snort. "Debt paid and accepted. Time to get back home. Some of us have to work early tomorrow." With one more quick look, she turned and sauntered off. Before she did something stupid—like kiss him again.

Damn, Taryn. You're playing with fire and bound to get burned.

Too bad the warning only heightened her desire.

Chapter 8

"Brandon isn't coming?" Taryn asked as she helped Meredith set the table for their usual Sunday family lunch.

"He's looking for a new truck," her father, Ben, answered.

Taryn grabbed the piping hot dish of green beans and set it on a hot pad near her father's seat. "His truck is only a couple of years old. Why is he getting a new one?"

Ben took his seat with a shrug.

Meredith carefully placed the ham in the center. Task done, she removed the protective mitts, grabbed a fork and knife, then began slicing. "He's trying to impress someone if you ask me."

"Jennifer putting pressure on him?" Taryn asked as she took a seat in her usual chair. She filled her glass with tea, then passed the pitcher on to her father.

"Maybe. He's head-over-heels for her. Been taking her out a lot, buying her presents." Ben's face clouded. "I tried to tell him that she's using him, but he won't listen."

Meredith passed out ham to each of them. "I don't know that it's all her. Brandon is climbing the ladder at the company. He wants the top position. I don't think he'll be happy until he owns the whole place."

Brandon took a job with the race car manufacturing

business right out of high school. He'd dabbled with college, finally getting serious on a degree when he landed an office job. First, he worked sales, traveling the country to attend races and speak to drivers and sponsors about the latest gadgets for the expensive fast cars. He soon tired of that, worked hard for a promotion, and now oversaw the sales line.

The whole system broke down pretty simply. The engineers fashioned new tools, parts, and components in order to make the cars faster and safer. After testing, if they showed promise, the owner and his support staff made a decision on their relevance. If it passed the grade, that item went out with the sales crew on the road. Since Brandon headed the sales department, he got a gander at all the approved stuff before it became available to anyone else.

Taryn never cared much for the automobile industry, but Brandon lived and breathed sports cars. He'd found his dream job, for sure. "He left his keys at work again the other day. Second time lately. I had to retrieve them for him." Taryn added beans to her plate, then a fried apple from another dish after her mother finished getting her serving with the dipping spoon. "I think he's too busy using his southern brain thinking of Jennifer rather than paying attention to his job."

Ben's gaze snapped over to her. "You shouldn't do that. It's too risky." Worry covered his face.

Taryn shrugged. "I waited for the guards to change shifts and slipped in after them. It wasn't a big deal." *Until they decided to get chatty. That just about got ugly.* But she wasn't going to tell her adoptive parents that. No way.

"Taryn. It's a big deal." Her father stared at her

with a firm expression. "Your abilities are great, but they're also dangerous. You take them for granted, treat them carelessly." His lips thinned. "What if they failed and you were caught? You'd go to jail."

"I'm always careful, Dad. Really." She knew the consequences, but she couldn't tell Brandon no.

Besides, they came in handy at the paintball course yesterday. She'd been able to tackle the shooter before he could lodge a bullet in her or Quint. He'd gotten away, unfortunately. Still, no one had been hurt, which was a blessing. Her nightmares had shown just what the potential outcome could have been instead.

She hadn't mentioned the episode to her parents. No sense in getting them riled and worried when they couldn't do a thing about it. *Besides order me to move back into their house.* Which wasn't going to happen, come hell or high water.

He frowned. "I don't care how careful you are; it's not enough." He blew out a breath and put down his fork. "Brandon is an adult. Stop bailing him out and risking yourself in the process. Let him make his own mistakes."

Taryn blinked at the leashed anger in his voice. "If I can help, then why shouldn't I?"

"Because." He opened his mouth then shut it again. After a quick shared look with his wife, he spoke again. "You're special, Taryn, meant for so much more. You have the motivation and intelligence to go far. Don't let Brandon ruin that."

Okay. What is that supposed to mean? She started to ask, only for Meredith to begin talking once more.

"How are the aerials going? You said you were working really hard to perfect them so you can start offering classes." Meredith changed the topic smoothly as she cut her meat into smaller pieces.

Nope. I'm not letting this go. She looked over at her father. "Wait a second. What are you talking about, Dad?"

Ben glanced at her then back to his plate. "Nothing. It's just that you're smart and pretty. You can go anywhere, do anything. It's a shame to risk such a bright future because Brandon can't get his head out of his butt."

"But..."

"Your mother asked a question," Ben reminded her.

Obviously, we're moving on.

Taryn sighed, sat up straighter, and began to eat. "It's okay, I guess. I've got a long way to go. Never considered myself klutzy until I started working on those silks."

"You'll get there. You always do." Meredith smiled softly. She chewed for a few seconds then swallowed. "Have you thought about going to graduate school again?"

Taryn shook her head. She'd earned her bachelor's degree at a small nearby college. Her field of study, psychology, didn't open a whole lot of doors. Although it did help her deal with clients better, see them in a new light, even the testy ones. "Not really. I'd have to go to a bigger city. And the money isn't there, either."

"So you get loans or grants. Don't they have student workers that get paid?" Meredith asked.

Ben nodded. "Graduate assistants. They get a stipend, and their tuition is covered." He brightened. "Why don't you look into schools? I'm sure you'll qualify for any of them."

Something's up. Her parents were acting a little odd, and she intended to find out why. Taryn paused with the fork halfway to her mouth. "Why do I get the feeling you're trying to get rid of me?"

"Oh, never that." Meredith took a sip of her tea. "It's just you're at an age where you can follow all your dreams. Instead, you're hanging around this one-horse town with little to offer."

Here we go again. "This place has a lot to offer. Peace. Tranquility," Taryn replied.

"Do you have those things?" Ben asked.

Taryn bit back the "no" before it slipped out. Especially considering yesterday's paintball outing with Quint.

"How are you ever going to meet a man, to fall in love, to really live your life, if you stick around here?" Meredith asked.

"There are guys here," Taryn pointed out. *Like Quint.* But she wasn't bringing him up in this conversation. No way, no how.

"Like Eric?" Ben asked with a hint of sarcasm.

That remark stung a little. Taryn narrowed her eyes at him. She'd also refrained from mentioning the jerk breaking into her apartment. All under the heading of taking care of herself and maintaining her independence without her parents on her back all the time.

"None to speak of," Meredith insisted, drawing the attention back to herself. "You know that for a fact."

Taryn dropped the food in her mouth, chewed, then swallowed. For a split second, she thought of telling them about Quint, then opted not to. That would bring up too many questions that she wasn't prepared or willing to answer. "I'm happy here."

Meredith shook her head slightly as if disagreeing. "Are you really?"

The deep question made Taryn stop and consider her present situation. "I'm not unhappy." Uncomfortable with the tone of the conversation, Taryn focused on eating, hoping her adoptive parents would take the hint.

"You've never left the state. Never really had a vacation. Work, work, work is all you do," Meredith pointed out.

No such luck. Damn it.

Taryn sighed heavily. "I have to work because I'm not rich. I like my job, too. Flexible hours, great people to work with." Totally on the defensive, she tried to keep her frustration in check.

"*If* the gym can remain open," Meredith retorted.

"I'm working my butt off to make sure it happens." Taryn wracked her brain, offered discounts, and uncommon classes to entice people to purchase a membership. Even if they only paid for a single class, it helped.

"What about your goals?" Ben asked.

"What goals?" Taryn asked.

"That's your first problem. You need dreams, challenging goals. Something that compels you to do something." Ben stuffed some food into his mouth and chewed. "Something besides spending your free time searching on that damn computer for ghosts."

Taryn's fork clattered to the plate. "It's not ghosts, and you know it." Anger surged as she stared at the man who had taken her in, supported her, and now seemed eager to send her on her way.

Meredith cleared her throat. "Would you like some more tea, Taryn?"

Taryn swiveled her head to stare at her. "Do you, too, think that it's stupid for me to be searching for the men that killed my grandfather?"

A long, silent pause followed. Meredith wiped her face with her napkin, then met Taryn's eyes. "No, it's not stupid, not at all. However, I see your life flashing by, all your time wasted on the effort that hasn't netted you anything." She reached over and patted Taryn's hand. "Honey, it's been years. Nothing has come to pass. Dead ends. *Endless* dead ends. Even the authorities have come up clueless." She offered up a small, encouraging smile. "Maybe it's time you let it go and focus on your life instead."

The words soaked in. Not like she hadn't thought of them a hundred times before. Every time she hit a road block, she questioned the sanity in pursuing, in spending so much time and energy trying to break a case that even the authorities had tucked away in a forgotten file cabinet in the cold case basement.

"I don't know." She dropped her face into her hands. "I promised…"

"You were a young child, Taryn. Sometimes mysteries just can't be solved," Ben added gently. "This is one of them. You need to let it go and focus on the living, not the dead."

Her appetite gone, Taryn rested her elbows on the table. She rubbed her forehead and tried to imagine a day without the relentless drive to discover the truth. "I don't know that I can. It's all I've really known."

Meredith smiled with understanding. "Sometimes we just have to break out of that old mold and create a new one."

"Could be." The admission added a flare of hope, along with a healthy dose of guilt.

How can I just let the killer walk free?

She considered the situation for a second longer.

What if there's no choice but to do just that?

"Just think about it, sweetheart. We'd love to see you making a difference in your own special way. Rushing River just isn't a place where you can really spread your wings and fly." Meredith gave Taryn's hand a squeeze. "We chose to move here to get away from the rat race, but even we're thinking of packing up and heading to greener pastures."

"Really?" Taryn never thought she'd hear those words. Her adoptive parents seemed perfectly content on their small square of earth.

"Yes," Ben affirmed.

"Where will you go?" Taryn just couldn't see the couple, both pushing fifty, picking up stakes and heading to the big city. They'd pecked out a living in rural America way too long to adjust to the commotion of urban life. She wasn't sure she could, either.

Meredith glanced to Ben and back again. "We're not sure. Just something we're discussing."

Taryn took a drink of her tea. "What about Brandon?"

"He's busy climbing the ladder of success," Ben answered.

There's that.

Taryn picked up her fork and started eating. She had much to think about, and none of those issues would be solved in a day. *Unfortunately.*

Another question popped into her mind, one she'd

asked before but had been shut down fast. "How did you end up with me?"

Ben stared at his plate after taking another bite. "A foster agency approached us. You needed a home and had no living family left. We had room and the want for more children. I believe we've gone over this a few times before." A hint of censure and warning entered his voice.

She took a second to process that. "How did I get from Texas to Minnesota?"

Meredith sat up straighter in her seat. "I don't know. The local agency contacted us."

"The agency? A state agency? There will be records." The wheels began to turn in Taryn's mind. Hope and excitement flared.

Ben's gaze flew to Meredith. "Not state. Private."

That didn't matter in the least. "They will have records," Taryn reiterated.

Meredith took another drink. "They closed years ago."

Too coincidental. Taryn paused eating and eyed one adoptive parent then the other. Realization struck as she easily read the hint of guilt on their faces. A warning bell sounded in her head. "You're keeping secrets. *From me.*" The statement came out with a healthy dose of tempered anger.

The room remained silent.

Not about to give up, Taryn pursued the topic. "Why did the agency approach you?"

Meredith squirmed in her seat. "We were on the list. Been wanting to foster or adopt for a while."

The answer sounded flimsy to Taryn.

A revelation occurred in the form of an epiphany.

Maybe I've been going about this all wrong looking for the tattooed killer. Maybe I should have been backtracking my adoption, instead. The new direction felt right. She latched onto it with near desperate strength and determination.

She folded her arms on the table and stared at Meredith. "Why didn't you freak out when you saw me go partially invisible the first time?"

Meredith took a long drink, then swallowed. She returned the glass to the table, then peered over at Ben. "I saw it before when you were young. As I told you before." There was a little bite in her tone this time. Defensive. A warning to stop the questioning.

Taryn ignored it. Her gut told her she was on the right track and that her adoptive parents knew a lot more than they were saying. "You didn't think about taking me to a doctor or the hospital when you saw me go invisible the first time?"

Meredith shook her head, then narrowed her eyes at Taryn. "What would they do? Besides use you as a lab rat? I protected you," she bit out, clearly becoming angry.

"Protected me," Taryn whispered aloud and mused, "From whom?"

Meredith's lips thinned as her eyes flashed. Ben's face turned sour.

Taryn sat back in her seat. "One way or another I'm going to get to the bottom of this. Either you can help me or not." She looked at one then the other.

No answers came. *Damn it.*

She scooted her seat back and stood, overflowing with exasperation at her adoptive parents—the same people that were supposed to support her, help her. Not keep closemouthed on secrets that could help her break open the past. "I thought you cared about me. Loved me. I guess I was wrong." Turning on her heel, she made a beeline for the front door.

"Taryn, wait!" Meredith called after her.

Taryn paused with her hand on the door knob. "What is it?"

"Can't you just let sleeping dogs lie?"

Slowly, Taryn swiveled to face Meredith. "What would you do if someone brutally killed your only remaining family member? What if you saw them do it? Would you sit on your hands and hope that God will finally sort it out in the end? Or would you work day and night to bring justice to your loved one?" She waited a couple of beats. "Just think about that for a while."

With those parting words, she left the house, slid into her car, and drove off.

Chapter 9

Immensely irritated with her parents, Taryn returned back to her apartment early. She let herself in, sat on the couch, and cranked on the television, for noise more than anything else. Fat rain drops serenaded her on the way home, nearly soaking her as she ran from her car to the front door of the apartment building. The thunder which followed echoed her rumbling emotions, as did the violent crack of lightning nearby. Ordinarily, she'd boot up the computer and commence her endless search. The storm made that an impossibility. The desktop required plugging in to work and for the modem to allow her to connect to the internet. Lightning ruled that out.

Instead, she grabbed a pen and a notebook, jotting down the ideas racing through her mind. Emotions welled up along with the memories of her hard promise.

"I'll hunt them down, Poppy. I will." The familiar vow steadied her, allowing her to think rationally, focusing on links from her adoption and backtracking from there. When all the queries exhausted themselves, she set the notebook aside, folded her legs under her, and watched the rain outside her window.

Her mind drifted back to the woods. Something nagged at her. Something she couldn't quite put her finger on. Not just with the suspect, but with Quint as well.

He'd led her to believe he wasn't a highly trained person in the realm of the military or as a policeman. However, everything about the guy screamed otherwise—the way he moved, his lack of fear, the way he took over, commanding her to stay down.

Then there was something else. His eyes. She swore she caught a glimpse of redness.

Surely not. People's eyes didn't change colors. It had to be a trick with the shadows of the trees. That could easily explain it. Much like the red-eye situation in pictures. A trick of the brightness.

A knock at her door interrupted her thoughts. She stood, walked over to it, and peered out. Quint, large and dominating the small hallway, stood outside staring at her door. The casual jeans and a deep blue oxford shirt provided flair to his physical features. Yumminess in a complete package. While not huge, he just had a way about him. And she was always a sucker for muscles. Of which, Quint had many.

Without hesitation, she opened the door. "Hi."

"Hi." He smiled at her.

Her heart skipped a beat. "Come on in." She waved her arm, waited for him to enter, then shut the door behind him. "Make yourself at home. Did you want something to drink?"

"No, thanks." He glanced around the room before turning his attention back to her. "I was just thinking about getting some lunch and wondered if you wanted to go with me."

She shook her head, returned to the couch, and sat. The last thing she wanted to do was go out in public with her emotions all out of kilter. Besides, she'd just eaten. Well, part of her meal, anyway. "No, thanks."

Quint strode over and sat next to her. "What's wrong?"

His presence alone soothed her, made her feel significant, cared about. None of the other guys she'd dated had that ability by just stepping in the room. She met his gaze and put on a brave face. "Why do you think something's wrong?"

"Because you look ready to either kill something or cry."

She shook her head. "Nothing important."

A few ticks of the clock passed before Quint spoke again. "One thing I've picked up about you is that you're afraid of nothing. Strong and independent. Hell, getting shot at in the woods didn't faze you in the least. So, I'd say it's something a bit more than nothing now."

"I really don't want to discuss it. If you don't mind." She pushed a wayward strand of hair aside.

He pursed his lips but didn't argue. "How about dinner? My treat." He checked his watch. "At five?"

Unable to resist his offer, she nodded. "I'd like that."

"Good. See you then." He exited, quietly closing the door behind him.

A wave of guilt pressed her shoulders down. He'd only wanted to help, and she'd shut him out.

As much as she appreciated his concern, she just wasn't sure how much to tell him. They were friends. Loose friends. His life was mostly a mystery to her. She supposed he could say the same about her. Thus, blurting out that her parents weren't coughing up the information about her adoption after her grandfather was murdered seemed a little heavy for their newfound acquaintance.

Loose friends could date, right? Sleep together? Get handsy on the couch? Quint had the ability to make her sorely pressed to forget her vow to lay off men, especially the bad boys. His intriguing, yet charming nature should set off warning bells in her head. Instead, he got her engine revved. When she didn't want to cuddle up in his arms, that is. Her feminine side sprang to life when he was around.

How much trust did she have to have in a guy to sleep with him? Because, boy howdy, she was so ready to throw caution to the wind. Especially today. When the chips were down, she needed consolation and a major distraction.

And the ability to live with myself the next morning. She shut down that train of thought, fast.

Time passed as a variety of thoughts raced through her head. Everything from the attempts on their lives to the mystery of Quint. The next thing she knew, he knocked on her door, signaling time for their dinner.

She opened it and invited him in. "Long time no see."

He offered up a small smile and stepped inside, shutting the door behind him. "Yeah. Ready to go?"

"Not quite." She walked to the bathroom and combed her hair. After quickly brushing her teeth, she re-emerged to face Quint. "I've been wondering. Any word on the truck that the guy was driving?"

"Well, yes and no. That's something else I wanted to tell you." He rubbed at his leg as if straightening out a wrinkle in the denim. "I spoke with the local police this morning. They said the truck had been reported stolen. They found it abandoned a couple of hours away. No prints. No gun. Nothing to give them further leads."

She nodded. Just the fact that the truck turned up surprised her. With the amount of acreage to cover and the potential for the suspect to be anywhere, it resembled searching for a needle in a haystack. "What I can't figure out is why someone wants to kill me."

Quint pursed his lips, opened his mouth, then closed it again.

She waited patiently, then saw him appear to change his mind. Oddly enough, that bothered her. "What aren't you telling me?"

He met her gaze steadily. "I spoke with Eric again."

She cringed. "I told you he wouldn't stoop to murder."

"Yeah, I know. He was shocked when I told him what happened. I don't think he's a good enough actor to pull off that kind of surprise. Anyway, he understood he was a potential suspect and really started babbling about how he was jealous of your winnings but is over it now."

"I'll believe it when I see it," she muttered under her breath. Eric wasn't able to conceive that losing was all part of playing the game. Good sportsmanship meant diddly squat to him.

"I think he'll keep his distance from now on. Probably would have before but will do so now to keep his nose out of the investigation and his hands clean." Quint rubbed at his forehead. "Which leaves us empty handed for someone else."

Taryn sighed. "Yeah. I know." She pushed her ponytail off her shoulder and behind her back. "I've run all kinds of scenarios through my mind, and nothing clicks." She looked at him. "Might as well have a seat." She took the corner of the small sofa, waiting for Quint to sit next to her. "Do you have enemies that would be so bold as to try to kill you in broad daylight?"

He sat still for several seconds. No finger or toe tapping. No squirming. Just frozen in place. "There's no one after me."

The words he spoke rang true. Yet, what lay between the lines? Another thought came to the fore. "Wait a minute. You're an IT consultant, yet you were checking on the police record of the incident?"

Thunder roared.

Quint peered out the window before focusing on her again. "I was involved in the situation, was curious what they'd found, and wanted to make sure there's no threats to us." He scratched at his forehead. "From what they told me, they're treating this as an isolated case. Wrong place. Wrong time. That sort of thing."

She picked up on the slight hesitation in his tone. "But you don't think it was?"

He shrugged one shoulder. "I don't have any proof one way or another."

"But?" she pressed.

"Why weren't they shooting at us with paintball guns?"

She'd already considered that. "Hunting illegally?"

"On a paintball course? Surely there's not that many deer or squirrels around when there's people visiting all the time."

"I know." She tucked one leg under her. "I haven't any answers, either. Just hope it won't happen again."

"Me, too." He looked out the window again. "It's really pouring."

"Yeah." Her stomach rumbled. "I've got a frozen pizza that I can stick in the oven. Saves getting soaked in the rain trying to go out."

Quint perked up. "Sounds perfect." He stood. "Point the way."

She smiled for the first time since returning from the visit with her parents. "I'll get it. You sit here and relax. It's not like it's that hard to open a box and punch some buttons."

Quint matched her grin. "I've got some soda in my apartment..."

"Got it covered." She stood, padded to the kitchen, and went about getting the pizza to cooking. That done, she pulled a couple of liters of soda from her small pantry. After setting out plates, glasses, and utensils on the small kitchen table, she returned to the living room to find Quint with her notebook in his hand.

She froze and sucked in a breath. "What do you think you're doing?"

He slowly placed the item on the coffee table. "I just picked it up to move it out of the way. Saw the questions, but didn't read it."

"Bullshit." She crossed her arms over her chest. "That's private."

"I gathered that, which is why I was putting it back down."

Incensed and embarrassed, she ground her teeth together. "My life isn't an open book for you to read whenever you'd like."

Quint stood, his hands hanging loosely at his sides. "Taryn, I know that. I'm sorry. I shouldn't have even touched it. But I did. I never meant to pry."

His tone and face conveyed contriteness and

uprightness. Still, it left a sting and a mark on her feelings toward him. *How can I trust him when he's busy reading my words at the first opportunity?*

She bit her lip and struggled with what to do next.

"I have no excuse other than I'm interested in you, want to know more about you." He sounded sincere, at least.

"Don't do it again." *I'm such a pansy pushover.* Those damn hormones were taking away her common sense.

She walked over and picked up the notebook.

"Why do you have so many questions about your adoption?"

Taryn swung to gape at him.

****

Quint mentally crossed his fingers and waited for her to answer. He'd been caught red-handed looking over her notes. If that wasn't bad enough, he was sure that just stung her confidence in him, which was the last thing he'd intended to do. If he was to stick by her side and protect her from Davis, he needed her trust—something she'd been reluctant to give up to this point.

"I just do."

He softly pursued the subject by offering a safe olive branch. "I know many people are eager to find their birth parents."

Taryn nodded. "I don't remember my parents. They were killed in a car wreck. My grandfather took me in and raised me until he…died."

That pause was telling. Quint, already knowing the story, didn't bother to mention the omission. That was her story to tell when she was ready. "Ah. So, you're wondering how you got here?"

"Yes." She met his gaze. "That's the start. I want to know what all happened. Fill in the gaps I can't remember."

From his briefing, he knew most of those gaps were indeed filled with traumatic events that she recalled vividly. There were likely a few more that piqued her interest, though. "Makes sense. Is there anything I can do to help?"

She bit her lower lip as if deep in thought. "No. This is something I'll have to do myself."

He nodded and released a breath. "I'm an IT guy. If you need assistance, just give a holler. I'll gladly give you a hand."

Her face relaxed into a small smile. "Thanks. I just might take you up on the offer."

He was afraid of what she'd ask in that direction. So, better to change topics before she decided to enlist his help to break into Dalliance's website. "You're upset. What happened today?"

She returned to the couch and sat, then crossed her legs. "I had lunch with my adoptive parents—the Golds."

"The Golds?" He already knew that information, but played along to maintain his cover.

"They adopted me, but I didn't take their last name."

"You didn't mention them as being a source of irritation before."

"Normally, they aren't. Today, they were. I asked about my adoption, and they kept shutting me down."

Damn. She's pushing the envelope. With such tenacity, she'd discover the truth sooner rather than later. And she'd most likely burn some bridges along the way through no real fault of her own. Some secrets were just meant to stay buried.

Despite the complications her curiosity presented, he respected her all the more. The odds were against her, and she'd hit some dead ends, but she persevered. That took fortitude, dedication, and guts. Those were rare in one individual.

"I'm sorry." What could he really say? *Just sit right down, and I'll tell you the whole thing? Not happening.* Most likely she wouldn't believe him. If she did and asked how he knew, he really couldn't throw his father under the bus. Which pretty much left little options—for now. With time and closeness, he could let some clues slide. Depending on what happened with Davis. That was the number one priority at the moment—earning Taryn's trust and keeping a look out for the man dogging her trail.

She rested her hands in her lap. "Ever since I was a little kid, I wanted to know the whole truth. I know I'm getting closer, but everywhere I turn, there's more questions than answers."

His stomach twisted at the hint of pain in her voice and on her expressive face. What she went through haunted her. Those answers she sought might allow her to fly free once more. Or they might be enough to squash her under their weight.

He studied her. *No, she wouldn't fold.* Not his Taryn. She'd stood up to a shooter without a tiny fuss. Surely, she could shoulder what lay in her future. "I imagine it's hard. The not knowing."

She nodded.

"As much as my parents drove me crazy, at least I had them."

"Were they good parents?" she asked.

He grinned. "Yeah. They kept me on the straight and narrow. Nose to the books all through college. Now, they pester me about grandchildren." He sighed dramatically.

She perked up with a grin. "What did you study in college?"

"Psychology."

"Me, too." A real smile appeared on her face, extending to her eyes. "I loved it."

He grinned back, genuinely thrilled to find some common ground. "So much to learn and think about. What was your favorite class?"

"Motivation. And yours?"

He debated for a second before answering. "Human sexuality."

She rolled her eyes. "Of course, that would be. Men. I swear. Every six seconds."

He chuckled. "You got it."

Scooting closer, she rested her hand on his knee. The green color of her eyes darkened to emerald as she drew in a breath. "What would your teachings tell you about this?" Slowly, she leaned in, paused, then brushed her lips over his.

The caress was so fleeting, he wasn't sure there'd actually been contact. Her touch on his leg was no question, though. It alone fired up his blood.

"I wasn't sure we were on the same page with this. I'm glad to know that you want me."

"There's no question about that. Who wouldn't want you?"

He didn't have an answer. Most wouldn't if they knew what his abilities were or what he did for a living.

That secret would have to say sealed for a while longer.

She sat back. "Well?"

"Well, what?" He'd lost track of the conversation.

"What would your human sexuality class say about that kiss?"

He kicked his mind back into gear. "That was definitely sweet. A tasty temptation." He lowered his cheek to rub against hers, a gentle caress of affection. Lifting his head, he studied her face before speaking again, "I was an 'A' student, by the way."

She smiled wickedly. "I'm sure you were quite the overachiever and got lots of practice."

"I'm not inexperienced, no. But I've never met someone like you."

"Meaning?" She met his eyes and held.

He ran his first finger along the curve of her jaw. "You're beautiful. Smart. Fun. And the knowledge that you can kick my ass just turns me on all the more." He paused for a second to trace her mouth with his thumb. "And I'd like more. Much more." This time he took the aggressor role, sealing their lips together, meshing, molding, and finally, licking. The second her lips parted on a gasp, he flicked his tongue inside, seeking a deeper exploration. Little cherry bombs went off in his mind.

A timer chimed.

Taryn startled, breaking the lip lock. "Umm."

"Pizza's done."

"Umm. Pizza. Yeah, right." She stood, checked her balance with a hand to the arm of the couch, and hurried into the kitchen.

Quint followed along, after taking a moment to cool his jets. He felt as shaky as she appeared. One fleeting caress and he was a goner. She was pretty damn potent.

Who knew one little kiss would set his libido free and instill a yearning for more? Hell, at this point, he'd be hard-pressed to resist the little vixen if she offered herself up for the taking.

Good thing one of them had sense. Taryn. Her bad boy past came in right handy.

He might be tasked with protecting her and taking out Davis. That role just became so much harder. She provided a distraction he couldn't afford. Her life depended on it.

She placed the pizza in the center of the table, grabbed the cutter, and sliced their meal into pieces. He filled the glasses with ice, poured them some soda, and took a seat after Taryn chose hers. He waited patiently while she selected her slice before grabbing a couple and placing them on his plate.

Taryn dug in, taking a large bite and chewing. He did the same, finding himself hungry enough to put the delicious food away and fast.

She finished her slice of pizza and took another.

Quint had already downed two and was munching on his third. Company was excellent, food not too bad. He couldn't complain in the least.

"So, the thought that I can kick your ass turns you on?" She tilted her head while a ghost of a mischievous grin flirted with her lips.

He groaned dramatically. "I let the cat out of the bag with that one."

She chuckled. "Yep. I'm not sure most guys, any guys, would want to date a woman who could wipe them on the floor."

Quint enjoyed her teasing. Much better than the

anger and downtrodden moods she'd ran through earlier. His manly pride took a stand. "Well, wiping the floor with me is a bit of a reach."

She arched an eyebrow at him.

"I'm a big guy."

"So is Eric," she pointed out.

"Yeah, well. I'm a hell of a lot smarter than he is."

She nodded. "I'll give you that." Finishing her slice, she wiped her hands on a paper towel. "Not sure what's on television, but you're welcome to stay and watch with me."

He didn't hesitate in the least. "I'd like that." He took the last bite, chewed, and swallowed. "You can quiz me about that human sexuality class if you want to." He grinned cheekily at her. "Test my knowledge."

She snorted. "I'm sure most of your knowledge was attained outside of class."

"You're probably right." He really didn't want to go into his previous exploits. Not kosher when dating a new person to start listing off his experiences before her. Still, he enjoyed this line of discussion, light and cheery with a hint of teasing.

Taryn gathered up the dishes and put them in the sink. Quint assisted by drawing hot water. "Detergent?"

She turned from stuffing the left-over pizza into a container. "You don't have to wash them."

"I'm not afraid of dishpan hands." He held them up.

She shook her head and grinned. "Now there's a way to a girl's heart. Any man who helps out with the household chores is a man worth keeping."

For you, I'd get down on my hands and knees to scrub the floor.

Glad he hadn't spoken those words out loud, Quint accepted the bottle of detergent and a washcloth from Taryn. No sense in making her leery or uncomfortable by spouting off such stuff, though it was true. "I'll remember that."

He made short work of the washing, setting aside each item in a plastic drainer. The entire time, he watched Taryn work, noted her graceful motions, her lithe body, and the power she possessed in those conditioned muscles.

Some might consider her dangerous. He found her attractive and alluring. She was strong, both inside and out. Yet he saw the cracks in her façade—the past that haunted her and pressed her to find those all-important answers.

He only hoped when she discovered what she'd coveted to know for the past eighteen years, she didn't break under the load. Or hate him for his part in the secret.

Chapter 10

The phone woke Quint the next morning. He rolled over in bed, checked the caller ID, then answered. "You're up early."

Reginald snorted. "Someone has to keep up with developments around here. By the way, no new bodies, but most likely a solid Davis spotting on the border of Minnesota and Wisconsin, northern edge."

"How long ago?"

"Couple of hours."

"He's sniffing, but not too close. Yet." Quint glanced out the window, saw the droplets of rain coming down, checked the clock, and sighed. He'd love nothing better than sleeping half the day away, but Taryn would be up and about soon.

"Yeah. It's just a matter of time, though. He's like a dog on a scent. Won't stop until he gets his prey."

Quint flinched at the terminology. "Not going to happen."

"How's she doing, anyway?"

Easily reading between the lines, Quint went for the vague, but truthful answer. "Fine. We were shot at while playing paintball in a wooded course. Nothing but a stolen truck so far."

"What? Why the hell didn't you tell me immediately?" Reginald's voice rose a couple of decibels in surprise and displeasure.

"I really don't think it's related to Davis. He's not going to spend all that time and energy just to shoot someone in the back. Not his style. He'll want to show off and take them down with his mental powers."

A couple of seconds went by. "So, who else is trying to kill her?"

"No clue. Figured it was her ex, but that didn't pan out."

"Do you need backup?"

"No," Quint answered right away, then winced at what he'd probably revealed in such a hasty response. "She's a smart tack. New people keep showing up in this small town, and she's going to get really suspicious."

"If you get in over your head, just say something. I'm not willing to risk you if things go to hell in a handbasket."

"I've got it, Dad." Quint recalled something bugging him. "Did her grandfather have paranormal powers?"

"Not that we know of."

"Her parents?"

"Again, not that we know of."

He could almost see Reginald tapping his fingers on the desk in concentration.

"She has them?"

"Maybe. I'm not sure yet."

"Interesting."

Quint knew what that comment meant—a long conversation he didn't want to participate in. "Got to go. Trust me on this one."

"I do. Keep in touch." Reginald clicked off.

Quint hung up, set the phone aside, and scrubbed

his face. Automatically, he listened for any activity in Taryn's room. A large twinge of guilt hit him with the knowledge that he'd invaded her privacy with the planted listening device. *Desperate times call for desperate measures.* He needed to know if Davis showed up. As good as Taryn was, she didn't have a chance against such a killer.

Clicking sounds, reminiscent of fingers typing on a keyboard, drew his attention.

She was on the computer, probably banging on the door of Dalliance. Again.

He flopped back in bed then ran his hands through his hair. *What the hell am I going to do?* He didn't want to lie to her, but telling her the whole truth wasn't beneficial. *Oh, by the way, your grandfather's killer is on the loose looking for you so he can blow up your brain from the inside out. How do I know? Well, my father was his partner when they broke in and killed your last remaining family member. He's the one that kidnapped you and took you to Minnesota.*

Yeah, that'll go over well. Not.

He hated that they were dancing around one another, neither reveling much. Tiny steps to getting closer. One small kiss aside, they were at a standstill. He wanted more. Needed more. Yet, his personal wants and his job tore him in opposite directions.

The more they were together, the more he realized the truth. She called to him. Her softness promised salvation. His soul cried out for the goodness, sweetness, and cheer she broadcast. It was as if he'd been in the dark too long and needed a beacon to bring him back to the light. The unending corridor of emotionlessness faded in her presence. To him, that was a miracle he couldn't walk away from. She reminded him how to laugh and how enjoyable life could be—a treasure worth fighting for.

If only he didn't have to hide his abilities and true reason for being there. If only he could level with her, throw caution to the wind, and take a chance on her. If only he could unload his burden and be a whole man again.

All of those things were pretty near impossible, leaving him in a sticky quandary that could suck the rest of his morality with the loss of the only woman who made him want to believe.

Awake and a little annoyed, he climbed from bed and headed to the bathroom. A hard workout would clear his head so he could plan how to progress. After all, he was good with details.

****

"Damn it." Taryn cursed under her breath. She'd been online for the past hour and a half, to no avail. There were no private adoption agencies in Minnesota that were around eighteen years ago. She'd queried the state website and came up empty as well. Not so much as a vaccination record. Which meant she'd have to call, but more than likely, drive down to the county seat to see if she could obtain any archives at all.

Doable, but on her lunch hour. Which pretty much took out her exercise time during the day. Unless she wanted to stay after her shift ended. It's not like she had much else to do, anyway.

Target practice rang a bell in her mind. She'd signed up at the local shooting range for the early evening. No way would she miss it. Shooting was like any other sport. Lack of practice led to a lack of performance. Besides, it helped eased her stress. Destroying targets, oddly enough, made her happy.

"Well, crap. There's never enough hours in the day."

She checked the clock and winced. Time to get ready and hurry to work. With just her and Macy, she had to be there to unlock the doors right on time.

In a rush, she dressed, brushed her hair, and put it up in the familiar ponytail. Hygiene taken care of, she slipped on her sneakers and headed out. There, she paused for a second, staring at Quint's door.

Last night had been fun. They chatted over pizza and soda. He'd ended up sitting with her on the couch and watching television until close to bedtime. Nothing fancy, but she'd found contentment with him, despite the anger at his reading her adoption notes she intended to pursue.

In frank honesty, she truly wanted to ask his help in tracking down some answers. As an IT person, he'd have far more ability to get to the right place with speed. But to ask for his aid meant to share her story with him. The whole thing. That stayed her hand and her voice. The only people that knew were her immediate family. To tell another person put a heavy weight on a relationship. He'd think she was crazy, even obsessed. And that's before she'd even hint at the invisibility thing.

Deep down, she wanted to trust him. Knew he'd have her back, just like he did at the paintball woods.

Maybe, just maybe, I should let him in a little more. See if he can handle the heat of my life.

She started to knock on the door, then paused when she glimpsed her watch. She was already late, and the early bird clients would be pissed if she didn't have the place open right on time.

With a silent sigh of regret, she hustled out of the building, into her car, and off to the gym.

An hour later, still drying out from the sprint in the pouring rain to get inside, Taryn glimpsed Quint enter the building. Despite wearing sweat pants and a short-sleeved gray t-shirt, he exuded sexiness. Just his demeanor and stride carried confidence and grace.

IT consultant, my ass. Quint had a background in something else. His power, regal carriage, and gliding ease spoke of years of training. She understood how it showed in a person's every move. Dancers had a certain way about them, as did advanced level military. Quint fell somewhere in the middle. He was observant, but not constantly searching for trouble. One glance seemed enough to assure himself that things were on the up and up.

Relaxed. That's how she'd describe him. He never appeared uptight, in a rush, or out of sorts. Even when they were getting shot at, he held himself together like a pro. She liked that in a man. Someone who kept their head under pressure made for a good man to have at her side.

It was his secretiveness that kept her guessing. Probably the reason she hadn't advanced further than the basics about her past. If he couldn't trust her, then how could she trust him? That was the supreme question. Her gut told her that Quint was worth the risk. Her cautious mind wasn't completely in agreement.

A knock at her door interrupted her train of thought. She glanced up to see her boss, Trent Dyson, standing before her. Shocked, she could only blink for a second. In her memory, he'd only visited the out-of-the-way gym twice. The fact that he showed up now made her stomach clench.

"Trent." She stood up to greet him properly. "What brings you by?"

He offered up a half smile at her, shook her hand, and entered the small office. "Kind of slow today, huh?"

"The rain always deters some." She latched onto the excuse, which was true.

He nodded and shut the door. "I wanted to swing by and talk to you."

"Okay." Taryn gestured to the extra chair. "Have a seat."

He did. She moved behind her desk and plopped down in her own, bracing herself for bad news. She folded her hands and rested them on her desk, sat up straight, and looked her boss in the eye.

"Taryn, this gym is barely making it."

She nodded. How many times had she pored over the numbers? Almost daily. They didn't change. Just squeaking by month after month. "I know, sir. I've tried everything to increase membership. The die-hards are the staple; it's getting the rest of the population to join and stick with it."

"You've done everything. I've noticed all the work you've done—advertising, adding classes, learning aerials just to be able to entice a few more people to walk in the door. Your dedication impresses me."

"But…" She prepared for the other shoe to drop.

"But we're not drawing in enough profit to pay your wage and Macy's, too. As it is, we're barely footing the electric bill." He leaned forward slightly and rested his hands on his knees. "I'm afraid we'll have to shut down."

Taryn's breath caught. Those words she'd had nightmares about had been spoken by her boss, the owner, and the one with the ultimate power to close the doors for good. Drawing in air, she wrapped her mind around the terrible news. "When?"

"The last day of the month is the official closing date." His voice held a steady tone, pure business, no sadness at all.

Taryn understood. Trent had several businesses to run, employees to hire and care for. He couldn't afford any single place to drain his assets. Profit was the name of the game, and her little gym wasn't meeting the mark.

One week. One week to start over.

"You're welcome to come to work at any of the other facilities. I'm not sure there's manager positions open, but you can teach classes. We always need that kind of help."

Taryn managed a single nod. Her mind whirled with the consequences of his actions. No job. No income. Moving hours away to work as a class instructor only, without steady work or benefits. The idea gave her a bad case of heartburn. "Is there any way to change your mind?"

He didn't even pause. "No. The numbers aren't getting any better. To be honest, I'm surprised they've held on for this long."

"What about Macy?"

"I'll let you tell her." He stood. "I'm sorry, Taryn."

"Me, too." She regained her feet and showed him out.

He hesitated only for a second, turned, and strode out of the building, taking Taryn's hopes, dreams, and stability with her.

"What's wrong?"

She startled at Quint standing so close. So focused on Trent and his awful news, she hadn't seen him approach. "He's closing the gym."

Quint frowned. "When?"

"One week." Her voice came out soft and lifeless. She heard it and cringed. Pride made her lift her chin.

"I'm sorry." Quint shifted weight from one foot to the next. "Is there anything I can do?"

She shook her head. "Win the lottery and buy the gym." Her attempt at humor fell flat. "No. It's a done deal."

Quint reached out and gently tugged until she bumped up against his chest.

With only a couple of people in the gym, she doubted anyone saw them or even cared. Relishing the solid comfort of Quint, she wrapped her arms around him and leaned in. Powerful muscles provided a cushion. The little kiss he pressed to her crown melted her heart.

Consoling. Soothing. In his arms, her worries dissipated. Unfortunately, she couldn't stay there forever.

Tears threatened. She blinked them back and swallowed hard. Pressing her face against his upper chest, she snuggled in. For once she gave in to the need to be held.

For however long she stood there, she drank in the scent and feel of Quint, confident in the knowledge that he'd be there for her. But all too soon, reality sank in.

She had work to do.

Stepping back, she wiped at her eyes. "Thank you."

He watched her with concern evident on his face. "Are you going to be okay?"

No. She couldn't even wrap her mind around where to go next. It was all too overwhelming. As long as the gym had struggled, she should have had a contingency plan in place. She'd never got around to it, and now she was scrambling because of it. "Yeah. I'll figure out something."

He rested his hand on her shoulder. "I'll help in any way that I can."

She heard the sincerity in his voice. "Thanks for offering. I just need some time to come up with a plan."

He nodded. "You know where I'm at."

"Yeah." She met his gaze. "Thanks. Really."

"Anytime." He grazed her cheek with his knuckles and sighed. "It'll be all right."

Unable to speak around the lump in her throat, she managed a nod.

Quint dropped his touch, backed out of the office, and returned to the free weights. His absence stole the warmth, leaving her cold and bereft.

He sat on the bench, picked up a weight, his gaze flicking back to her.

She felt his stare, knew he was concerned, and realized she needed to pull up her big girl pants.

After blowing her nose, she sat back down, pulled out a piece of paper, and started writing a to-do list. With the freedom from a full-time job, she had the ability to focus on the one burning item in her agenda—revenge.

Chapter 11

First things first.

She'd told Macy. The girl wasn't surprised, a little sad, but seemed to brush the bad news off. She was young and planning to go to college in the fall anyway, so she had the freedom to enjoy a handful of weeks' vacation before hitting the books. Great for her.

Next, she took the time to pick up the phone and call the Texas State Department of Health and Adoptive Services. She'd hoped to net a birth certificate and adoption request all in the same place.

"Central Adoption Registry. Can I help you?"

"Yes. I'm trying to track down my birth certificate and adoption records."

"Your birth certificate can be requested online. Fill out the form, print it, and send it in with the processing fee."

Taryn jotted the instructions down. "What about the adoption records?"

"Adoption records are sealed. Permission has to be given from all parties before they can be opened."

She wanted to bang her head on the desk. "What if my biological parents are deceased and my adoptive parents aren't willing to get involved?"

"You can petition the court in the county which has your records. There's a fee for that, but a judge can order the records opened. Some of the data will be marked out to protect the other parties, but the basic information will be available." The woman rattled on.

Taryn crossed her eyes. So much red tape. Yet another dead end.

"I was adopted from Texas to Minnesota. Will that make a difference?"

The lady paused for a second. "Then you need to contact ICPC, Interstate Compact on the Placement of Children. They oversee all adoptions crossing state lines."

Taryn sat up straighter. Finally, she might be getting somewhere. "Okay. How does that work?"

"Well, they do have a website that answers a lot of your questions, and a phone number. But basically, they do a home inspection to make sure it's appropriate and verify that all laws are being followed covering adoption in both states."

"Okay."

"They don't work with the families themselves, but through a state-licensed adoption agent with each state involved. They make sure the adoptive family has training and the best family situation for an adoptive child to enter."

A red flag waved in her head. "You said they have to have a state worker on both ends and be checked out and trained *before* they can assume custody of the child?"

"Yes, ma'am."

Taryn processed that little gem.

"You can look at their website. It has all kinds of information."

"And the adoption records?"

"Will stay sealed unless you get a court order in the

county of your adoption."

"Got it. Thank you so much for your help."

"You're very welcome." The lady hung up.

Taryn disconnected the call and sat back in her chair.

There was no way her adoption went through regular channels, like her adoptive parents claimed. There wasn't time for state workers on both sides to get all the required investigation done ahead of time, let alone the training. She'd had suspicions about the immediateness of the actions but didn't bother to question things. Even if they were foster parents, they wouldn't have taken her directly from Texas into their home and adopted her a day or three later. No way.

Now she had yet another mystery on her hands.

The chances of getting that adoption record unsealed were slim to none. If it even existed in the first place.

The question became who had enough power to rush through the process in a matter of a few hours?

One step forward and a half one back.

She glanced down at her list, wiggled her mouse to wake up the computer, and went to the search engine. Using a variety of keywords, she searched once again for a tattoo matching the one from her memory.

An hour passed before a picture caught her attention.

She clicked on the image and expanded it. Her heart pounded as she peered at the identical drawing from her kidnapper's wrist. Excitement flushed through her at the small breakthrough.

A few clicks later, she backtracked the picture to a tattoo studio in New Jersey. Grabbing her phone, she punched in the number supplied with shaking fingers.

"Tattoo Studio."

"Yes, I have an odd question. I was looking at tattoos online and found one of a black widow spider on a web."

"Oh, yeah. That's a great one. Creepy, but damn fun to do."

It takes all kinds…

"I'm into research and saw this tattoo on a man's wrist. It's real important that I can identify this man, and this is my only lead. I'm hoping you can help me out in telling me a name or a location. Anything will help."

The guy snorted. "Listen, lady. Do you know how many people come through here every day? Like I can remember them all."

She cringed. "Do you keep records? This would have been at least eighteen years ago, maybe more."

He murmured under his breath. "My father copyrighted the image back in the sixties. That don't mean other places didn't borrow it. But no, we didn't keep any records back then. You wanted a tattoo, sit down, flash the money, and pick your art."

She rubbed her forehead. "Would it be possible to speak to your father? Perhaps he'd recall this man."

"He died a year ago."

"Oh. I'm so sorry."

"Look. Even if I had any records, they'd be private. Even the cops have to have a court order to come in and peek at them. Happens now and again when a John Doe ends up dead. They try to trace tats. Don't have much luck with it, either. Not with everyone and their cousin owning a business."

"Of course. Thank you for your time. I'm sorry to have bothered you." She hung up and let out a long breath.

Face it, Taryn. Today just isn't your day.

Unmotivated to work with the impending close, Taryn marked off her to-do list while trying to focus on the past while planning the next step in her future. She'd struck out on both.

"What am I going to do?"

No words of inspiration came.

Fate had spoken. She had to move with the punches. The world was an open door and all that. An upbeat saying, but she didn't feel that way in the least.

And possibly worst of all, she'd have to leave Quint.

The guy said he could work from anywhere. Nice for him. She, on the other hand, needed a full-time job somewhere within decent driving distance. In such a rural area, those were rare, indeed. While the summer sun beat down and sizzled the land, winter snows would arrive in due time, making long drives precarious and even impossible.

They hadn't confessed undying love. She wasn't even sure they were officially dating. But the idea of leaving the one man who'd impressed her with his chivalry made her heart plummet.

She considered what her parents recommended, going back to college for a graduate degree. The thought didn't even appeal. It hadn't before, either. Her degree, something she enjoyed, really didn't open many doors. No fast-track to a career. Unfortunately.

Then there was the mystery behind her adoption. Her parents had lied to her all these years. *Why?* She'd confronted them a few days ago and got nowhere. Doing so again probably would net the same outcome. *So where does that leave me?*

Face it, Taryn, you've been given a batch of lemons with no idea how to make lemonade.

Restless, she cleared out her office and carried her few belongings home, leaving Macy to run the place in her stead. Since Macy already had posted the impending closure announcement everywhere and figured out how to refund gym memberships, Taryn felt pretty useless.

So, after dropping her belongings off, she grabbed her rifle, in its case, from under the bed, and drove back to the shooting range. Going through a box of shells would clear her head.

It had helped, but as soon as she entered her apartment, the weight of her burdens pressed her shoulders back down. A little lost, she sat down on the floor and cleaned her rifle. The familiar task at least kept her hands busy while her mind bounced around ideas like a pinball machine.

Too bad she couldn't snag a single one and put it to good use.

Face the facts. You're a mess.

And she no longer knew which way was up.

After finishing cleaning her rifle, she carefully returned it to its case and tucked it under the bed. It was her pride and joy, the weapon that allowed her to win numerous target shooting events. And the gun that would be an instrument in her version of justice. *If I can ever find that bastard.*

A sigh of sheer frustration slipped from her lips.

Her phone rang. She picked it up, glanced at the

caller ID, recognized her brother's name, and silenced it. The last thing she wanted at the moment was to talk to him. She preferred quiet time by herself without a gazillion questions that she didn't have any answers for.

Flicking on the television, she halfway listened to the background noise until a rapping at her door drew her attention.

Knowing it had to be Quint, she went to answer. After peeking through the hole, she unlocked and opened it. "Hi."

He'd recently showered, his dark hair still damp. Jeans covered his lower body while a dressy pullover fit well enough to show off his chiseled chest and hint at the six-pack abs she knew he'd possess.

"Hi. Can I come in?"

"Sure." She waited for him to cross the threshold before closing and locking the door behind him.

Quint glanced around the room before turning back to face her. "You left early today."

She nodded. "Had things to do. Do you want something to drink?" Making her way over to the kitchen, she pulled two sodas out of the fridge knowing he wouldn't turn the offer down. He met her at the junction of the kitchen and family room and took the offered drink. "Thanks."

"You're welcome." She returned to the living room and took a seat on the couch. "Thank you for what you did earlier today. I really needed that hug."

He eyed her for a few seconds before unscrewing the lid on his bottle and taking a sip. "I want to do more."

She shook her head, her independent nature rearing up. "There's nothing to do. I'll find another job. Simple as that. People do it every day."

His lips thinned slightly.

Her phone rang again. She looked at the number, scowled, and hit the mute button.

"Avoiding someone?"

"My brother. He's probably wanting a favor, and I'm not in the mood." She set the phone aside.

"You need to get away for a few days. Clear your head."

She closed her eyes for a second and savored the thought. To just drive off into the sunset, leave her worries behind. To actually enjoy some down time. It sounded like heaven. "As much as I'd like to, I'm not sure I can." She had so much to do with announcing to the gym patrons about the closing and perhaps attending a target shoot in a couple of days. Not to mention the constant pull of her team to sign up for and attend yet another paintball tournament. At least with those, she could earn a small paycheck.

The news came on television with pictures of people, dressed in summer shorts and t-shirts, hauling bags of sand. Video of a raging river followed. The story snared her attention and held it.

"The floods? Yeah, I heard about that. Down south. Everyone is chipping in to try to save the town." Quint's soft voice carried easily through the room.

Inspiration hit. "That's what I can do. I'll take a couple of days off, go help them, and figure out my problems later."

Quint tilted his head. "You wouldn't rather hang out at a pool at some resort?"

She smiled. "Nope. I want to help. Down time is bad. Work is good. Besides, it's not too far from the bigger cities. I can spend a couple of days getting dirty, then head to the city. If I remember right, there's a target shooting contest this coming weekend that I can enter." For the first time since Trent stepped into her office, Taryn felt something positive click into place. "Macy is already running the gym. I'm sure she won't mind covering for the last few days. Let me just text her." She retrieved her phone and quickly sent the message.

"River rescue it is." He stood up.

She blinked at him. "Where are you going?"

He smiled at her. "To pack, of course. I'm going with you."

A part of her put on the brakes. The rest leaped for joy. "Are you sure?"

"Absolutely." The grin on his face released butterflies in her stomach. "Anywhere with you will be fun."

She chuckled. "You might not be saying that after a day of lifting sandbags."

"I bet I will." He took her hand and helped her to her feet. She left the phone behind on the couch.

"What are we betting?" Her question came out a little breathless. Not surprising since she could hardly breathe with the sensual look in his eyes.

"A kiss?"

Sensual delight flared. She wrapped her arms around his neck and pressed her lips to his. The tender caress soon deepened into something more. Heat. Searing heat flowed over her, setting her on fire with undeniable need.

Rational thought fled under the onslaught of passion.

Quint took control of the kiss. He bracketed her head, then delved deep when she parted her lips. Gentle, molten pleasure followed as he kissed her with wild abandon. She gave back, taking her turn to taste, to tease. Only when the need for air broke them apart did she pause in her exploration.

He peppered kisses along her cheek and chin while trailing his fingers from her shoulders down her arms and back to her sides.

Her phone rang. She reached for it, hit a button, and turned the annoying interruption off. After tossing the phone back onto the couch, she immersed herself back into the moment.

The caress only whetted her appetite for more. Words failed her as she tried to make him understand the burning need by licking his neck and nibbling on his ear.

A low groan filled the air. Belatedly, she realized it escaped from her throat. He was driving her that crazy and distracting her way too much to care.

His hand slid under her shirt, lightly brushing over the skin of her belly before moving upward. Large, calloused hands, but filled with infinite tenderness. So perfect, she almost forgot to breathe.

Lust spurred her onward. Her clothes were a burden that simply had to go. "Off." She tugged at his shirt, needing to return the favor and finally both see and feel those hard muscles she so craved.

"Patience, Taryn."

Way too worked up, she knew she'd burn up if he didn't escalate the pace. "Off. Now." Grasping the bottom of his shirt, she pulled until he relented. As soon as he tossed the shirt aside, she reached for him, letting her curiosity guide her over the hills and valleys of his toned torso. His pecs intrigued her nearly as much as the bulge in his pants.

Unable to help herself, she focused her attention on his jeans. By the time she'd unfastened the button, he'd taken over, sliding the zipper down with practiced ease. In one fluid motion, he shoved the denim down, revealing nude skin underneath. Nude, tanned skin, and one impressive cock.

"Oh, my. You go commando."

He chuckled. "Sometimes. Now, I really think you're overdressed." He closed the distance with a single step, latched onto her shirt, and assisted her to remove it. Her pants followed, leaving her standing in her underwear. Not one to be shy, she reached behind to unsnap her bra.

"Let me." He molded one hand over her breast, using the other to slip behind, pinch the material, and let it loose. She slid it off and tossed it to the side.

His hands immediately covered her. Lightly tweaking, he rubbed his thumbs over her sensitive nipples, sending a shivery wave of delight coursing through her. She arched into his touch, needing more. So much more.

As if reading her mind, Quint leaned down and flicked his tongue over a peak. The slight brush drew another slight whimper from her. She wrapped an arm around his neck for support and used the other to follow an imaginary line from his ribs down his flank, and around to his perfect rear. Giving in to the overwhelming urge, she squeezed.

Quint moaned quietly. He rewarded her by sucking at first one side then the other.

Taryn savored his feasting on her. Yet, it still wasn't enough. "Please, Quint."

He released her nipple with a pop and kissed the area between her breasts. "Please what?"

"I need you." The statement came out breathlessly.

He lifted his head and stared down at her for a few seconds. "Are you sure?"

"Yes." She didn't even have to think about the answer.

As if he didn't hear, he returned his attention to her breasts. One hand teased the other mound while the other drifted farther south, dipping under the material of her panties.

She squirmed, needing his touch more than she needed a new job. And that happened to be paramount.

Impatient, she brought her hand from his backside, wrapped her fingers around his shaft, and lightly stroked. The hardened flesh was silky to the touch. And responsive. Jumping with her lightest stroke.

His groan echoed hers.

Without further ado, he swept her up in his arms, carrying her back to the bedroom. She'd never experienced anything so romantic in her life. All she could do was stare at him like he was King Arthur himself come to carry her off to Camelot.

Ever so gently, he laid her in the center of the bed, then followed her down.

A single rational thought surged to the forefront. "I don't have any condoms."

He stretched out alongside her, cupped her breast, and pressed his lips against the sensitive flesh. "I don't need one. This time."

She opened her mouth to protest, when he slipped

his fingers under her panties until he found her slit. The slightest brush against her clit sent her hips to bucking.

"Shh. This time is all about you. For you."

She blinked, trying to decipher his words as he strummed her body with expertise. Small tremors of need came on the heels of every brief tease of her nub. "But…"

"Let me give to you like I've been wanting to. Savor you. As you so deserve."

She didn't have the words to complain. Not when he lavished such wondrous attention on her.

Not to be denied, she took advantage to explore his body, invariably returning to his erection. Intrigued, she played with different grips and motions, trying to determine what he liked the best. The way he pressed into her hand and jerked now and again told the story—he pretty much liked it all.

"Enough, Taryn. This is for you." He gently removed her hand and scooted around to settle between her legs. Grasping her panties, he tugged them down as she lifted her rear to help relieve her of her final garment.

Nude, she watched his face, easily reading the tightening of the lips, the flaring of the nostrils, and the darkening of his chocolate eyes. All those hints signaled he liked what he saw.

"So beautiful. Perfect." He ran one hand up her left side from calf to thigh, then lightly pushed. "Open for me."

She hesitated only a second before complying. As soon as she bared herself, he returned with his fingers, dipping one inside while using his thumb to seek out her nub.

Throwing her head back, Taryn's breath hitched then sped, matching her heart. The gentle touches aroused her as nothing had before.

Then, Quint lay on his stomach, lifted her thighs to rest on his shoulders, and licked.

She saw stars.

Never before had anyone done such a thing for her. It was intimate. And oh so sexy.

He repeated the caress, causing her thighs to tighten, her body to tense, and a feeling of impending explosion to rush over her. A sound escaped her lips.

"Taryn. Look at me."

She shook her head, riding the tide of a huge tsunami wave she knew she couldn't control.

"Taryn." He pressed on her sensitive button and rotated.

Her eyes flew open as she met his gaze.

"Trust me. I'll take care of you. I'll always take care of you." His eyes and tone made the promise written in stone.

"I know you will." It was true. Deep down, she trusted him. Sure, much of his life remained a mystery, but actions were more accurate and powerful than words. She put herself into his hands and didn't look back.

When he lowered his head once again, she grasped the bedcover and held on for dear life. He sucked. He laved. He worshipped and feasted. She squirmed and lifted her hips, needing more. Something more.

He pressed two fingers into her slit and slid deep. The welcome pressure jacked up her arousal to a fevered pitch. Then, he lowered his mouth over her clit.

One kiss, a lick, then a tickling that ended with

gentle sucking.

Her world exploded.

One second, she hovered on the edge, the next she rocketed into orbit. Her hips jerked, and breathing came in great gasps. All the while, Quint stuck to the course, riding that high tide with her, then easing her back down with tender caresses and quiet murmurings of praise.

A minute or two passed before she could get enough air to speak. "Oh, my."

He rubbed his cheek over her thigh and smiled at her. "You liked?"

"Is there any question?"

He chuckled. "I told you. I'm good with details."

Boy howdy, was he.

"Ready for round two?"

She blinked at him. "Again?"

"Yep."

She thought for a second. "It gets better?"

"Oh, yeah."

She doubted at first. Then he showed her how good at details he really was.

Chapter 12

Quint woke earlier than usual, opened his eyes, and took in the situation. Taryn slept next to him, spooned, with her back to his front. He curled around her as if protecting her as she slept. The softness of her skin, the warmth of her body, even her pretty butt pressed up against his morning wood simply felt right. They fit together like she belonged there. He didn't question it any further than that. Didn't need to. He knew perfection when he saw it.

Carefully, he unraveled himself from Taryn and exited the bed. Padding into the living room, he rounded up his discarded clothing, slipped his jeans on, then went directly to the kitchen. A man made breakfast for his woman after a night of sex. He knew that much.

Unfortunately, this particular woman lacked much in the fridge for him to make her a morning meal.

The fridge contained milk and juice, but that was it. He wasn't even sure the milk was still good as the expiration date passed two days before.

He shut the door and trod quietly from her apartment and into his. There, he gathered up a few items and brought them back to hers. He set everything down, returned to lock the door, then began to mix up some pancakes for their meal.

He'd just added glasses and plates to the table already sporting drinks, butter, and syrup and taken the last pancake out of the skillet when Taryn appeared wearing an oversized t-shirt. The ends covered all her essentials, though barely. He wished she'd bend over so he could see if she'd bothered to slip panties on or not.

She walked over, a lazy gait which could only be called sensual. Her hair had been brushed and now hung loose down her back. Even devoid of makeup, she glowed with magnificence. A vision filled with sex appeal and one that he knew he'd fantasize about for nights to come.

Grace showed in her gait as did the raw beauty she possessed. Even more, he saw and understood the goodness carried all the way inside. Not everyone would put their life's troubles on hold and dash off to help a small town prepare for a major river flooding. She certainly had enough to deal with, yet chose to go help others. He respected her all the more for her generosity.

"Hungry?"

She smiled at him. "I thought I smelled breakfast."

"Pancakes. Hope you like them."

"Oh, I do." She took a seat at the table. "Milk or juice?"

"Milk for me."

She poured both glasses, placing one in front of his plate.

Quint carried the platter over to the table and lowered it to the table in front of her. "Breakfast is served."

She grinned. "Thank you." After forking a couple of pancakes, she added butter and syrup.

Quint did the same before taking his seat.

Hungry, he dug in, though he struggled with

keeping his attention on the food rather than the lady sitting across from him. He could easily envision the very same situation repeating itself most mornings.

It was a novel thought for him but one that took a solid foothold.

"Why didn't you...you know...go all the way last night? I wouldn't have protested at all. Was it because I didn't have any condoms?"

Quint jogged his attention back to the moment and took a drink of milk. "No. You were upset. Had a lot on your mind and your plate. I wanted our first time together to be because we wanted it, not because you needed comforting." He returned his glass to the table. "I'll hold you any time, but I want that special moment to be because we're on the same page and can't keep our hands off one another."

Taryn smiled softly. "A knight in shining armor, full of chivalry. Never thought I'd find such a thing."

He shook his head. "Don't paint me in too bright a picture."

"Why?" She tilted her head and met his eyes.

"I haven't told you much about myself. I think it's time I share some parts."

"Okay."

"I work for a worldwide security company." He watched closely for her reaction. Her face didn't change in the least. "Basically, we track down criminals and put them out of commission."

"Like Interpol?"

He shrugged. "Sort of, I guess. We cover the world as well, but focus on certain types of criminals. What I said before was true. I used to work in IT, but now I'm a field agent."

She rested her elbows on the table. "Like James Bond?"

"Less gadgets, wealth, and prestige. More secret black ops."

"Which is why you move and handle yourself like a Navy Seal."

"Yeah." He chose his words carefully. "I track down rogues with special abilities. Called para—"

A loud banging at the door interrupted.

Taryn spared him a glance before getting up to look out the peep hole. She sighed heavily, unlocked the door, and opened it.

A man barged right in. His brown hair appeared freshly cut. Slacks and a fancy oxford shirt spoke of a nod to fashion or wealth, or an attempt to make others believe those things. His loafers were new, bright, and lacked a single scuff. While none of his appearance really stood out, the rage on his face did. Harsh disapproval rolled off the guy.

Quint took to his feet.

"Brandon, what's the emergency?"

Brandon glared at Quint. "Who's he?"

"Quint. Brandon, my brother. Brandon. Quint." She pointed to each in turn. "There. Now what is so important that you have to show up here at the crack of dawn?"

"I need your help."

Taryn lowered her chin, and her shoulders sagged. The body language said it all. Another bitter chunk of coal on her plate stood before them.

Quint approached to stand next to her.

Brandon eyed him with a sneer. "Have an aversion to shirts?" The sarcastic remark fell flat when Taryn stepped from behind the door, allowing both men to see her completely. Brandon's mouth dropped open at the sight of Taryn dressed only in a rumpled shirt. Shock came first, followed quickly by fury.

Quint brushed up against Taryn's side. The hairs on the back of his neck stood up. A warning. About Brandon. Just because Brandon was her brother didn't mean he wouldn't harm her. Quint prepared to intervene should that happen.

"You didn't answer your phone last night."

"I was busy, Brandon."

"Yeah, I can tell." He crossed his arms over his chest and snarled his face.

Quint resisted the supreme urge to punch that demeaning look off Brandon's face. "Say what you came to say, then get out." He bit off the words.

Brandon dropped his arms and narrowed his eyes. "Big words coming from a jackass taking advantage of my sister."

"Both of you. Stop it." Taryn stepped in the middle. She put her back to Quint and faced Brandon. "What do you want?"

"Like I said, I need your help. Your *special* help."

Quint picked up on the badly covered hint.

Taryn stiffened. "What this time?"

Brandon glared at Quint. "Maybe he should leave so we can discuss this?"

Tension filled the air as they waited Taryn's decision.

"No."

Brandon's face furrowed. "No what?"

"No. I'm done bailing you out. You're a big boy. Figure it out, whatever it is." She straightened her back and didn't flinch when Brandon tightened his fists.

"It's because of him. You'd rather get screwed than to help out your family."

She said nothing, just stood still.

"Whatever happened to blood is thicker than water?"

She planted her hands on her hips. "You tell me since you've been using me to clean up your mistakes. I'm done."

"But Taryn."

"No." She pointed to the entryway. "Go away. And stop calling me."

Brandon's scowl landed on Quint. "You haven't heard the last of this."

Quint wrapped a supporting arm around Taryn's shoulders. She reached up and rested her hand on his, a show of unity.

Brandon hissed, jerked open the door, and stormed out.

Quint caught the door before it slammed shut behind him. Calmly, quietly, he shut and locked it before turning to face Taryn. "That was intense."

She rubbed her head. "I'm done helping him out. Said that last time. Guess he didn't take the hint."

Recognizing her upset, Quint pulled her into his embrace and simply held her. When she wrapped her arms around him, he pressed his lips against her temple. After a few seconds, he both heard and felt her weary sigh. "Ready to get out of this place and go help some deserving people save their town?"

She lifted her head and looked up at him. "More than ready."

****

An hour later, suitcase in hand, Taryn stepped out the exit of her apartment building, spotted Brandon leaning against her car, and slowed her steps.

Quint, right behind her, pulled abreast. "Doesn't take a hint well, does he?"

Taryn grinned at his whispered remark. The amusement faded immediately when Brandon turned in her direction. He leveled his gaze at her, then glared outright at Quint. Gathering her fortitude and irritation with her brother, she walked toward Quint's car, ignoring Brandon in the process.

Good plan except Brandon cut her off. "Taryn. Just listen to me for a second."

Taryn blew out a breath. "I thought I told you no."

"Look. I know I surprised you and well, the timing was bad. Now, I thought we could talk, get things straightened out." He rested his hand on her arm.

Taryn could have sworn Quint growled. As it was, he stepped close, snagged her bag, and deposited both suitcases in the trunk. "Thank you, Quint." She returned her attention to Brandon. "The answer is still no." She tried to push past him only for him to grab her arm.

A second later, she was free and Brandon had to catch his balance a few feet away. He banged into a parked car, frowned, then stared at them in shock. One glance told her Brandon was rattled. Quint, on the other hand, looked like he'd just stepped out of a spa. Calm. Centered. Relaxed.

If any man could handle himself, it was Quint. She appreciated that, especially in this particular scenario. No one had ever stood up for her. The knowledge that Quint did cracked open the wall around her heart quite a bit more.

She didn't believe in love at first sight. Lust, sure. More than that, she figured it took time to fall head over heels. Now, she wasn't so sure her rigid beliefs would hold up against reality.

Quint brushed his hands together as if they had gotten dirty from manhandling Brandon. "I believe the lady told you no."

Brandon swiveled to glare at Quint. Taryn had never seen such an expression of fury and hate from her brother. "Who the hell are you?"

"We've been introduced already. But in case you don't remember, I'm Quint."

"My boyfriend," Taryn chimed in.

Brandon swung back around to gape at her. "You mean your bed buddy, don't you?"

Taryn fought the urge to break Brandon's knee. She could do it. So easily. Instead, she counted to ten, found it didn't help in the least, and opted to just get the hell out of Dodge.

She didn't bother to answer his rude statement. Brandon was already worked up enough for the both of them and would take it out on Quint if given a chance. That much she understood about her brother. He'd always been spoiled but lately had gotten much worse. Things didn't fall into place for him, and he became angry. While her mother thought Jennifer was pressuring Brandon to climb the ladder and bring home more money, Taryn wasn't as sure. Regardless, something had Brandon tied up in knots.

Brandon eyed him with malice. "Butt out. This is between her and me."

"Actually, it's not. We're just on our way out. Appointment and reservations to keep and all." Quint stepped in front of Taryn and ushered her around to the passenger's side of the car.

"Taryn. You can't leave. I need your help."

She shook her head, tired of his insistence that she use her abilities to help him out of a jam again and again. "Sorry, Brandon. Not this time."

He threw his hands in the air. "But I *need* you."

She hardened her heart. "No, Brandon. You *need* to get your head on straight. Bailing you out isn't the answer. Not anymore."

"It's him. This bastard is filling your mind with crap when all he wants is to screw you."

Quint stepped forward in obvious defense. The expression on his face and position of his body told Taryn all she needed to know. If pressed, Quint would do more than take Brandon's knees out. He'd send him straight to ICU.

Taryn stopped him with her hand to his chest. She turned her anger on her brother. "Brandon!" Taryn gasped at his implication. "It's not your damn business who I date, or sleep with, so get over it."

"When did you turn into a selfish harpy?" He flung the insult with obvious rage.

Taryn ignored him, opened the passenger's side door, and slid into her seat. She shut the door and clicked her seat belt. Quint took the driver's side, buckled up, started the engine, and drove off, leaving a fuming Brandon in their rearview mirror.

"Want to talk about it?"

Taryn considered his offer.

"I don't know what's going on with him, but he has no right to treat you that way."

She folded her hands and settled them in her lap. "I

know."

"I'm glad you stood up to him."

"It's about time. I've been bailing him out lately. He has to live with his mistakes at some point."

"Exactly." Quint reached over and laced his fingers with hers. "You always do for others. Sometimes you just have to draw that line in the sand and take care of yourself."

"You're right." The feel of his hand holding hers offered comfort and support, something she'd both craved and needed. There might be several unanswered questions about Quint, but she knew one thing—he was a rock for her. He didn't ask for favors. He accepted what she offered and made for a great guy to be around. Considering her track record with men, that ranked right up there with a miracle. "How did I get so lucky to find you?"

He'd never pushed her for intimacy, always letting her set the pace. She was slow about some things until last night. Heck, last night she'd practically jumped his bones. He'd taken it all in stride and set the night afire. It had been the best sex she'd ever had, even if they hadn't gone all the way. From what she'd experienced during the night, when that time came, they might just burn down the apartment building.

He smiled over at her. "Fate works in mysterious ways."

"I guess so." She brushed aside her hurt feelings and her unending curiosity in order to just enjoy the moment. The man she wanted, respected, and trusted was at her side. They were on their way to help out some less fortunate people and spend a couple of days away from the chaos that had become her home life.

That was the next best thing to a Hawaiian vacation in her book. At least right now.

Several miles passed before Quint spoke. "It's none of my business, but why is he so demanding?"

Taryn peered out the side window, pondering how much to say. "I've been helping him out of jams. He's obviously accustomed to me bailing him out. Like a child, when told no, he's acting out."

"Bail him out? You mean financially?" Quint held the steering wheel with lazy confidence, glancing her direction now and again.

"No. He's been distracted lately with his girlfriend. He's…forgetful. His job doesn't allow for forgetfulness."

Quint rubbed his chin with one hand before returning it to rest on the top of the steering wheel. "Why you?"

She found her feet enthralling. "Because I can."

"Seems to me he's old enough to handle his responsibilities." Quint's tone lacked bite or censure. It was as steady as if he were discussing the weather. Certainly nothing to put her on the defensive.

"I agree." She turned to study him. "How did you get him to release me and send him flying without jerking me along in the process?"

His lips twitched in the slightest. "An old martial arts move. I'll teach it to you if you'd like."

"Definitely." She hadn't had the pleasure of sparring with Quint yet. The idea excited and thrilled her. He had some moves. She did as well. Whoever came out on top could be considered a toss-up at this junction.

Her thoughts returned to their breakfast. He was

telling her about his job when they were rudely interrupted. "You were saying, at breakfast, that you're a field agent, tracking rogues, for an Interpol-like agency."

"Yes."

"So, you're not really here for some R and R?"

"I'm on assignment." He kept his attention forward on the road.

She glanced down at her hands then back up again. "Who are you after?"

"A man called Davis."

"What did he do?"

"He—Son of a bitch." Quint jerked the wheel and stomped on the brake in order to avoid being plowed into by a black SUV trying to pass them, then cutting too sharply back into the lane. Their car went to the shoulder and then some, with a steep drop off mere feet away.

Taryn grabbed onto her seat belt and braced herself as the vehicle tilted up on two tires. Her heart stopped as Quint battled for control. Instinctively, she leaned inward, trying to tip the balance in the right direction.

Life moved in slow motion. Yet, at the same time, in the blink of an eye. She stifled a scream as the car teetered, then fell back onto the four tires. Quint's knuckles whitened as he gripped the wheel so tightly she was afraid it might break. "Quint!"

He punched the gas, jerked the car back onto the road, and darted forward.

Her heart pounded in her ears, and her stomach rolled. The seat belt dug into her chest, but she was alive and the car upright. That meant something. A big something.

"Are you okay?" His question came out a little clipped.

"Yeah." She sucked in air, trying to calm the jitters. "What the hell happened?"

"Stupid black SUV decided to cut me off. Just about knocked us off the road for good." Anger coated his words.

She empathized. If she had the guy in her sights, she'd shoot him in the foot.

The landscape shot by at an alarming speed. She glanced over at the speedometer. "Um, Quint?"

"Yes?"

"Think you might slow down a little? I'm not certain, but going one hundred in a sixty-five might be a bit much. Not to mention jail time if you're caught."

"Right." He eased up on the accelerator.

She noticed he fell into line with the rest of the traffic, motoring just over seventy. At least at that speed she didn't have near as many concerns. "Think we should report him? Maybe he was having a heart attack?"

Quint checked the rearview mirror. "Nope. He corrected as soon as he hit the other lane. If it were a medical emergency, he wouldn't have been able to do that. I vote for distraction."

She nodded slowly. While that excuse sounded as good as any, she was beginning to see a scary pattern. They were shot at, now about run over on the highway. Certainly, they could be random events. Her intuition told her something could be up.

Her phone dinged. She plucked it out of her purse, scanned the caller ID, then put it back on mute.

"Anything going on?"

"Looks like my brother tattled on me to my parents. My mother left me a text, saying, and I quote, 'What the hell is going on? You're living with a man and didn't bother to tell me?' "

Quint winced.

Taryn shrugged. "Family drama is so much fun."

"I hope that's sarcasm."

"Yep."

"Seems like a good time for you to get away."

Now that's an understatement. "Whisking me off is a little romantic." She peered over at him. "A romantic knight in shining armor. Very interesting indeed. Wonder what adventure awaits me?"

He grinned at her. "I keep telling you, I'm good with details."

Her stomach flipped over in a delightful twist. "Yes, you are."

Chapter 13

"Here. Let me help you." Taryn rushed over to assist an older lady as she tried to lift one of the heavy sandbags.

The gray-haired woman smiled at her. "Thank you, dear, but I think I've got it." She hefted the heavy load up and around to the side.

"Wow." Taryn blinked. "I'm impressed."

The lady chuckled. "Use it or lose it."

"Yep. You're an inspiration."

The woman winked at her. "I'm just chipping in, like everyone else."

"How do you stay so upbeat in times like this?"

"Life's too short to let these kinds of things ruin my day or my week. Heck, I don't know how much time I have left on this earth, but I'm not about to spend it pouting because Mother Nature is in a fit. What can't be changed, you just have to let it go. Forgive and forget if you can."

The words resounded with Taryn. "You're quite the lady."

"I'm just little old me." She picked up another bag and hefted it to the side.

"Well, thank you for being you." Taryn sent her a genuine smile and returned to her spot next to Quint, who was busy lifting the half to two-thirds full bags and carrying them to a nearby pallet. Once enough of those were loaded, someone else on a forklift carried it off, and left an empty one in its place. That had been the routine for most of the day.

What surprised her the most was the people, standing shoulder to shoulder, working their butts off, for the good of the community. They didn't complain. They didn't fuss. Heck, they smiled in appreciation for the free lunch and frequent bottles of water passed around. Each one potentially could lose their home, their business, or their job if the river rose high enough to wipe out part of the town. Yet, they put their backs into the effort with dignity and grace.

They had their own personal issues, and the weight of Mother Nature's wrath had to threaten to send some of them to their knees. Instead, they put one foot in front of the other, seemingly grateful for what they had.

Taryn took a lesson from them and tried to incorporate it into her own life. Times were tough, but she'd keep fighting. There was nothing else really to do.

Taryn used her wrist to wipe the sweat from her face. Thick leather gloves protected her hands from the rough sand. She stretched her back and winced at the tightness.

"You okay?"

Quint filled another bag, then propped his shovel up to lean on. Sweat dripped from his hairline and soaked his dark colored t-shirt. Clouds blocked out the sun, but the oppressive humidity made up for it. A slight breeze was the only salvation. Otherwise, she'd have melted into a puddle by now. As it was, she'd need an hour in the shower to get clean and sand free. "Yeah. You?"

"Getting my workout, that's for sure." His arm muscles bulged and flexed with each shovelful. She knew his back would be the same. She just wished he'd strip down enough for her to watch the fascinating play of roped, leashed power in action.

"Why don't you two take off for the rest of the day?" Roger, the foreman for the operation, patted Quint on the shoulder. "New replacements are here. Besides, you guys have been here all day long and look bone tired."

Taryn glanced over, saw more people approaching. Their clean clothes proclaimed them as fresh. "Are you sure?"

"Yeah. We've got enough to keep up production just fine."

Quint handed over his shovel. "We'll be back early tomorrow."

"It's supposed to rain all day tomorrow." Roger frowned.

"I'll wear a trash bag." Quint offered up a small grin.

"Okay. If you insist. We'll take any help we can get. Get some rest while you can. Oh, and thank you for helping out. That means a lot." Roger waved, then headed off to greet the newcomers.

"Ready to go?" Quint asked.

Taryn nodded. "Yeah." She took off her gloves and laid them on a nearby bench. "Somewhere we can clean up."

"There's some hotels not too far away. I asked earlier, and some of the locals gave me a rundown of the better ones."

"Sounds like heaven right now." She didn't mind

getting dirty and gritty, but the sand that managed to hide away in her tennis shoes was driving her crazy. Combined with the sweat and dirt, she itched and scrunched her nose at her own body odor. "I hate to get into your car being this grimy."

"It's a rental. It'll clean up just fine."

She paused and stared at him. "You haven't bought a car yet?"

He slapped sand off his jeans. "No. Got this one for a few weeks. Figured if I decided to pull up roots again, it would suit well."

Her heart skipped a beat as a spike of concern shot through her. "Are you going to pull up roots again?"

He closed the distance between them, lowered his head, and brushed his nose against hers. "No way in hell. I've got something in Rushing River worth staying for."

Her spirit buoyed. She couldn't help but smile. "I hope you're not talking about the fine food at Bobbie's."

He chuckled, the sound musical and compelling. "It's a far second." A quick kiss followed. "You're it in my book." He wrapped an arm around her and escorted her back to the car. "Don't fret about the upholstery. I'll swing by a car wash somewhere along the way."

"Okay." She noted he wore just as much sand and grime as she did. Maybe more. Oddly enough, that addition made him all the sexier. Like a gym workout, sweat did something for a man. The muscles stood out, bulging with each movement. Or perhaps she just noticed them more.

She'd seen her fair share of toned, exquisitely molded bodies in the gym. Quint, wearing his jeans and a perspiration-soaked t-shirt still took the cake. Hands down.

After sitting down in the passenger's seat and getting buckled in, she stretched out her legs and sighed. They'd been at it for nearly eight hours straight, a marathon by the way her body protested.

"That was tough work." He settled in next to her and snapped his seat belt. "Going to be able to walk tomorrow?"

She turned to look at him. "Yeah. I'll take a hot shower, then stretch out. It does wonders."

"I'll take your word for it." He started the engine, pulled out of the parking area, and hit the road.

A couple of miles passed in silence. She ended up dozing off, not waking until the car pulled to a complete stop and Quint nudged her.

"Taryn. We're here."

She opened her eyes to find a large building directly in front of the car, presumably a hotel one of the locals recommended. "I guess we are." She unfastened her seat belt and stretched. "I'm sorry. Didn't mean to nod off."

He smiled softly at her. "No problem. You're beat and needed the nap. How about we get settled in a room, get those showers taken, order room service, then hit the sack early?"

"That sounds perfect." She pursed her lips, wondering what his accommodation plan might be. One room or two. King sized bed or two doubles. So many options, and his choice was of utmost importance to her.

"Do you mind sharing a room?"

"Nope. Not at all. I mean, we've been together,

so…" She closed her mouth to prevent any more faltering words from escaping.

His eyes lit up. "I remember it vividly."

She did, too. All day long today and in her dreams last night. Boy, did she remember.

"So sharing a bed won't be a hardship?" he pursued.

"Not in the least." She hoped for that option.

"Good." He climbed out of the car, went around to the trunk, and gathered up their suitcases. She followed his example, taking her bag and her rifle in hand. Normally, carrying her weapon in didn't cause a stir in Minnesota, especially with a tournament nearby. She expected it to be a non-issue this time as well.

He shut the trunk, beeped the car locked, and looked around before ushering her to the front door.

As many times as she'd been around him, he always had that same habit—lift his head and search, as if scanning the area for threats. Probably a habit developed way back when that had never gone away. Perhaps, in his occupation, it came in handy. She didn't know, but it proved interesting.

The clerk didn't look twice at her rifle case. Instead, he pulled a key from a shelf behind him, handed it over, and pointed the way. The older man seemed too engrossed in his newspaper to pay them more than a smidgen of attention.

They made their way up on the elevator, found their room, and entered. Taryn took a quick gander, finding the typical hotel features. A large bed covered in a bright, tropical-colored bedspread dominated the room. A loveseat sat opposite and a little forward, while a round table and two matching chairs were stationed near the large window. A bedside table matched the décor while a single picture of a sunset complemented the medium blue walls. Two doors were to her left. Probably a bathroom and a closet, if she had to guess. Next to the window, a glass sliding door led to a balcony.

She walked over and peered out. It overlooked the parking lot. Not much of a view, but she didn't mind. They weren't there for more than a night or two, anyway.

"Not too bad."

Turning, she found Quint setting down his luggage and looking over the area.

"Not bad at all." She agreed completely. Although, she really meant the man standing before her rather than the hotel room.

He picked up a menu left on the small table and held it up. "Why don't you choose what you want from room service? While you're in the shower, I'll order.

Or we can shower together. She bit back the thought, glad she hadn't let the suggestion slip. He was tired, sore. Worn out. Tonight wouldn't be the best time for sex. Tomorrow, though… "You can clean up first."

He shook his head. "Ladies first." He handed over the menu, dropping a kiss to her cheek in the process.

She smiled at the small act of affection. "Okay. Then I'll give you a backrub after your shower."

He stilled. "You don't have to."

"I want to." And it was the truth. She'd yearned to run her hands over his body, to explore to her heart's content. The small opportunity before only whetted her desire for more. Like a grand, amazing sculpture, she wanted to admire and touch, to learn about Quint in more ways than one. Art hadn't been one of her hobbies, until now, and just when it came to Quint.

"Then it's a deal."

She pointed out what she wanted before digging through her suitcase, grabbing what she needed, and entering the shower. Determined not to take too long, she hurried through. Less than thirty minutes later, she emerged wearing yoga pants, a stretchy top, and white socks. She'd combed out her long hair and tucked it back into a ponytail.

Quint glanced up at her. His eyes darkened just a bit, a sure sign he liked what he saw.

She smiled warmly at him. "Your turn."

"Food is on the way. I'll eat first." He stood and met her halfway. Reaching out, he paused, frowned, then dropped his hand.

"What's the matter?"

"I'm still dirty. You're clean."

Relieved, she grinned. "That's fixable."

"Yep." His face relaxed before he dipped his head in the direction of her rifle case sitting on the floor. "I guess you went ahead and signed up for the target shooting competition?"

"I did. Figured we're close by, and I might as well try to earn a paycheck. It's the day after tomorrow. I hope you don't mind staying that long." She kicked herself for not asking before.

"Not at all. It'll be fun to watch you shoot."

She sat on the edge of the bed. "Do you ever pack?"

"Rarely."

"Are you packing now?"

"No." He turned back toward her, meeting her

gaze.

When he didn't elaborate further, she opened her mouth to ask. A knocking at the door interrupted her.

Quint covered the distance in long strides, checked through the hole, then opened the door. A busboy of sorts pushed a cart into the room. A large tray with covered plates held the top position. He unloaded each one onto the small table before pulling out glasses, filling them with ice from a bucket, and adding a two-liter bottle of soda to the offering. He collected the unneeded supplies, returned them to the cart, and pushed it back to the exit.

Quint pulled money from his wallet and handed it over.

"Keep the change."

The young man smiled widely and nodded to him. "Thank you so much. If you need anything else, just let me know."

A twinge of guilt hit. She'd always prided herself on independence. Yet Quint was footing the bill for their meals, their hotel stay. The gas for the trip. "I'll pick up the tab for breakfast."

He closed the distance between them, collected her hand in his, and kissed the back of it. "It's my treat. Let me take care of you."

Those familiar words caused a flare of heat in the pit of her stomach. "Let's eat so you can get cleaned up, and we'll move on to that rub down."

"Sounds like a plan." He waited for her to take her seat, then sat in the one opposite.

Hungry, she ate quickly, noting he did the same. By the time she'd finished, he'd cleaned his plate.

"Want some dessert?"

She shook her head. "I'm full. Besides, that giant chocolate chip cookie covered in ice cream is too damn tempting." Although she had a decent metabolism, she didn't dare press her luck.

"I'm sure it's still available."

"No way. Unless you want some?"

"Nah. Not a huge sweet fan."

She gaped at him. "Are you even human?"

He chuckled. "I'm pretty sure I am."

"Let me guess. More meat inclined?"

"You could say that."

She'd noticed his protein-rich meal with a side of veggies. All had been eaten, leaving an empty plate in front of him. "Ah." She leaned back in her seat. "More caveman, less uptown guy."

"Are you calling me primitive?" He stared at her with an amused expression.

She sipped on her soda. "If the shoe fits."

"Uh-huh."

She couldn't take her eyes off him. He dominated the room. Not the best dressed or the worst, his presence simply drew attention. Taryn knew the women checked out his body. The men read Quint's projected confidence and left him a wide berth.

The little spark in his gaze proclaimed his enjoyment of their banter. She knew it reflected her own.

"Maybe you were hatched from an egg?"

He snorted. "Now, you're going a bit far out on a limb."

She finished her drink and set the glass back on the table. "I know we're both beat, but I want you to know that I'm having a great time."

"Good. You deserve a break." He studied her for a long moment.

Her stomach flipped over in a sensual manner. Flashbacks of the last time they shared a bed sent her blood to pumping and her feminine parts to yearning. "I bet you're good with your hands."

He grinned cockily. "Goes right along with those details I'm good at."

Holy, moly. Was he ever good at those details. She resisted the urge to fan herself at the mere thought.

He'd had plenty of unselfish playtime before, letting her lie back and just enjoy. Now, she wanted to return the favor. Well, she'd given back some the last time, but a quick hand job wasn't even close to the reward she truly believed he deserved.

She couldn't wait to finally get her hands on his body and appease her curiosity and hunger. At that moment, she wanted nothing more. "My turn to treat you." She grinned over at him. "You did all the work, and I had all the fun. It's time to flip the tables."

His face took on a sultry expression, one that set her heart to thumping. *Oh, my.* His bedroom eyes were her undoing. She knew if he asked her to swing from a trapeze wearing nothing but a purple monkey suit and a bright red wig, she'd give it her best shot. In private, of course.

And why is that image not as distasteful as it should be? She mentally shook her head at such ridiculousness.

"You didn't have all the fun. I recall having a ball."

She pursed her lips. "Nope. Not going to say it."

A saucy grin appeared on his lips. "I guess I should be getting to that shower?"

"Yep. I can't wait to get my hands on you."

He closed his eyes as if savoring a perfect chocolate cake. "You're a temptation, vixen."

She blinked innocently. "Who, me?"

"Uh-huh." He leaned in close and caught her lips in a delectable kiss. "I'll be out soon." With that promise, he stood, dug a few items out of his suitcase, and disappeared into the bathroom, softly closing the door in his wake.

She watched him go. *Damn, Taryn. You've got it bad.*

The truth said it all. She'd known the guy for less than a month. In that time, they'd been shot at and about run off the road. Then her brother had harassed her to save his butt. Yet she'd jumped in the car with Quint, rushed down to the southern part of the state to help sandbag the river, and ended up in a hotel room with a single bed. Quite the adventure thus far. And Quint was, by far, the best of it.

The sound of running water drew her attention.

I'm pretty damn tempted to go in and join him.

She sighed heavily. *When exactly did I turn into a walking hormone? Oh, yeah. The moment he walked into the gym, that's when.*

With an amused shake of her head, she stacked up the dishes on the tray he left and placed everything outside their door. A quick call to the desk notified the staff that they were finished with the meal and it was ready to be collected.

Task done, she sat on the floor and began to stretch. Her back protested, as did her hamstrings. They were tight after a full day of dealing with those heavy sandbags. If she didn't get them loosened back up, she'd be walking stiff tomorrow.

Out of routine, she moved from one pose into another, yoga positions which allowed her to relax and ease the tension.

She was so involved with her activity, she didn't notice the shower had ceased and the bathroom door had opened. One minute she was alone in the room, the next, she glanced up to see Quint staring at her with an expression that could only be called appreciative hunger on his face.

And she stared back until she realized the wide-legged forward-bend pose was a bit awkward. After all, her legs were spread wide, her butt was in the air facing him, and her head was down low, watching him from literally between her legs.

He grinned wickedly. "Never knew yoga to be so interesting."

She snorted, her momentary hesitation forgotten. "Every six seconds again, huh?"

"Something like that."

Something like that indeed. With him standing there wearing only a towel around his waist, she understood the strong power of want. Her libido landed smack dab in the same ballpark as his. Maybe on the express lane. Three seconds tops. *Cool your jets. Tonight is for him.*

She stood back up. "Ready for that backrub?"

"You can finish, first."

"I'm good. Really." She rubbed her hands together. "And you'll be just as good in a few minutes."

The corner of his lips curled up slightly. Instead of saying anything, he stretched out on the king-sized mattress, stomach down. He rested his arms alongside his head and turned to face her. "Do your worst."

That was all the invitation she needed.

She crawled on the bed and took up a kneeling position next to his right hip. The abundance of muscles fascinated her as much as the way they began taut before loosening under her ministrations. He was a big guy, but if there was an ounce of fat on him, she didn't see or feel it. Just roped, powerful, conditioned muscles. And plenty of them.

She worked on his shoulders first, rubbing and kneading, using her palms to dig in when she felt a knot.

He groaned softly.

She smiled. "Tell me if I get too rough."

"Not happening." He sighed as she worked. "Did you do this for all your boyfriends?"

The query surprised her. He hadn't really asked much about her romantic past. Probably didn't want to know. Not that there was a lot to tell. "No. The only two guys I dated weren't really touchy-feely. They were athletes and addictive bad boys, but lacked in other departments."

"Like in bed?"

She shook her head at his obvious curiosity. "I didn't sleep with Eric, if that's what you're asking. I was stupid enough to go out with him, but that's where it ended." She moved down his spine, lightly massaging every inch of the way. When he said nothing more, she decided that turnabout was fair game. "And you, sir. How many women have you been with?"

He buried his face in the mattress. "I thought talking about past relationships was a sure way to mess up the present one."

"Probably. So just answer me this. Why me?"

He tilted in order to be able to look up at her. "Because you're a spitfire who reminds me about the meaning of life."

"Thank you." Sincerity carried easily in her words.

"No, thank you." He reached up and ran his hand lightly up her thigh and back down again. The tender caress left a heated trail in its wake. "You've got talented hands, Taryn. No one has ever given me a backrub. No one cared enough."

She bit her lip, her emotions riding high at those sage words. Obviously, he'd been dating the wrong women. While she couldn't change the past, she could influence the present. "Well, you're in my care now, and I'm going to make sure you're a puddle of mush when I'm done."

He smiled and rolled back to his belly. "Keep this up, and you'll put me to sleep."

"That's okay." She leaned down and pressed a kiss to his shoulder blade. "You've worked hard all day long. Rest. Sleep. I'm not going anywhere."

He blew out a breath and relaxed.

She continued with her task, making sure to hit every single spot on his back, shoulders, and hips. Over and over she went until his muscles were like pancakes, soft and supple.

Pour some syrup on him and commence eating.

She snorted at the silly idea. *Not now. Tonight is for him.*

As she continued, she let her thoughts run free, thinking about the man who showed up out of the blue and made such an influence on her life. He'd rescued her during that first meeting, stuck by even when she rebuffed him, and rode with her on this impulsive road trip, footing the bill thus far. It was like he couldn't get enough of her and planned on being her shadow until he'd had enough or gotten the answers he sought.

She knew all about unanswered questions. She also knew her track record with men stank. Yet, this diamond in the rough had stolen her heart.

A soft snore escaped him.

She grinned, her heart thudding against her ribs at the cute sound.

"It's been a whirlwind, but I know what my heart says. It says I love you." She whispered the words softly, knowing Quint wouldn't hear, especially in his sleep. There were times for blurting out things and times for more subtle approaches. This was one of the latter.

The sentiment was solid, as were the feelings. This wasn't just about falling head over heels for the new stud in town. This was getting struck with Cupid's arrow for the guy who had a tender heart and a few mysteries yet to solve.

It would come in time. Hopefully, so would his love for her.

Chapter 14

"How do you like Rushing River so far?"

Quint offered up a small smile. "Better with you there."

Taryn snorted. "A little cheesy."

"But true," Quint countered as he took her hand in his.

"And kind of cute." Taryn grinned up at him, soundly interlocking her fingers with his.

They'd bonded on this trip. He'd felt the change in the air, especially this morning. Taryn had snuggled up against him during the night and stayed there. He'd never label himself a cuddler, but damn if it didn't feel good to have her in his bed and at his side.

The back rub she'd given him was top notch, as relaxing as it was stimulating. He'd let himself go, falling asleep before she finished. In a sense, he felt a little guilty for not staying awake to return the favor. On the other hand, the evening ended perfectly just the same.

So perfectly, he could almost forget the threat that stalked them. The only sour lemon in the whole scenario revolved around the inability to know when or where Davis would strike.

And Quint was finding it increasingly hard to keep his attention off her and on the job at hand. She unknowingly distracted him with a simple look, a glance, a movement. He struggled to keep his senses open and observant around her. His instinct to keep her safe won out, but his masculine inner self vowed to pursue the sparks between them in the future.

She squeezed his hand. "What are you so deep in thought about?"

He glanced over at her. "Nothing, really."

"Obviously something."

They continued down the street, heading back toward the hotel. The half-moon broadcast some illumination through the darkness. Widely spaced street lights picked up the rest, allowing for decent vision despite the late hour.

He grappled with the great urge to spill the secret and fill her in on the situation. The fear he'd slam into her life held his words in check. Yet, he needed to ease her into things. To let her take it all in. To be honest with her. "There's something I've been meaning to tell you."

"Yes?" She continued with the lazy pace of their steps.

"It's about my job."

"Okay."

"I'm on assignment to find someone." He chose his words carefully.

"Someone named Davis. I remember. Why would he be hanging out in Rushing River? It's not like there's much going on in that sleepy town."

"It's not because of where, it's because of—"

A thin, scruffy man with unkempt clothes and greasy hair stepped out of the shadows of a building's doorway and shoved a pistol toward Quint. "Hand over the wallet." The guy's hand shook slightly, altering the aim of the weapon from Quint to Taryn.

Son of a bitch. Quint's heart nearly stopped.

Get your head out of your ass, Quint, before you end up getting her killed. He chided himself while formulating a plan of action. Protective instincts roared to life, threatening to shove common sense and rational thought to the wayside.

While he could invade the man's mind and shut some thoughts down or plant an idea of rabid panic, he didn't dare project too much for fear of inadvertently including Taryn in his spray of mental power.

He released Taryn's hand and stepped to the forefront in order to shield her with his body. Slowly, he raised his arms. "Anything you say; just calm down." No other people were in sight, lessening the chance of an intervention or someone to call the authorities for them.

Sweat dripped down the young man's face. His black leather jacket appeared fairly new and fancy, with all kinds of snaps and pockets. Denim covered his lower body, minus tears or bald spots. Even his sneakers were of a name brand and looked new. Yet, it was the guy's wide eyes, filled with wildness, that most concerned Quint. They spoke of desperation and a mighty need—most likely for more drugs, judging by the guy's dilated pupils—or just an idiot on a high that was out of his league. Tremors wracked the man's body, causing the gun to veer once again back to Quint.

"Don't try anything stupid," the robber gruffly warned.

"I won't. I just need to reach my wallet." Quint tried to appease the man, more worried that he'd end up bobbling the gun and accidentally pulling the trigger in the process. If he were alone, he'd have broadcast a mental shard and taken his chance to knock the guy down and out before he had time to pull the trigger. Taryn's presence changed things in a major way. *Better to live to fight another day.* His gut told him the guy wasn't looking to kill in cold blood; he just needed money to secure his next fix.

He reached for the man's brain waves, found them chaotic, and knew there'd be no way to control the frenzy quickly enough to prevent him from pulling the trigger. Adding a heavy charge to the mix would be unpredictable at best, an explosion that could backfire at the worst.

Quint sensed a movement from behind him. He dared not take his eyes off the robber to check it out. Instead, he cautiously stepped back, expecting to bump into Taryn. When he didn't, his senses cranked into high gear.

Taryn appeared next to the guy, though not in full form. She hovered like the spirit of Christmas past. A ghostly apparition. The next instant, she disappeared, completely invisible.

Before he could process seeing her in such a state, the man's arm jerked downward, sending the gun's muzzle pointing toward the sidewalk. His grip wavered a little.

"What—"

Quint jumped toward the man but stopped just as quickly when he heard a crunching sound, and the man crashed to the ground. The second he hit the cement, he hollered, his wrist flattened, and the gun fell from his lax fingers. Immediately, Quint kicked it well out of reach.

"Stop it." The man held his wounded leg, stared up at him, his eyes now showing plenty of fear. "Whatever the hell you are, just stop. Leave me the hell alone. I didn't do nothin'."

Another thud sounded.

The guy cried out in pain. He managed to gain his feet, hobbling when he tried to put weight on his injured knee.

"I suggest you hang around for a while. I'm sure the cops might like to have a chat with you." Taryn reappeared.

If possible, the man's eyes grew bigger. "No. You can't be."

Taryn crossed her arms and smirked down at the guy. "A ghost?" She went invisible once more.

The guy screamed and gimpily hopped off, moving as fast as he could to escape, the gun obviously forgotten in his haste.

"Oh, no, you don't." Quint hurried over, grabbed the guy by his shirt, and dragged him back to the sidewalk. He dropped him down heavily next to fence, well away from the discarded weapon, and scowled at the man. "Move an inch, and you'll regret it."

Judging by the sudden terror clearly written on the man's face, Quint knew that his eyes had briefly turned red, a little side effect of his mental abilities. A power surge, so to speak, which changed the color of his eyes to a molten crimson. Nothing he could do about it, though he'd tried to eradicate that tell-tale sign over the years.

"What...what are you?"

"Your biggest nightmare." Quint smirked at his own inside joke. Satisfied that he'd stay put, Quint pulled out his cell phone and called the police.

Taryn came back into normal view, drawing Quint's attention as he spoke to the dispatcher. She appraised the guy with an expression of gratification on her face.

She seemed to be enjoying herself. *Go figure.*

Quint stared at her with newfound interest. As far as he knew, the ability to go invisible fit under the heading of extremely rare on the paranormal skills list. He'd never met anyone else that could achieve such a state, and he'd been pretty much raised in the Dalliance world.

The paintball woods incident came to mind. She'd gone invisible then; he'd just been too distracted to catch it when it happened. Nowhere in the reports on her listed anything about her being other than an average human. His father didn't mention it, not even in passing. Which meant, her secret was just that—a well-guarded secret. Another puzzle piece or two fell into place. He didn't have everything figured out yet, but slowly and surely was getting there.

And one that he could appreciate—later, after his heart stopped racing from the realization that she'd taken on an armed man, risking her life in the process. Again. He knew he'd have nightmares for days to come because of it. Frustration and left-over fear kept his pulse rate up and the knot in his gut.

A short siren drew his attention away from her and to an approaching police vehicle. As soon as it parked, an officer stepped out. The man's badge read Officer Harrison. Quint quickly greeted him, explained the situation, and pointed out the gun still lying on the sidewalk.

"You know it's recommended that you do what they want. It's safer that way."

Taryn walked over, keeping an eye on the would-be robber. "Where I come from, you fight tooth and nail for everything. So when someone tries to take it from you, then you have to stand up to them."

The cop shook his head. "Choose your battles, sure, but if you didn't have him with you, then I'd recommend you just comply." He gestured toward Quint.

Quint frowned. "Actually, she was the one who took him down."

Officer Harrison's eyebrows shot up. "No kidding?"

"No kidding." Quint gave a sheepish shrug. "She's a barracuda when she has to be."

Respect and appreciation lit in Harrison's eyes. Quint knew his reflected the same.

Taryn drew an imaginary line with the toe of her shoe. "About time all those self-defense lessons paid off."

Quint chuckled. He caught a movement out of the corner of his eye.

"Brown, if you so much as lift your ass off that concrete…"

The robber, presumably named Brown, settled back down. Resignation covered his face.

"You know him?" Taryn asked.

"Yeah. Frequent flyer. He's on probation. Let's just say this will break it big time." Harrison stared at the miscreant for a long moment, then turned his attention back to Quint. "I just need a contact number in case we have more questions."

"Sure." Quint rattled off his phone number.

"Thanks." Harrison strode over, put Brown in handcuffs while reading him his rights, then collected the gun. He noticed Brown's obvious limp. "Hit him in the knee, huh?"

Taryn grinned. "Yep."

Harrison nodded. "Nice." He loaded up his prisoner, placed the gun in a plastic bag, and then climbed back into the driver's seat. With a small wave, he drove off.

"Well, that made for an exciting evening." Quint looked back to Taryn.

Slowly, she turned back to him, her eyes dulling with worry. She chewed on her lower lip and wiped her hands on her jeans. "Maybe I should explain…"

Once more, he became aware of their location—standing on the sidewalk after dark. They'd been lucky once, but he wasn't willing to take another chance on the next mugger that might happen along. Not to mention any other innocent bystanders walking along that might catch sight of Taryn doing her vanishing act. Neither would be a good thing.

"Hold that thought." He took her elbow and tugged her along.

"Where—"

"We've got a few things to discuss. *Inside.*" He quickened his strides, thankful that Taryn didn't balk. Instead, she remained at his side despite the hastened pace. That fact offered a bit of relief.

However, it was the look on her face that foretold of a storm to come.

Quint didn't stop until he stood in front of their hotel room. He dug out his keys, shoved the correct one in the lock, then pushed the door open. After Taryn stepped inside, he followed suit, shut the door, and locked it.

Taryn halted in the middle of the room, her attention focused on the floor in front of her. She fidgeted with her shirt and peeked up long enough to eye the exit behind him. She began to pace, not once lifting her gaze to look at him. "You're angry."

"No. I'm not. Not about what you think. However, you just about scared the shit out of me."

She halted and looked at him. "I had to do something."

He narrowed his eyes. "I had it under control. Damn, woman. You can't keep charging into battle without running the risk of getting killed."

Taryn scowled, threw up her arms, then marched across the floor. The people in the room below could probably hear her stomping. "You were just going to appease the idiot. There was no reason for that when I could put him down and out in less than thirty seconds."

Quint shook his head even as he respected and appreciated the spitfire side of her personality. Meek and mild, she'd never be. Good, since that was not what would keep her alive in this fiasco. That was also not what he ever wanted. Give him a woman who fights back with everything she has. Give him a woman who charges ahead in a crisis. *Give me Taryn.* "There was good reason. I'm not about to stand by and let some moron jacked up high on drugs shoot you because he's got a hair trigger and you've got a temper."

"Temper? That's what you call it?" Her voice rose in decibels. "I'd call it survival instinct."

"And what if he blabs to his friends about you? What then?"

She spun around so fast her hair slung. "No one would believe him. Like you said, he was high. They would just jot it down as some sort of bad trip."

Quint swore she growled at him. "Once the adrenaline wears off, we need to have a talk."

"I might not be around," she retorted.

Hesitant to leave his position blocking the door lest she decide to bolt, Quint casually leaned back against the wall and folded his arms across his chest. He aimed for relaxed in hopes of quelling the enormous amount of worry radiating from her. "Got it. Talk now." He watched her agitated movements, knowing that her barracuda side had made an appearance once again. He aimed for tactful and non-threatening. "Nifty trick you have. Can't say as I've ever known anyone that can go invisible."

She spared him a quick peek filled with stubborn determination. "I need to go." She tried to slip past him.

Quint was having none of it. "I didn't take you for a runner. Thought you had more guts than that."

She stilled and met his eyes. Curiosity and realization shone in their depths. "Why aren't you throwing me out? Packing a bag and getting out of town? Why aren't *you* running from *me*?"

Quint stilled. "Maybe because I'm not quite normal either."

Her eyes widened and her mouth fell open. She closed it right back and tilted her head. "What do you mean?" Her words came out quieter and more controlled.

He stood up straight. "There's always been a

segment of the population that had extra abilities. We're all a descendent of them."

"We?"

Quint motioned with his hand. "There are quite a few of us around. Different powers and abilities, too."

Intrigue fully replaced the earlier concerns in her expression. "What's your power?"

"I'm able to figure out puzzles. Follow a pattern, I guess. See connections."

Her face scrunched. "That's a gift?"

He ignored the slight slap inherent in the question. It wasn't the first time someone had hedged that mystery solving was more of a hobby than an inherited talent. Besides, he understood Taryn didn't mean it in a derogatory way. She wasn't that kind of person. "Yes." He started to speak of his other gift, but shut his mouth instead. The last thing he needed was to terrify her when he admitted he could squash her invisibility trick or steal it from her, splintering her paranormal power in the process. It wasn't something most people wanted to hear.

"Oh." She pursed her lips. "You're a detective of sorts, then."

"I guess you can loosely call me that. But I don't work for the police."

"Then who do you work for?"

"A group of people with paranormal powers. We intervene when regular humans can't get the job done. I mentioned them before."

"You said you traveled the world to track them down." Much more composed, she exuded curiosity rather than hostility as she took a seat on the small sofa.

Quint followed suit, turning to face her from the

opposite end. "There's some real monsters out there—anything from psychopaths to rogues with supernatural powers. We keep tabs on certain people and step in when they cross the line."

Taryn peered at the coffee table. "You investigate murders." She made it a statement, then lifted her chin as if a light bulb just turned on. "So maybe you can look into a murder for me." Hope flared in her eyes.

Well, hell. I just stepped into that one. Quint ran his hand through his hair and pondered how to tactfully get out of this bind. "I don't freelance. Everything comes from the board at the office. We don't get involved in regular murder cases."

"Oh." Her face fell and she slouched.

I'm a rotten bastard. Quint's shoulders sagged under the guilt of shutting her down. "Was it someone close to you?"

Taryn nodded. "My grandfather. Two men broke in one night. They argued with him, then killed him."

"I'm sorry. That had to be tough. How old were you?"

"Six." She blew out a breath and sat up straighter. "The police found nothing. Chalked it up to a robbery gone bad or even a rival businessman taking out the competition. I've been trying to find some answers all my life. Swore to bring his murderers to justice. I promised him as he lay on the floor dead that I'd make those responsible pay. I won't quit until I do." Determination came across thickly in her tone.

Quint resisted the urge to say anything more. He never knew keeping a secret could be so hard, especially when it would ease the burden she placed on herself years ago. "That's a lot to put on your plate at such a young age."

Taryn blew out a breath. "It's the right thing to do. He loved me just like I loved him. He cared for me, read me bedtime stories. He was the best grandfather a girl could have."

That image warred with the real portrait of Ruford Dyal. The man was singly responsible for a dozen or so murders. Anyone that represented a barrier to him, in any way, ended up floating in the sea. No one was safe. Not political figures or millionaires. Even a handful of assassins ended up meeting their demise when they turned their focus to him. Rumors proclaimed Ruford trusted no one and was quick to put out a contract on anyone that tested his ire. He managed to keep his hands clean through hefty bribes and unveiled threats. The combination landed him with more power than a person should ever hold and a circle of people around him that both feared and admired the mob boss. His sharp wit drew in abundant profits which he shared with those backing his ventures. For those few, he was generous. To others, he was the devil walking.

Quint nodded. He didn't dare douse her memories. Not now, anyway. A nagging detail drew his attention. Something about Ruford Dyal and Taryn didn't mesh.

He studied her, comparing her features with a picture of her grandfather seemingly permanently stamped in his memory. She had more of an oval face, a slight tilt to her eyes which made them appear catlike, especially with the vibrant green color. Ruford had a longer face, ordinary brown hair, and dark eyes. He lacked the finer lines that Taryn possessed.

Not everyone looks like their grandparents. Yet, he couldn't seem to miss some blaring discrepancies, namely that his father didn't believe that Ruford had paranormal powers. Taryn could have received them from the other side of the family, certainly, but the connection appeared flimsy to Quint. Too flimsy.

"Let's talk about your invisibility trick."

She lowered her gaze.

"How long have you been doing that?"

"Since I turned fifteen or so. I just woke up one day and noticed my legs were gone. I could feel them, just couldn't see them. I was so frightened I screamed. My mother rushed in, showed me that they were still there, and told me that it had been happening since I was a few years younger." She lifted her head again. "I practiced, worked hard to control it."

"That's an amazing gift you have. Useful in many ways." Quint tapped his chin. "Did you inherit it?"

She shrugged. "I have no idea."

He pondered that for a moment. Reginald said he had no record that her parents or grandfather had any paranormal powers. That didn't mean anything, though. Plenty of others could be walking around with all kinds of abilities, and Dalliance had no clue they existed.

A small smile appeared on Taryn's face. "The only advantage it gives me is sneaking past the guards at my brother's work to collect his forgotten keys." Her amusement fled just as quickly.

"That's what he became so distressed over? Because he'd left his keys at work and you refused to sneak in and retrieve them?"

She sighed wearily. "In the past, yes. I don't know about this last time. He was always forgetting them when he had to open up another office. If he was caught leaving them at work, he'd be in trouble. Same for misplacing them at home. He works for a company experimenting on perfecting racing cars and their efficiency. Big stuff from what he's said."

Something clicked in Quint's mind. The situation with her brother didn't ring true. His gut agreed. The coincidences stacked up with Brandon, his often-missing keys, and the need for an invisible woman to help him out. Not so strange except for the place he worked. "He'd forget his keys where?"

"In his desk." Taryn frowned. "What are you thinking?"

Brandon's aggressive behavior and incensed anger when Taryn refused to help began to make sense. The little black spot grew exponentially where Brandon was concerned. "I'm not sure. Just seems odd that he'd keep his work keys on another ring than his car keys."

Taryn appeared thoughtful. "I mentioned that. He said he wasn't allowed to, in case his car keys were lost."

"Yet he was always forgetting and losing his work keys but not his car keys," Quint said quietly. "And why couldn't he just call a buddy to let him in instead of having you sneak in and put yourself in jeopardy?"

She shrugged. "He was afraid he'd be in trouble. I guess if anyone else knew, he'd be worried they'd blab or hold it over his head. This way, I snuck in when the guards changed shifts. No harm, no foul."

"Uh-huh." He didn't believe it. Something fishy was going on. He just needed time and a little insight to figure it out. "You said never again. I take it you mean it?"

She nodded. "I like using my abilities, but enough is enough." She blew out a breath. "The last time, the guards got chatty instead of immediately swapping out. I was pushed to the limit before the off-going one decided to leave. I was so afraid I'd become visible again and be arrested."

He bit back a growl. "Bastard." The idea of Brandon putting her in such a position sent shards of fury racing through him. He'd be hard pressed not to punch the guy in the face next time he saw him. "He has no right putting you through that."

"I know." She lifted her chin. "He's on his own. It might take another time or three for it to sink into his thick skull, but it's true."

I'll be there when you face him. The silent vow quelled his burning anger. For now. Still, he didn't utter those words aloud. She'd club him for stomping on her independent nature again.

Studying her, her he found a hint of uneasiness, possible wariness in her eyes. He knew he bore responsibility and moved to erase any doubts in whatever way he could considering the circumstances. "You were amazing out there."

A slow smile crept back on her face. "All those karate lessons did pay off."

"I'd say so. Smack, thunk, and he was down. I don't think he's going to mess with another woman again."

She laughed. "I wouldn't go that far. But yeah, it felt good to turn the tables and knock him on his ass."

"You're a hell of a lady," he said sincerely.

Her eyelids lowered a bit. "I could say the same for you."

"I didn't do anything."

"Uh, huh. Not buying it. Yeah, I know you were

trying to keep him calm and keep from getting anyone shot, but I know you were about to go all berserk on his ass. Would have if I weren't in the way."

"Think so?" He found her perception amusing.

"Oh, yeah." She scooched closer, rested her hand on his knee, and leaned in until she was inches from his face. "I think you're pretty spiffy."

"Spiffy?" He chuckled. "That's the first time I've been called that."

She wound her arms around his neck. "Get used to it then." She sealed her lips over his, aggressively taking the leading role.

He encircled her waist with his arms, lifted, and set her gently on his lap. She sat crossways, so turned her head in order to maintain the lip lock. Allowing her to play, he worked on slipping his hands under her blouse and unsnapping her bra. Task done, he collected both cups in his hands and boosted until she broke away just enough so he could rid her of them.

Taryn returned the favor.

He sat forward to allow her ample room to get his shirt over his head. She dropped it to the floor, forgotten. She adjusted her position to straddle his lap.

For an instant, he considered balking, to lay her down and pleasure her and avoid taking her fully. Maybe, just maybe, in the end, she'd forgive him a few kisses and an orgasm or two. Full on sex might be another story. Once he plunged deep, any perceived betrayal would surely slash his chances of keeping her. That, he feared the most.

Then she rubbed her bare chest against his. All other thoughts flew from his mind. His shaft, already quite interested, hardened in an instant and began to ache.

He molded her breasts with his hands, enjoying the feel of her soft skin and hardened nipples. After pressing a kiss to each one, he sucked the tips, lashing his tongue gently over them.

Taryn's quiet moan encouraged him to seek more as did her grip on his head, holding him close. She pressed her pelvis downward, rocking against his cock, which throbbed to be released from his jeans.

He bit back a groan of sheer need.

With leashed passion, he tipped her head down for a meeting of their lips. He plundered, he explored, he mimicked what actions he'd be taking shortly, revving her hunger to a desperate pitch to match his own before he took her.

She broke their kiss on a gasp and heavy breathing. Her lidded eyes spoke of intense arousal, as did her near frantic rubbing of her body against his.

"Bed." He gritted out the word, wrapped his arms around her, and stood. She clung to him like Velcro as he carried her a few steps and deposited her in the middle of the mattress.

Her hair spread out around her head, adding a glow to her already beautiful body.

He tightened his hold on his control, stripped off his pants and boxers, and grinned when he saw the lustful appreciation flare in her eyes.

"Oh, my."

Pride straightened his shoulders, padded his ego, and reinforced his vow to send her over the edge in an unforgettable way—to give her so much pleasure she never wanted to leave him, no matter what happened in the near future.

"Your turn, Taryn." Without waiting on her, he rested a knee on the bed, assisted her to unsnap her pants, and tugged them free. He hooked her panties and tossed them to land on the growing pile of discarded clothes.

He trailed his fingers up the inside of her thigh, thrilled when she spread her legs, giving him ample room to reach her folds. Slowly, tenderly, he immersed one finger inside her while using his thumb to stroke her clit. The heat and abundant moisture told him she was just as turned on as he was. The realization went straight to his head. "You're so hot for me."

She wiggled, pressing closer. "And you're moving too slow."

He managed a rough chuckle while he played her some more. "Patience is a virtue."

"Don't make me kick your butt right here." Her eyes snapped with sensual cravings and a banked fire mixed with a hint of frustration. "Please, Quint. I'm burning up."

The plea lashed him into action. He quickly backtracked, found his wallet, and pulled out a condom. With practiced ease, he rolled it on before returning to the bed. Once there, he covered her, enjoying the sensation of skin to skin contact.

She widened her legs. He occupied the spot, rested his arms alongside her head, and nudged his cock against her.

She lifted her eyes to meet his.

"You sure?"

"Absolutely." Her smile could only be called wicked.

Satisfied she was ready, he gradually connected

their bodies. The initial resistance gave way quickly, allowing him to slide deep. Slickness and heat surrounded him, along with a snugness he knew he'd crave from here on out.

"Damn, you feel good."

She grunted in reply, embraced him with her arms, ran her hands down his back, and lightly slapped his rear.

He jumped at the unexpected gesture and looked down at her.

She grinned ruefully. "Did I mention you're going too slow?"

He laughed, thrilled with her exuberance in bed and willingness to not only participate, but to make her demands known. "I'll see what I can do about that." He buried his face in her neck, found her earlobe, and nibbled. At the same time, he set a steady pace of thrusting, languid and smooth.

She explored with her hands, ran her nails down his flanks, and cupped his ass. Every touch left a fire in its wake, escalating his pleasure by large leaps and bounds. Taryn lifted to meet his thrusts, locked her knees against his sides, and made the sexiest little sounds along the way.

"Bear with me, Taryn. Just a little longer. I'm going to make sure you fly. Just trust me."

She opened her pretty eyes to meet his. "I do."

"Then hold on." He picked up the pace, careful to not get too reckless.

Taryn dug her short nails into his skin and bowed her back. Her breath came in pants.

He knew she climbed fast to the pinnacle, but strove to hold her there, for just a little longer.

Switching from long thrusts to shorter, harder jabs, he added power.

Her body tightened.

He sucked in much needed air, brushed his lips over hers, and let himself go. His penetrations became more frenzied. Deeper, then shallow. Long, then short. Light, then heavy. He thrust over and over again, his gaze fixated on Taryn's face.

Electricity sparkled in the air.

Mentally, he both saw and felt the glowing particles. With a psychic leap, he grabbed them all up, adding them to his own, and used the extras to feed back into Taryn. She projected so loudly, he easily absorbed her energy, mulled it around, then sent it back to her.

Never before had such a thing happened. Yet he found it to be right. Perfect. It heightened his senses and cranked up his already supreme pleasure.

Taryn cried out as her body grew taut. Her face screwed up as her channel clutched his cock like a steel glove covered in velvet. Tight. So tight that he could barely move. It was as if she needed to hold onto him forever.

Quint panted and threw himself into the sexual frenzy. He couldn't hold anything back, had to give it all to her, everything inside of him and out. Including his heart and soul.

Taryn clung to him as if expecting a stout hurricane force wind to rip him away. If possible, her body tightened even more. Then, strong ripples massaged his cock, the walls squeezing with surprising power. Quakes cascaded through her body and ignited him into orbit.

With a muted shout, he followed her into rapture.

A couple of minutes passed before he came to his senses enough to roll off Taryn, taking her with him. He tucked her against his chest and savored the aftermath of the best sex he'd ever had. All because of Taryn.

The bright sparks of psychic energy no longer danced in the air. Peace and tranquility replaced them. He soaked up the last remaining ones and offered them up to a quiet, still Taryn. His gift to her.

She'd amazed him last night. The beauty, grace, flexibility, and strength she displayed transitioned from one complex yoga pose to the next. Watching her bend and flex so smoothly, so effortlessly, impressed him. He marveled at her skills and found her enticing and alluring. Simply beautiful. Inside and out.

She reminded him of a doe in that regard— exquisite and pretty, delicate yet powerful. Just like that deer, the threat of her being in the crosshairs angered him. She deserved none of it. And the thought of some horrible person snuffing out her life made him want to rip Davis apart with his bare hands.

I'll take care of you. Protect you. With my life. He'd never said those words to another person, but there was no doubt in his mind about them this time.

Taryn held the darkness at bay, gave him sunlight and humor. She reminded him of the good times. Also, she kept him hard as a rock and fantasizing about the possibilities her flexibility presented in bed. That particular item fell down the totem pole a step, though, compared to the other pieces she offered. Salvation. A re-ignited sense of purpose. A reason to embrace his abilities, as they were what stood between her and Davis. Her generosity touched him. She'd given of herself to him and others, asking nothing in return. That trait had become increasingly rare.

She gave him hope, peace, and fun. She gave him love.

The elusive emotion evaded him before. Now, he soundly understood what it meant and felt like. There was no time table, no hoops to jump through. It just was. All because of Taryn.

****

Taryn opened her eyes, looked up at him, and smiled a grin of feminine satisfaction and fulfillment.

His pride leaped at seeing the positive results of his lovemaking.

Then her face scrunched, and a slight frown appeared on her lips. "Why are your eyes red?"

Uh-oh. He cleared his throat. "Well…"

"And what just happened?"

Oh, hell. He wasn't sure she picked up on that little extra. Trying to explain it all would only make him sound like more of a freak. "We had sex. Great sex."

She sat up and cut him a look. "Not that."

It was the best he'd ever had. If she classified it as only mediocre, his confidence would take a huge hit, not to mention his dignity. Guys prided themselves on their prowess in bed. He was no different in that regard. "You didn't think it was great?" He waited impatiently for her answer.

Her eyes deepened in hue. She cleared her throat. "That part was incredible."

Pleased, he was all too tempted to puff out his chest, then take her on another magical ride until the serious bewilderment pasted on her face stopped that idea in its tracks.

"That…" She fanned her hand in the air as if trying to find the right words. "That wave thing at the end. It was like you…intensified things…in my mind. Back and forth. Light, then heavy. I don't know what or even how to describe it."

"It's okay. We're okay." He tried to reassure her, doubting she'd drop the topic, but giving it a try anyway.

"Your eyes turned red about that time. Deep crimson red." She sat up and pulled the sheet over her nude body. "No more secrets. Tell me."

Quint rolled off the bed, discarded the condom in the bathroom trash, and cleaned himself off with a washcloth before pulling on his jeans and striding across the room. He stopped at the sliding glass door. Sheepishly, he tucked his hands in his pockets. "First of all, I'd never hurt you." When she said nothing, he bolstered his courage and prayed she wouldn't freak out and run for her life. *Nah.* She was more likely to squash him like an ant instead. Attack first, mortally wound him second. "I have a second ability."

"Which is?" The way she gripped the sheet against her chest marked a line between them. Always before she'd been open and giving. Now, she hunkered in the bed as if only the linens protected her from the monster that was him.

He grimaced. "I'm able to dim the power of another person or borrow it when needed."

"Such as?"

"Your emotions were running high, which made you put off mental energy in abundance." He ran a hand through his hair. "I'm able to absorb that energy and either use it for myself or feed it back to another person.

In this case, you were projecting. I collected it and fed it back into your climax."

A slight blush covered her cheeks. "You can do that during sex?"

"Well, I've never tried it before. Never had the situation or opportunity. With you, it's different." He cringed inwardly at his lack of finesse in handling the situation. *I'll be damn lucky if she doesn't karate chop me in the crotch for such a lousy explanation.*

"Different?"

"I don't know how to explain. You're powerful. The energy was there for the taking. It wasn't something I consciously did. It just happened naturally. Gathering it up is second nature. Not that I've ever fed it back to someone in that same way." He drew in a calming breath. "My eyes turn red when I'm using my powers. Nothing more exciting than that."

He knew he'd just dug the hole about four feet deeper. *Shit. I told Reginald I sucked at these kinds of things. Yet, here I am, anyway.*

She sat up straighter. "So, you steal the energy from another person with paranormal powers and either take their abilities or crush them for good?"

He hated hearing it put like that. So black and white. Calculating. Emotionless.

Isn't that what I'm becoming? She just read the writing on the wall. Nothing I haven't known for a while now.

His morale slumped all the more.

She stared at him. He could almost see the light bulb click on. "Field agent. You're a hunter." Her eyes widened.

He lowered his head. "Yeah." Worried, he turned

to meet her eyes. "I'm not a monster, even though I hunt them."

Taryn remained mute.

Damn it. Say something. He pulled on his patience and continued to explain. "Others track them down. I'm sent in to collect them."

"You mean kill them." Shock and hesitation laced her quietly uttered statement.

"Not always. Some are sick. Really sick. They want help. By the time I've caught up with them, they're more than ready to come in for medical attention."

She stared at him, unblinking.

"They're offered state-of-the-art care. Many are helped."

"If they can't be?"

He looked up at the ceiling. "Imprisoned."

"Why do I hear a 'but' in there?"

Slowly, he lifted his hands and braced them on the sliding glass door. He looked out, not really seeing the balcony or the city below. "Some have no intention of returning or seeking help. Those are like rabid animals. There's no cure."

"I see." The whispered words barely carried to him.

"I'm not a psychopath. I don't enjoy what I'm forced to do. But the lives of innocent people outweigh the rights of another to slaughter them. The job found me long before I perfected my skills. It's my gift. And my curse." He lowered his head.

The creak of the bed and soft footfalls announced Taryn approaching.

Quint didn't move. He didn't dare.

She halted behind him, leaned into his back, and wrapped her arms around his middle. Soft kisses rained over his back.

Surprised but afraid to sabotage the moment, he stood completely still, absorbing her affection as a balm to his soul.

"I'm sorry. Your load is too heavy. Isn't there anyone else to share in it?"

He shook his head. "No. As far as anyone knows, I'm an original."

She gently squeezed in a supportive hug. "Then I'll share it with you."

Turning, he returned her embrace, thrilled when she didn't budge. If anything, she pressed closer. His soul buoyed at her acceptance, something he never thought could happen. "I…"

"Shh." She pressed her lips against his for a brief moment. "Let me take care of you. Trust me."

"With all my heart." He swooped down to seal their lips together, maintaining the contact as he scooped her up and gently deposited her on the bed.

Chapter 15

"I have so many questions." Taryn bit into her banana as she watched Quint finish his toast. The hotel offered a free breakfast bar, the least they could do for the prices they charged to spend the night. And the company wasn't bad. *Not at all.*

Rain poured down and thunder rumbled across the land making neither in a hurry to scurry out into the deluge. The storms were bad enough to cancel the shooting competition for the next day as the area was flooded with more rain to come. Taryn didn't mind. While she lost an opportunity to make some extra money, she gained so much more, namely, several hours with Quint. Alone. In their hotel room.

They'd gone downstairs, loaded up their plates, then escaped back to their room to eat in peace. The small living area contained a work table. They didn't even bother moving the furniture around. Instead, they just parked themselves on the bed to eat—the same rumpled bed after their long night of lovemaking.

Taryn's heart skipped a beat at the delicious memory.

Quint grinned. "Fire away."

She smiled in return. "Where did these powers we have come from originally? How many different types are there? Do they get stronger as we age? Level off? Weaken?"

He held his hands up and chuckled. "Whoa, whoa. Slow down." He tapped her lightly on the nose. "It's widely believed that some segment of the population has always carried a genetic propensity for paranormal powers—ESP, premonitions, even seers. Those have been mentioned in documents for as long as there's been human civilization."

"But nothing like what we have." Taryn tried to wrap her mind around all this.

Quint shrugged. "Maybe. Maybe not. If so, it was kept hushed. Modern theory is that people with innate powers gravitated toward one another, whether due to some natural pull or because of the social need for acceptance, maybe both. Anyway, as people with these powers hooked up and started having children, they passed those traits to their kids, but in a higher dose than before. Take that forward a few generations, and voila, you get some pretty strong individuals with some interesting abilities."

Taryn cocked her head. "Makes sense."

"Yep. As far as your other questions, we aren't sure how many different types of powers there are. Some people have more than one. I'm sure there's a list somewhere if you really want to look it up. As for if the powers wax and wane, it seems to be individual-dependent. Certainly, as kids the powers will be weaker and inconsistent. By the time adulthood hits, the power should reach peak levels. Some argue that it doesn't get stronger, just that the user learns how to adapt and customize their abilities as they go, tweaking them into a finely tuned skill."

She'd pondered the same questions for years but didn't really know how to go about researching them.

Even with the internet, she doubted she'd get a solid response. Now, Quint gave that to her.

"So, do your parents have the same abilities?"

"No. My father can read minds. My mother has telekinesis."

Taryn's mouth fell open. "Reading minds? Holy crap. Please tell me he only has a mild ability."

"Nope. Strong. Very strong."

"Whew. I bet you didn't get by with anything growing up."

Quint grinned a little. "Nope. Not a single thing."

"Telekinesis? Moving things, right?"

"Yeah. Mom can make pretty much any object move. It's a little daunting to walk into the kitchen to find spoons stirring pots without a hand attached to them."

"Uh-huh. I bet." She couldn't imagine such things. Heck, going invisible was pretty advanced, but nothing compared to those people. And Quint. "So, where did your unique power come from?"

"I have no idea. The overseeing body doesn't have record of anyone with my power."

Something about his tone and slowing of words clued her in. "But?"

"But I'm not sure someone with my gift would make himself known and studied. Hunters are just that. We go after people. Why would you want your name splashed across records so the world knows you're a highly skilled killer? Talk about a fire and pitchfork-carrying mob just waiting to happen."

That made complete sense to her. "Any siblings?"

"Only child."

"Let me guess. You were groomed for this kind of

job since you could walk?"

Quint ate another couple of bites before answering. "My skills didn't appear until around puberty, but essentially yes and no. My workplace employs people with all sorts of extrasensory perception. It wasn't a big leap of faith that I might end up there. What they didn't know was my particular type of ability. When it became apparent as a teen, then I was recruited by my father, who heads the company right now."

"Meaning your father locked you into a job and tossed away the key?"

"Something like that. But I always had a choice. Unfortunately, the job chose me. Being the only one with the ability to handle the rogues, it's not like I could just walk away. In a sense, I was their only hope. Sure, they could have an assassin take them out. But with my ability, I can approach them, try to reason with them, and possibly save their lives."

Taryn grasped new understanding of him. "That's a hefty load to carry."

"It is what it is." He took a few more bites and cleaned his plate.

She watched him with a bit of concern. He'd pretty much spent his whole life "hunting" others. Maybe he inspired a few to seek help and escorted them there. Most, likely, he had to kill. For the good of society. For the good of the people. For the good of everyone else except for him.

Her heart melted at the load he carried. Just like last night, she needed to soothe the hurt, to show him that he mattered. To her, he mattered most.

Somewhere along the way she'd fallen for him. Craved him. Wanted him. Loved him. Their time together had been short and tumultuous, but that didn't matter to her heart. Not in the least. For her, he was it.

While she might not be able to admit those feelings openly, yet, she could damn well show him.

She gathered her dishes, stood, and carried them to the small table near the window. "Are you finished?"

"Yes." He handed his dishes and utensils to her when she held out her hands. She stacked them on top of hers.

"What did you have in mind?"

She smiled wickedly. "Oh, I don't know. I have this gorgeous man in my hotel room. It's storming outside. Hmm." She tapped her lips. "What would any sane woman do?"

A grin slowly appeared on his lips. "And the answer is?"

"I'm going to jump your bones, of course."

He chuckled. Happiness and sexual want flared in his eyes. "Since you put it that way…" He moved to stand.

She placed a hand on his chest and eased him back down. "My turn to be on top."

Excitement flashed across his face. A quick glance found a bulge in his pants, a sure-tell sign that he was up for a little fun. Both figuratively and literally. She grinned at the pun.

"I think you're wearing way too many clothes."

"No problem." He sat upright, tugged his shirt off, tossed it to the side, elevated his hips, and quickly removed his pants. When he sat naked, he let his arms hang out to his side. "Now what?"

Oh, my. She had to kick her brain into gear. "Lie back down."

While he did just that, she quickly removed her garments. Naked, she joined him on the bed, sitting next to his hip, facing him. "Did I mention how excellent you are in the sack?"

The corners of his mouth curled up in a wicked way. "You keep forgetting. I'm good with details."

"Yes, you are." She ran her fingers over his chest and down his stomach. "You're also a good man." She punctuated the statement with a kiss to his chest, then to both pecs. "A sweet man." Another caress, this one to his mouth.

When he lifted his head, their lips clung for a moment longer.

She smiled at his enthusiasm. Scooting lower, she left a meandering trail along his body. "A caring man."

He rested his hand on the back of her head. "Singing my praises?"

"Uh-huh." She nibbled his six-pack abs. "A strong man who stands up for others." She arched her back in order to lightly lick up the inside of his thigh. "A brave man who keeps the rest of us safe."

His hips jerked.

She lapped at his balls. "A sexy man who I can't get enough of."

He moaned low, spread his legs more, and caught his breath.

"A man that I'm honored to be with." She nuzzled his shaft. "A man that makes me bold, hot, and needy." She ran the tip of her tongue along the underside of his shaft. "The man I want to be with because he's pretty damn amazing." She opened wide and took his shaft into her mouth, then treated him to a tongue licking along with a bit of suction.

"Oh, yes. Taryn, damn." He gripped the bedspread in his hands so hard his knuckles whitened.

She bobbed her head and added a little hum.

He cried out in a hoarse, muted shout. His breath became erratic. "You're going to make me come."

For a split second, she considered doing just that, wavering between pleasing him this way or another.

"You're special, Quint. I…" She stalled on the words, unable to toss them out there lest he not return the feeling. Instead, she focused on the moment. "This time is just for you. And for all that you do." She resumed lapping at his shaft, working her way over the tip and along the length, nearly to the base. Finding his balls, she lightly weighed them with one hand, adding a little caress in now and again.

Quint's body tightened. His face screwed up. "Taryn."

A moment later, she experienced his release. Still, she continued showering him with pleasure until he sat up with a flinch. "Sensitive."

Pulling away, she smiled up at him, kissed him quickly, then retreated to the bathroom. She warmed the water, dampened a towel, and returned to wash him off.

"Thank you." His sincere words came out a little breathless.

"Oh, don't thank me yet. I've got all kinds of expectations for round two."

He groaned dramatically. "How did I know you were insatiable?"

She smiled. "Only with you. Only with you." She set the towel aside, grabbed Quint's wallet, and handed it to him. He pulled out a condom before setting the wallet on the bedside table.

She climbed back in bed and urged him to lie back down. When he did while rolling on the rubber, she straddled him. "You haven't seen anything yet. I've got a hankering for a ride. A long, hot, hard ride." She studied his face. "Think you're up for it?"

"Oh, yeah."

"I knew you would be." She leaned over and sealed their lips together. His aggressiveness and passion told the story—he wanted her as much as she wanted him.

Now, if that could only be true in other ways.

He'd stolen her heart. She only hoped he'd be willing to share a little of his in return.

His fingers found her slit, then her nub. All thoughts vanished under the unrelenting pleasure. He touched. He caressed. He rocked her world. Then, he bonded with her in a psychic meteor shower rivaling and surpassing the brilliance of the great northern lights.

She knew love. Quint had shown it to her in every way imaginable. Everything except the words.

They'll come. They have to.

Chapter 16

The next morning, reality returned. They climbed out of bed, ate breakfast, showered, dressed, and reluctantly gathered all their belongings before the eleven o'clock checkout time. Since the target shooting competition had been canceled, they opted to simply return home, a bittersweet end to the all-too-short vacation.

Taryn hated to leave but made a promise that they'd do something like this again soon. A weekend trip. Just the two of them.

"I hope the town is okay with all that flooding."

"Me, too." Quint reached out to take her hand in his. "I'm sorry you have to go back to a mess."

"It is what it is." Taryn's attention turned to the scenery outside her passenger window. Her mind locked onto her troubles and spun them around. No epiphany occurred.

A couple of hours later, Quint pulled into the parking lot of their apartment building.

Taryn sighed. "I guess we're home."

"Yeah." He cut the engine and turned toward her. "I'd rather go back to the hotel and not stick our heads out the door for another week or so."

She smiled at the thought. "Me, too, but I suppose we have to be responsible adults. Like it or not." She climbed out of the car, waited for Quint to open the trunk, then pulled her suitcase and rifle out. Quint followed suit, carrying his suitcase in one hand.

He led the way toward the entrance. She followed along.

Movement in the parking lot drew her attention. A man stepped between cars and dipped out of sight. Taryn paused.

Quint stopped. "What is it?"

She stared a bit longer, didn't see anything more, then shook her head. "Just thought I saw a man, someone that rang a bell."

Quint stood up straight and stared in the direction she'd been looking. "Taryn, get inside."

Confused, she did as he commanded. "What's going on?" His protectiveness came out at odd times, sometimes stepped on her independent toes, but she never complained. He had her best interest at heart, the same as she had with him.

Quint ushered her inside the building before returning to the lot. She watched from inside the front door, bewildered with his actions.

After a few minutes, he entered, shutting the door firmly behind him.

"What was that about?"

"Let's get in the apartment first, and we'll talk." He urged her ahead with a hand on her back.

She entered her home, glanced around, found nothing amiss, and put her things down. Curious as to what caused Quint's concern, she left her home, locking the door behind her, then nearly bowled over Quint, who stood just outside her door as if blocking anyone else from entering.

"What's going on?"

He put his finger to his lips. Pausing for a second, he dug out his key and let them both into his apartment.

Automatically, Taryn glanced around. He'd always visited her apartment, never the other way around. She'd been afforded a peek inside now and again, but that was all. She hadn't thought anything about it. No biggie. But now that she had the opportunity, she checked it out.

"Did you want something to drink?"

"No, thanks. I'm good." She raked the area with her gaze. The furniture mimicked hers. Basic. Nothing fancy. A deep brown sofa with a matching recliner occupied most of the living room while a small, deep walnut-colored coffee table added a touch of class. Large windows oversaw the front of the building, with beige colored curtains hanging on either side. A mid-sized television sat in the corner. The kitchen appeared clean, like the rest of the place. The countertops were bare of clutter, and the hardwood floors shone as if they'd been dust mopped recently. A hallway led to presumably his bedroom, if the rest of the place had been set up in the same pattern as her own.

She considered his bedroom, wondered if he had a king-sized bed and masculine colors that proclaimed the area entirely male-dominated. Curious, but mannerly, she resisted the urge to take a gander.

The whole place appeared a little cold. Nothing warm or personal. Just somewhere that he lived. She found the realization sad.

Turning, she discovered one item which snared her attention—a picture sat on a mantel. It drew her. The need to understand more about the man compelled her to walk across the room and pick it up for a closer inspection.

The photo had been taken years before, showing Quint as perhaps an early teenager. Presumably his parents stood behind him, his father's hand resting on his shoulder. That hand and wrist led to his exposed forearm.

Her breath seized and her stomach dropped as she focused on that hand. Bringing the picture closer, she studied the tattoo on the man's lower arm. A web, with a black spider to one side. The all-too-familiar red spot and eyes peering back at her mirrored her nightmares.

Oh, my God. It can't be. Her mind swirled into chaos at the finding. Questions fired like bullets across a battlefield, bouncing and ricocheting in her mind. *How? Why?* She bit her lip as the deep hurt stabbed through her heart.

Grappling for calmness, she managed to swallow past the lump in her throat. "Who is this man?" The words came out a little hoarse. She turned around and held up the photo for Quint to see.

Quint smiled slightly. "That's me and my parents. I was maybe thirteen or fourteen at the time."

Her heart crumbled at his words. Quint's father was the killer. There was no mistaking the tattoo or its location on his body. Memories flooded her. She closed her eyes, pictured that horrifying moment, then opened them again. Certainty came to her along with a rush of leashed rage. "He sent you."

"What are you talking about?" Quint's lips flipped upside down into a frown. His expression became one of cautiousness as he stared at her with a hint of guilt reflected in his gaze.

She shoved the evidence toward him. "Your father.

The man with the black widow tattoo. The same man who killed my grandfather in cold blood, kidnapped me, then took me to live with the Golds." She pointed to the mark on the guy's arm. "This man is responsible for murdering my grandfather, and he sent you after me."

"No, Taryn, wait. It's not like that." Quint's voice took on a soothing quality.

Too bad she was way past that. She saw a red haze as years of fury clashed to the fore. "Then what the hell is it?" She forced herself to drop the family portrait into a nearby chair rather than throw it at his face like she wanted to. "Never mind. Just answer me this. Are you here to kill me?"

"No." He strode to her. "I'm here to protect you."

"Yeah, right." Trust in him crumbled like a cookie in a toddler's hand.

"Just listen," he pleaded. Concern and pain dominated his expression. None of it mattered. Just the knife sticking out of her back did.

"No, I'm done listening." She glared at him. "That's why you're here. Because of me. I knew it. Knew people don't just show up in Rushing River to get away from it all, not like you. You said you were looking for someone. Me. You were looking for *me*." She threw her hands up in the air. "All of this was an act. You sticking to me like glue. The sex. All an act to…draw me in." Emotion caused her words to falter and crack.

"Taryn. No. That's not true." He approached with his hands hanging loosely at his sides.

She took a big step back, maintaining the distance between them. "How could you be so callous? So heartless? I thought you cared for me." Tears overflowed.

"It's not what you think. I'm here to protect you. Dalliance is tracking Davis—"

"Dalliance?" She gaped at him. "You work for Dalliance?" It all came together. She'd been so close. If only she'd known that Quint would arrive and save her all kinds of trouble trying to discover what she'd always sought. Of course, he'd broken her heart in the process.

"Yes. If you'd just calm down for a second and listen, I can explain." He reached for her.

She dodged his hands, retreated to his door, and slid out. A few steps later, she entered her apartment and slammed the door shut behind her. Her heart completely shattered, she drew in air, wiped at the tears, and tried to kick her brain into gear. *What am I going to do now?*

Glancing around the room, she saw the familiar surroundings blur under the onslaught of tears. She wiped them away angrily, walked to the bathroom, and blew her nose on a tissue. She spied herself in the mirror and looked deep, deeper than she had in a very long time, and didn't like what she saw.

Years ago, she'd made a vow. Recently, it had lessened in importance and became like a side hobby in her busy life. Shame pinched her for that neglect. Add in the fact that her job at the gym had just been chopped, her adoptive parents wanted her well away from them and couldn't be bothered to answer a few questions about her adoption, and the writing was on the wall.

It was time to get the hell out of Dodge.

With Quint living just a few steps down the hall, she knew he wouldn't allow her to hide for long. Which meant she could either confront him and kick his ass or pack another bag, this one with clean clothes, and hit the road.

She would have flipped a coin if she'd had one. Instead, she decided that she'd feel too guilty if she actually hurt Quint. Thus, the only option was to leave.

Twenty minutes later, two suitcases and her rifle in hand, she quietly snuck down the hall and to her car, thankful that she'd parked in the back and Quint's apartment oversaw the front. She made quick work of loading up, then drove straight for the gym. After all, she needed to turn in her keys and ask Macy to take over for the last few days of the gym's existence.

She parked in her old spot on the side of the building away from the glass door and entrance. She didn't have to, especially considering the lack of cars. But once a habit, always a habit. Obviously, word had gotten around and people had called it quits early. No matter. What was done was done.

She entered, found Macy at her usual station just inside, and smiled. "Hey, Macy."

"Taryn. How was your trip?" Macy smiled genuinely. She was young, pretty, and friendly, which was why she'd made for a perfect greeter.

"It was fine. Listen, I'm kind of in a hurry. I wanted to let you know that I'm going on a road trip. Figured no sense in working the last three or four days since I'd already packed up my stuff."

Macy tilted her head. "Vacation?"

"Yeah, I guess so. Just taking some time to figure out my next step." *Well, that much is the truth.*

Macy nodded. "I understand. This is the perfect time to do it before finding and starting a new job. Where are you going?"

"That's the fun part. I haven't decided yet. Figure I'll start heading one direction and see what looks good when I get there." She offered up a smile.

"Wow. Footloose and fancy free."

"Yep." Taryn removed her gym key from her ring. "Here. Can you turn this in when you do yours? Trent will be back the last day to collect them."

"Sure." Macy accepted it and stuck it in her pocket. "I'm going to miss working with you. You've been a great boss and an inspiration. I don't know another woman who can shoot like you do."

"Thanks." Taryn hugged her. "I've enjoyed working with you, too. Enjoy the rest of your summer, and good luck in college. I know you'll do great." She released her and walked back to the door with a small wave. "Take care."

"Bye, Taryn."

Taryn hurried to the side of the building where she'd left her car, only to slow her steps as she noticed Brandon leaning against her driver's side door with his arms crossed over his chest. *Well, hell. Just what I need. Not.*

"Brandon. I'm in a hurry, if you don't mind."

"Where have you been?" He stared down at her with a stern expression.

"None of your business. And like I said, I've got things to do, so please move."

"Where's that jackass boyfriend of yours?"

Inwardly, she flinched. "Why do you care?"

His face clouded. "Because you're my sister and

he's just hanging around to screw you a few times before hitting the road again."

Wow. For once Brandon is right. Sort of. She schooled herself to keep a straight face and not show how he'd hit the nail a glancing blow. Deciding to cut to the chase, she planted her hands on her hips. "What do you want, Brandon?"

"I need your help getting something back."

She sighed heavily. "I told you no before. I haven't changed my mind."

"This is really important. The last time, I promise."

"Uh-huh." She didn't believe him. He'd only gotten worse and worse lately. The chances of him turning around and flying straight were slim to none. "Your keys again?"

"No, my laptop."

A memory snagged her attention. Brandon once told her he couldn't work from home because no computers were to leave the workplace. His boss worried about them being stolen from cars or homes, which set up the possibility that secret information could get out there. That's why, no matter the weather, Brandon always had to go into work.

"Your laptop?" She played innocent, wondering where this conversation might lead. Her gut told her that some major insights were right around the corner.

"Yeah." He ran his hand through his hair. "I misplaced my laptop."

That didn't make much sense to her. "How did you 'misplace' a laptop?"

"It was a crazy day. We had meetings here and there. I was all over the place. I realized on Friday evening that it wasn't on my desk. I searched around my department, but it wasn't there. Which means I probably left it in the research area's conference room. It's black with a red Porsche decal on it." He smiled charmingly, but it didn't quite reach his calculating eyes.

She realized that he'd changed from the brother she'd grown up with, and not in a good way.

"Why can't you just go down there and retrieve it when you go back to work?" She checked her watch. It was just past noon.

"My boss is watching me. He's such an obsessive freak. The cameras. The guards. He watches over us all the time. If we leave even a pen out of place, he's liable to fire us."

"I'm sure Mr. Hanks has a reason to be so obsessive, considering the kind of company he runs," she pointed out.

Brandon frowned. "One of the guys lost his keys. He was canned immediately. If he figures out that I misplaced my laptop, I'm sunk."

She scoffed. "It's not like you lost your laptop when your car was stolen." She waved her hand. "Just go back to work and track it down."

He stepped closer. "You don't understand. I have to have that laptop. Today."

She blinked at his low, snarly voice. "I just said go back to work and get it. No biggie."

"You don't understand." His face scrunched up into a mean scowl. "That laptop has the blueprint for a new design on a high-flow fuel pump. If it works in tests, it can revolutionize the industry. That's millions of dollars."

A red flag waved in her mind. "You're in sales.

Why do you have a research blueprint on your laptop that isn't available for sale yet?"

He lowered his head and met her eyes firmly. "Because I want my cut of those millions. And I'll get it when I deliver that information to Seamless Industries."

She gawked at him as the puzzle pieces fell into place. "You're selling research information from your company to another?"

"So what?"

"That's called industrial espionage." She shook her head. "I can't believe you'd stoop that low. It's a felony, Brandon. Did you consider that?"

"I call it payback and my due," Brandon snapped back angrily.

"No. I won't be a part of this." She brushed past him.

He grabbed her arm hard enough to bruise. "Oh, I think you will."

She glared at him. "What happened to you? You used to care about people, to put others before yourself. Were dedicated to your job. One that you loved."

"I got fed up with coming in last all the time. Now, I'm in the driver's seat." He gave her a small shake. "You're not going anywhere. You'll do what I tell you to do."

"Go to hell." She kicked him squarely in the knee. Immediately, he released her to grab the wounded area. The moment he bent over, she nailed him in the groin with another kick, then used her clasped hands to come down on his upper back. He crumpled to the asphalt.

Not bothering to check on him, Taryn jumped into her car, fastened her seat belt, and backed out of her parking spot. She sped by just as Brandon regained his feet. The expression on his face made her shiver. He was pissed. Pissed enough to do more than bruise her arm.

Once she hit the highway, she realized she had nowhere to go. Quint was probably still in his apartment waiting for her to get over her mad and give him a second chance. Fine and dandy, except that she didn't want to ever see him again. Brandon would pursue her, fearing she'd go to the cops. The aggressiveness she'd never witnessed in him before frightened her. Sure, she could go to her adoptive parents' house, but honestly, her faith in the people that had taken her in had crumbled greatly. Who was to say that the Golds weren't supportive of Brandon's actions and would back him to the end? The thought might be a stretch, but they'd shown their true colors by refusing to spill the beans that would fill in some immensely important gaps in her timeline. She hadn't been able to bring herself to forgive them just yet. Maybe never.

No. I just can't.

Her once stable world had fallen apart. The dream and goal she'd endeavored toward for so many years had finally come true—she'd found one of her grandfather's killers. However, that had backfired as well, tearing a big chunk of her heart out with the realization that the murderer was Quint's father. She truly had no safe house, no escape or hiding place. Quint and Brandon might pursue her, adding to the realization of how dire her situation had become.

She tightened her grip on the steering wheel, then blew out a breath. Tears threatened. She blinked them back.

"Now what do I do?"

A picture of her grandfather's mansion popped into her mind. *There's one place I can go.* She hadn't been back since she'd been ripped away at the age of six, didn't even know what had become of the place. But she'd recalled the address. Written it down as soon as she reached her new home with the Golds. After all, she believed she'd return there one day. Times had changed but that address remained etched in her memory.

Now, she wondered if it had been sold, remodeled, or just left vacant all those years. Certainly, she never saw her belongings again. Either they were sold or trashed. The thought stung. After all, those were the happy memories of her youth, the only real family she ever had.

She stopped at a crossroads. Left took her back to town. To Quint. To her crashing life and joblessness. Back to her home where Brandon could track her down and threaten her to obey. She shuddered at the thought of what he might do. Only the immediate family knew about her ability to go invisible. If Brandon told, people might not believe him. That's all she had going for her. Otherwise, he could ruin her.

She shook her head, unhappy with that particular scenario.

A black SUV with tinted windows approached, pulling up behind her. She tried to wave him around, but he didn't budge.

Decision time.

Right led to the interstate and south—to Texas.

It's not like I have anything to lose. The decision felt correct. Not only to get away from the chaos in Minnesota, but also to get back to her main goal in life—discover who killed Poppy and why. And to make someone pay. Finally.

Without bothering with the turn signal, she hooked a hard right. "Spontaneous road trip it is."

She had clothes, her purse, a credit card, and her cell phone, presently turned off to avoid anyone she didn't want to speak to from harassing her. Inside her purse, her Glock 19 rested in a special compartment. She'd obtained her conceal and carry license ages ago and felt much more comfortable having the handgun with her at all times. A woman alone, especially at night, couldn't be too prepared for unsavory happenings. Sure, she could go invisible. That might work fine and dandy, as did her background in karate. Unfortunately, when faced with worse situations, she might need more protection. That's where her Glock came in.

With those tools, she could make it.

"Maybe, just maybe that's where all the answers await."

The optimistic thought both encouraged and worried her.

****

A banging on the door a few minutes later drew Quint's attention. He stepped out to see Brandon.

"I know you're there. Open this fucking door right now."

Quint's radar told him something big was up and Brandon was in the mix. He stepped out of his apartment and into the hallway. "What do you want with her?"

Brandon swiveled his head and glared at Quint. "You. This is your fault."

"What is?"

"Taryn. I just saw her at the gym. She blew me off and left. She's upset, and I need to speak with her."

Quint read between the lines easily enough. Yes, she was upset. Brandon probably wanted another favor and met up with her resistance again. His aggressive reaction spoke of desperation. Whatever he'd gotten himself mixed up in, he expected Taryn to bail him out. When she refused, he'd lost his mind.

"I thought she told you no?"

Brandon swung around, stepped forward, and limped heavily on one leg. It just about buckled at the next step, effectively halting his forward momentum as he steadied himself against the wall.

"What happened to your leg?"

"None of your fucking business. Now where's Taryn?" His growl didn't go unnoticed.

Quint widened his stance and released his arms. If Brandon wanted to go another round, he'd be ready and willing to lay him out. "Why do you think I know?"

"Because you've been attached to the hip with her for the past few days. You've been screw—"

Quint punched Brandon in the nose. "You won't speak of your sister that way." He lowered his voice and added enough command that even an idiot would take the hint.

"Go fuck yourself." Brandon took a swing at him.

Quint ducked and came back with a hard front-kick to Brandon's knee. He fell to the ground clutching the injured leg. "Son of a bitch. Same damn knee as she hit."

"Taryn hit you?"

"Shit. Yes."

"Why?" Quint narrowed his eyes. Taryn cared for

her brother. She had excellent common sense and restraint. She didn't go around beating up people for no reason. Which meant that she had to defend herself from Brandon.

"No reason. She went off on me. Stupid woman." Brandon struggled to his feet, cut Quint one more look of fury, and walked off with a decided gimp.

Taryn? What the hell happened, and where are you?

He returned to his apartment, shut the door, and picked up his cell phone. Worry hastened his movements. The knots in his stomach told him things just went straight to hell in a handbasket.

Quint dialed Taryn's cell phone number, cursing when it went straight to voicemail.

"This is Taryn. Leave a message."

"Taryn. It's Quint. I know I screwed up. You're upset and hurt, and I'm sorry. I should have handled this differently, but I didn't. We can work this out. I promise. What's most important right now is that you know something I've been trying to tell you and haven't been able to. Davis, the killer I'm hunting. He's after you." A beep ended the recording.

Quint paced the room, agitated and anxious. She was out there alone, somewhere, with Davis. *If I don't find her soon…*

He tried her number again.

"This is Taryn. Leave a message."

"Damn it, Taryn. Pick up."

Still nothing.

He hung up and forced himself to think. *Where would she go? The gym?* It would close the doors for good very soon. She'd told him that she'd packed up her belongings the day she'd learned of that fact. There was nothing pressing left for her there. Besides, Brandon just said she was there but had come looking for her at her apartment, meaning she'd left. Her brother was nothing more than a bully and source of irritation for her. She'd avoid him like the plague. *Her adoptive parents.* There had been a recent falling out. He wasn't sure if they were even to the level of speaking much at this point. In her degree of upset, going there might be like tossing gasoline on an inferno.

"Where?"

His phone rang. Immediately he answered. "Taryn?"

"No. What's wrong?" Reginald's voice came through like a beacon, calm and clear. A guiding light to rational thought.

"She's running."

"What in the hell happened?" Reginald's surprise warred with frustration in his tone.

Quint rubbed his forehead. "She saw a family picture of us. Recognized your black widow tattoo. That jogged some memories, I guess. She knows you were one of the men there when her grandfather was killed and that you're the man who took her to live with the Golds."

"Shit."

Quint couldn't have said it better.

"Her timing sucks. Davis has killed again. Just twenty miles from Rushing River. That's what I called to tell you. He's closing in."

Those words sent cold chills down Quint's spine. "He'll follow her."

"Where would she go? To the Golds? To see her brother? Maybe a friend?"

Quint had already thought about all those options. An answer popped into his mind. His gut agreed. Instinctively, he knew he'd guessed right. It all made sense now. "None of them."

"What do you mean?" Reginald asked.

"Something's going on with her brother. He was livid with her. Banging on her door. Said he'd left her not long ago at the gym. They'd had a confrontation, it seems. He was limping around a little, too. My money's on the fact that she defended herself to get away from him."

"So if he's after her or even out of the picture, where else would she go?"

The final puzzle pieces filled in quickly in his mind. "To her grandfather's house."

"Why there after all these years?"

Quint grabbed his duffle bag and started packing. "That's where all this began. She's been searching for answers. She has a few already, as well as the eye-opening realization about you and me and that her brother isn't who she thought he was. Her job ends in a few days, and she's at odds with her parents. Her world is shattering. Human nature is to return to a safe and familiar place, especially at times of duress. She's going home."

"Get to the airport. I'll get a company jet there as fast as I can."

Quint did the time calculations in his head. "She'll have to spend the night somewhere. I just hope to hell Davis isn't hot on her trail."

"Me, too." Reginald paused. "Check in as soon as

you get there."

"Will do."

"And, Quint?"

"Yes?"

"I'm sorry. You were right. I should have approached her years ago."

Quint held onto the phone with one hand and used his knee to stabilize the bag while he zipped it up with his free hand. "Water under the bridge, Dad. Water under the bridge."

Chapter 17

"Poppy, let's go outside. Walk along the road. See where it leads." She clutched his hand and tugged.

"No, Taryn. You must never go through those gates. Never." He latched onto her upper arms so tightly, she winced. His severe frown hurt her the most. She'd never seen him so angry.

"Why, Poppy?"

"Because there are bad people out there that will try to take you from me. That must never happen. And the only way to prevent it is for you to stay safe behind the fence at all times."

The memory of that day made the moment all that more surreal, almost as if she could peer down at her young self and view that very instance all over again. "You were wrong, Poppy. These fences didn't keep me safe at all."

She didn't know what exactly she expected to see as she pulled into the long, winding driveway to the mansion, but a freshly mowed yard and clean windows reflecting the bright sun wasn't it. Dilapidated or perhaps overgrown and unkempt, yes. Pristine, no.

Unless someone bought the place.

The thought, formerly just a vague possibility in her mind, rushed to the forefront, leaving a sunken feeling in the pit of her stomach. If the place had been sold, everything inside would have been auctioned off or simply thrown away. As much as she'd told herself that it didn't matter, in the end, it did. Her chance at re-grasping her past, even for a few minutes, shattered.

Stoically, she lifted her chin, pulled up in front of the detached garage, and parked. She sat there a few moments, collecting her courage and formulating what to say when some stranger answered the door. *Hi. I used to live here until my grandfather was brutally murdered in the living room. Do you mind if I have a look around?*

She snorted to herself. *Yeah, right. That will get a police visit and questioning for sure.* Nothing else came to mind. Winging it won out.

No time like the present.

She gathered her courage and quelled her nerves with a couple of deep breaths. Getting out of the car with her purse on her shoulder, she beeped the car locked from habit, walked up to the front door, and rang the bell. She waited and waited. No one answered. She tried again, along with knocking, with the same result. She checked her watch. Just after noon. People should be home at that time of the day, right? Unless they were at work. Which was a good possibility, but one she couldn't wait on.

She glanced at the rock bed to the right of the door. A recollection struck as she recognized a particular stone, one left over from her time there. After a quick look around, she hurried over, picked it up, and immediately noticed the light weight. *This is it.* Flipping it over, she pushed on a small door, then disconnected it entirely. She tapped the bottom of the rock against her hand, smiling ruefully when a key landed on her palm. Without further pause, she stuck the key into the lock and turned. Holding her breath, she let it out when a click sounded. She turned the knob and pushed. Easily, the door opened for her.

I'm not breaking and entering. No breaking. Okay, I'm entering, but I have a key, so it's okay.

The small pep talk didn't quite settle her high-strung nerves.

Hurriedly, she stepped inside and shut the door behind her, automatically locking it in her wake. No alarms went off. No one rushed to the entry way. The house was simply silent. It either bode well or really, really bad.

"Hello? Anyone here?" Her voice echoed through the large open area.

There was no answering call or footfalls. Nothing. Just silence.

Intrigued, she slowly wandered around, taking in the layout of the house, the furniture, and the wall hangings. Memories assailed her every which way she looked. An old picture hanging on the dining room wall caught her eye. Kittens were drinking milk under their mother's watchful eye, a watercolor she adored as a kid. Poppy mentioned getting rid of it in favor of something more expensive. She'd begged for that to stay. And so it did, and still did to this day. She turned toward the living room. It remained the same—the leather couch, the recliner, under the coffee table the area rug with swirls of bold reds and blues on a black background.

Excited and intrigued, she kept walking, taking in one room after the next.

A few minutes later, she froze. Her heart sped as she stood at the entrance to her old bedroom. Peeking in, she gasped. Her bed, neatly made, centered the room. Her stuffed teddy bear, Milo, sat at the head in between the pillows. Her dresser and even the bookshelf with a couple dozen children's books were completely untouched.

Stepping in, she ran her hands over the wood of the dresser, then the end of her bed. Unable to resist, she picked up Milo and hugged him to her chest. Tears threatened to overflow.

How many times had she thought of this place? Wondered what had been left behind never to be seen again?

Now, she'd returned to find the place a time capsule. It was as if she were six years old again and just came in from playing outside.

The closet drew her attention, the same one she'd hidden in, only to be found. Her stomach knotted at the memory that was as fresh as if it happened yesterday.

Oddly enough, nothing seemed to have changed from eighteen years ago. As far as she could tell, not a single thing had been moved, removed, or replaced. Nothing. *Why?* Her grandfather was dead. The house was kept up. Surely, it had been sold? Perhaps rented out? No other reason came to mind where all the furnishings would remain just as before.

Overwhelmed and exhausted from driving over thirteen hundred miles for twenty hours to get there, she sat on the bed and curled into a ball with Milo. She'd stopped at a hotel for some much-needed rest and food before hitting the road at three this morning. Never before had she driven so far or so long. Not to mention the emotional rollercoaster which zapped her energy and sucked the life out of her. Now, this. It was almost too much.

The tears took over. Tears of heartache, pain, and relief. Tears of loss. She cried until she fell asleep in a bed she hadn't slept in for so many years.

The squeak of the door opening woke Taryn. She blinked awake, sat up, and returned Milo to the head of the bed. Brushing her hair out of her face and over her shoulder, she listened carefully, trying to determine what woke her. Another sound of the front door shutting and footsteps over the hardwood floors alerted her that someone else had arrived. Her heart stuttered as she wondered if the other killer had returned as well.

That's crazy talk, Taryn. It's probably just a housekeeper. Or a robber. The killer has no reason to come back here after that many years.

She debated, uncertain if she should go invisible, try to catch a peek of the newcomer, or simply run. Courage returned, pushing aside everything but caution. She needed answers, and to leave without them would be a total failure. If one of the two men had come to kill her, then she would just thwart his plans. *Simple.*

The little voice in her head reminded her that denial was never a good thing. She ignored it.

Hesitantly, she made her way back to the kitchen, where the sound originated. As soon as she stepped into the room, she halted.

An older woman with salt and pepper hair, wearing loose tan slacks and a matching blouse, stood near the sink, her back to Taryn. She unloaded some cleaning supplies and placed them on the kitchen counter.

Taryn cleared her throat. "Hello."

The woman spun around in a rush.

Memories returned in an instant as Taryn stared

into the face of the woman she hadn't seen in eighteen years. "Nana Mary?" The name came out as a whisper.

Momentary fear and shock gave way as Mary's eyes lit up, and a gentle smile appeared for a second before she sobered once again. "Taryn. Child. I thought I'd never see you again."

"Oh, Nana Mary." Taryn hurried to close the distance and to embrace her. "I'm so glad to see you."

Mary hugged her back, then held her at arm's length. "Let me look at you. So grown up and beautiful." She pushed some hair away from Taryn's face. "Just like your mother."

Taryn's mouth fell open. "You never said you knew my mother before. Why now?"

Mary sobered. "I couldn't say anything as long as he was alive."

"He?"

"Ruford."

"Grandfather?"

Mary's face pinched. "Let's go to the library and sit down. I think there's some things you should know."

A mix of trepidation and excitement coursed through Taryn. Finally, all the questions she had might be answered. She tilted her head and stared at Mary. "You waited this long to tell me?" A hint of anger entered her voice.

"Come, child. I have something to show you that might help you understand." With a quick look, Mary led the way through the house to the quaint room filled with shelves of books.

Taryn bit her lip as Mary moved aside a foot stool, pulled a piece of wood out of the floor, and dragged out a small trunk. She placed it on the stool and gestured toward a nearby overstuffed chair. "Have a seat. It will take a while to go through all this."

Taryn did as bidden after she assisted Mary back to her feet. The older woman pulled up a wooden chair and sat before opening the trunk. "I know you've got many questions. The answers are all here." Sure enough, papers, photos, and a couple of photo albums filled the small trunk. The amount surprised Taryn. "Well, most of them anyway."

"Where did you get all this stuff?"

"Your grandfather threw them away. I saved them from the trash, hid them away so he never knew. If he found them, I would have been considered a threat, one that he would have spared not a moment to rid himself of."

Still perplexed at this twist, Taryn studied Mary, resisting the great urge to dig in for the moment. "Why did you keep this?"

Mary's expression remained sad, her eyes dulling. "I both feared and hoped you'd return. You'd been through so much already. I hated the thought of you left without answers. Yet, I knew those same answers would spin your world around once more." She sighed. "I tried to locate you at first. When there were no crumbs to follow, I hoped you'd make your way back. The house was paid for and yours. It couldn't be sold without your permission, though it could go through probate after a while. So, I took care of the house, paid the electric bills, kept up the appearance that it was lived in hoping that you would return one day."

The generosity touched Taryn. "That's a lot of money you spent on this place. I don't know how to thank you or to pay you back."

Mary waved her hand. "You don't have to worry about money, child. This house, the other assets, and the bank account are all yours. You're loaded."

Taryn's mouth fell open. "My inheritance. I'd never even thought about such a thing, about why I hadn't been getting it. It just never came up."

"Yes, dear. It's yours. All yours." Mary grinned, but the amusement didn't reach her eyes, which were filled with worry. "My salary was set up as an automatic payment from the bank. I've been collecting it all these years. I covered the electric bills myself and any repairs. Leo took care of those. We didn't know what else to do besides keep the estate going. I didn't question the fact that the money kept coming. In truth, I was thankful. Without it, my husband and I couldn't have made it. With his medical bills, we would have been forced into bankruptcy, homelessness even. With my salary, we pulled through. I'll always see that as a blessing, even if it came from a man you have yet to really know."

When Taryn sat there with her hands folded on her lap, Mary reached out and pulled out a picture. "These are your parents." She passed it over to Taryn.

Her hand a little shaky, Taryn accepted the old photograph, gazing at it in awe. Faces she'd only imagined before stared back at her. They seemed happy, in love, as both held hands and looked toward the camera. The woman wore a long, white lace gown. He, a black suit. Youth and a carefree attitude radiated from them, as if they were just about to take the first step in a great journey filled with joy and enthusiasm. A life together.

Her long brunette hair matched Taryn's in color

and nearly in length. All the facial features except for perhaps the lips were nearly identical, including her bright green eyes. The striking appearance proved beyond a doubt that this woman was Taryn's mother.

"Too short." Taryn cleared her throat. "Their lives were too short." She touched them with her fingers, wishing she could have one chance to meet them, to hug them, to learn about them, to make up for the time they should have had together.

"Yes, they were." Mary's tone carried much sadness. She reached in the box and pulled out another photo. "I remember your mother well. So vibrant and beautiful. You're the spitting image of her, but I'm sure you've noticed that. Observant and quick. You reminded me so much of her, even when you were very young."

"They were killed in a car wreck. I remember hating cars after that."

Mary's gaze dropped. "They didn't die in a wreck, Taryn."

Perplexed, Taryn turned her attention to Mary. "Why would Ruford lie about that?"

Mary sighed, her eyes beginning to water. "Because he had them killed."

Taryn couldn't believe her ears. She stared at Mary, trying to decipher truth from fiction. The woman, with lines of age covering her face, could have lost her sanity along the way. Making up stories could be part of her dementia.

Yet the longer she studied Mary, the more she realized Mary had told her the facts. Her stomach fell. Instinctively, she braced herself for the harrowing story to come. "Why?" The single word slipped out as a plea.

Mary pulled a kerchief out of her pocket and wiped at her eyes. "Your mother and father both worked for Ruford. That's how they met. Lisa and Shawn. Such a beautiful couple. Perfect for one another and so in love." She held up another picture, tilted her head, and a sad smile appeared on her lips. "They were always upbeat, eager to face another challenge, until Ruford changed their jobs."

Taryn glanced at the picture Mary held, feeling a connection between the couple and herself. "What was their job?"

"Initially, he used them to sneak into places, to procure valuable items."

Taryn gasped. "My parents were thieves?" Her stomach tightened.

"Yes, dear. High-end thieves, but thieves, nonetheless. Expensively priced gems and collectibles were their specialty." Mary handed over the picture and picked up another. "Not an ideal profession, but one they were suited for."

Taryn's gut seized. "Suited for?" She held her breath waiting for the answer she already knew.

Mary lowered her hand to her lap and used her free hand to pat Taryn's arm. "They both could achieve invisibility."

Taryn's heart skipped a beat or two as she gasped in a breath.

"Yes, I know about that. Ruford boasted about their talents and how efficient they were. He was jealous at first, but then realized all they could do for him." She pulled out a scrapbook of sorts and opened it. "Jewelry heists made the front-page news. Private collectors on the black market paid huge sums for those items. Ruford never had a problem getting top dollar. That's how he made his fortune, by your parents stealing for him."

Taryn's mouth started to water as queasiness set in. She forced herself to breathe through it, needing to know the rest of the story. "What went wrong?"

"He pushed them to do more and more, until he found their hard line." Mary sighed. "I remember coming to work that morning with your mother yelling at Ruford. She told him under no circumstance would she kill another person."

Taryn focused her attention on her mother's face. Even a thief had principles, or so it seemed.

"He wanted them to use their invisibility in order to assassinate his enemies."

Taryn shuddered. "But they said no?"

"Yes. You were three or four at the time. Just a little tyke. They wanted to spend more time with you and less time on assignments. Ruford wouldn't have it. He manipulated them, held up grand prizes for them, and finally threatened them." She turned the page of the book. "They refused. Ruford knew they'd go to the police. So, he ordered them to be taken out." Mary paused as a tear fell from her face. "They were here one day, gone the next. He had you brought to him and told me that it was my new job to raise you."

Overwhelmed, Taryn could only listen and soak up what she could. "But he was so kind to me. Read me stories." The image of her loving grandfather warred with the picture Mary painted, like they were two very different people. She reeled from the revelation.

"You killed them," a strange man hollered.

"You don't know shit," Poppy answered.

"Yes, we do. Evidence enough to send you away for a lifetime," the other invader answered heatedly. *"Dalliance? Ring a bell?"*

The memory flooded back.

Mary nodded. "I can't say he didn't have feelings for you. Maybe he did. I hope so. What I do know is that he had an ulterior motive when it came to you."

"I was to take my parents' place in his organization." The puzzle pieces fell into place.

"Yes. He hedged his bets that you would develop the same ability."

Taryn's heart splintered. The man she thought loved her above anyone else was nothing more than a deceitful mobster who murdered her parents.

Mary rested a hand on her shoulder. "I'm so sorry, dear. I wish I could have done something sooner. Said something. But one rule anyone who worked for Ruford never forgot was he considered betrayal the ultimate sin. Not only would he make you pay, but your family as well. No one dared to cross him without facing the consequences, including your parents."

Feeling like she'd been kicked by a mule, Taryn could only sit and stare at the picture. Too shocked to do anything more, she took in the evidence before her, listened to the words, and saw what remained of her life crumble to a pile of ashes.

A lifetime of questions had been answered. Except one. She knew it was Quint's father, but she didn't have a name or a reason. Nothing except the memories and the picture in Quint's apartment. "Who killed him?"

"I don't know. He had enemies. Many of them. The case was never solved, and no witnesses ever came forward."

That's because I'm the only one. Taryn kept the thought to herself.

Mary patted her arm. "Have you eaten?"

Taryn shook her head.

Mary *tsked.* "There's sandwich makings in the kitchen. It's not much, just what I keep here to have when I'm working, but it's filling—bread, milk, juice, peanut butter, lunch meat. I think there's even some chocolate cake."

"Thank you." Taryn's stomach growled right on cue.

Mary chuckled. "How about I fix you something and bring it to you. I know you have so much to go through and so many questions."

Taryn beamed at her. "That would be perfect. Thank you so much. For everything."

Mary stood and looked down at her. "It's the least I can do. I didn't do anything before, something I'll regret to my dying day, but I can do something now." She left the room.

A few minutes later, Taryn finished scarfing down the meal and wiped her hands on a paper towel Mary also had provided. Full, she returned to searching through the contents of the box, paying attention to each slip of paper, no matter how small.

"How do you know the house and his assets are mine?" Taryn asked.

"He has a living trust. There's a copy of it filed with his lawyer and another in a safety deposit box. You are the one listed as beneficiary. The only one."

"How do you know so much?"

Mary smiled ruefully. "I was everything to Ruford, except his lover." The last part she tossed out in a hurry. "Housekeeper. Secretary. Nanny. Anything he needed done, that I could do, he assigned to me. I looked over everything closely. Once I knew what the man was, I started hedging my bets. Nothing went past me without my understanding everything about it, perhaps even making a copy of it. I just knew that one day I might have to appear in court and needed all the evidence I could get—" She sighed. "—or end up dead, and none of it would matter."

Taryn gave her a hug. Mary had bargained with the devil in dealing with Ruford.

She glanced back at the paper in her hand. Certainly, she didn't know diddly squat about inheritance legal issues. Still, she couldn't believe it was easy to walk in and take over everything. "But the lawyers know he's deceased. Didn't they petition the court for something? Try to seize the land and sell it?"

Mary shook her head. "You are the only one he had. So he had you put on it. Since you were a child, he added the stipulation that nothing could be done, sold, liquidated, or touched until you were twenty-five. At that time, you'd be able to settle the estate as you saw fit." She set another item to the side. "I'm not a lawyer, but that's the way I understood it when the lawyer contacted me. He was looking for you. Needed to notify you. Since you weren't declared dead, only missing, their hands were tied. You were young when it happened, and the statute of limitations could carry on for a hundred years or so I understood."

Taryn blinked. "So things continued on status quo?"

"Yep. If I remember right, the original lawyer who drew up the trust has passed. I think his partners run the company now. They'd still have the trust, but it's probably filed under old news that no one has looked at in many years."

The enormity of what Mary told her boggled Taryn's mind. The house, the land, the money was hers—money stemming from her parents stealing jewelry and other items so Ruford could sell them on the black market. Blood money, as they'd died over it in the end. "I can't take it. It's what killed my parents."

Mary frowned. "It's your inheritance. Ruford stole your life from you. Your parents were the ones who provided his fortune, or most of it. He murdered them and stole you. I'd say whatever you netted from his assets is still not enough to offset the pain and suffering he caused you and your family."

Taryn nodded slowly. It was too much to handle at the moment. Her mind whirled with all the news. This decision could easily be placed on the back burner until a later date—after she had a chance to process everything else first and seek advice from those trust lawyers.

Mary glanced up at the grandfather clock in the room. "I know you have so much to go through, so many questions."

"Yes." Taryn glanced inside the box. "I'm sure more will come as I read through all this."

"To be expected, dear." Mary rested her hand on Taryn's shoulder. "I can't believe you're here. You do an old woman's heart good."

Taryn smiled softly, recalling Mary uttering that expression more than once to her as a kid. "You do mine as well."

"I need to get back home and get Leo's supper

ready. I'll be back tomorrow morning. Save up those questions for then."

"Will do." Taryn regained her feet and hugged Mary. "I'm so glad you saved this stuff and that you're still here. I wouldn't have known any of this without you. It was a big risk you took. I can never repay you."

"You already have." Mary waved, collected Taryn's trash from her meal, and started out of the room. "I'll lock the door behind me."

"Thank you. See you in the morning." Taryn waved, picked up a small photo album, and opened it. The clicking of the front door a little later announced Mary's departure. Taryn made a mental note to check it in a few. After all, she needed to retrieve her suitcases and rifle from the car. She wouldn't need the rifle, but didn't dare leave it behind. If anyone broke in, they'd steal the expensive gun and sell it on the black market.

She decided she'd be staying put for the next few days, learning about her past and making plans for her future. With nowhere else to go and nothing pressing, she had the luxury of spending time learning about a past she'd never known.

Chapter 18

The clock struck ten p.m.

Taryn stretched. She'd been sitting in the library for hours just looking through all the information Mary had thoughtfully collected over the years and ferreted away. A lifetime of memories she should have lived through now only existed in scraps of papers and photos. *At least I have those.* If it weren't for Mary's bravery, determination, and caring nature, Taryn would have none of it. For that, she owed Mary in a big way.

Tired, she rubbed her eyes. With nowhere to go and in no hurry, she could return to her bedroom, get some rest, then start fresh in the morning.

The idea had merit. She left everything as it was, exited the library, closing the door behind her out of habit. She'd just passed the laundry room when the unmistakable sound of a door opening drew her attention.

Her mind raced. *Did Mary forget something? Not this late at night.* Fear rushed to the fore.

Finding her purse in her bedroom, she dug out her Glock. The familiar grip reaffirmed her confidence. *No matter what it is, I can handle this. I've worked my entire life to be able to take care of myself and take out those killers. A little robbery is nothing. Just ask the stupid idiot with the ball bat.*

Her bravado didn't equal her words. Still, she

walked slowly toward the front room, preparing herself for what she might find.

She stopped at the junction of the living area and the hallway, spying a man standing as if he owned the place.

Slowly, he turned, stared at her, and a gradual, sinister grin appeared on his face.

Her breath caught, and her stomach dropped as she recognized his features and the blatant cruelty in his eyes. He was the other one here that night, the one that bragged about killing her grandfather.

"About time we meet again."

That voice. That same voice. He definitely was the man who wanted to kill her on the spot. No doubt existed in her mind. Suddenly, she was that small child again, frozen in terror. *Get a grip, Taryn.*

He approached with confident steps, his footfalls loud in the otherwise silent house. If her gun pointed at his chest concerned him, he sure didn't show it.

"You remember me." He made it a statement.

"Yes," she whispered.

She pulled on her courage, stood tall, and faced the demon that bore responsibility for all the nightmares over the years.

"I knew you would. Told Warren that. He wouldn't listen." The man *tsk*ed. "That's why I had to come back and finish what I started."

Davis. The man Quint sought. Davis had been after her the whole time. Quint clung to her, knowing that Davis would show up sooner or later. More questions were answered, though they caused her heart to rip open once again. Quint had used her as bait. Worse, he'd never told her about the man who hunted her.

Anger flared, only for a moment. Survival instincts kept her attention on the crisis at hand.

Another memory clicked. She recognized his build from the day at the paintball course. "Why didn't you just shoot me in the woods that day? A fast, easy fix to your problem."

"That wouldn't have been much fun." He leaned back against the door jamb. "Taking out that hunter was my goal that day. Then, imagine my surprise when you pulled your disappearing act." He smiled wickedly. "The way you handled yourself and those martial arts moves. Impressive. You made me rethink my plans. I'll give you credit for that."

"So what did you decide?"

"Well, when running you off the road and getting rid of Warren didn't work, I decided to make this a grand overture." He waved his arm in the air. "Fitting, don't you think? We're back to where it all began. And I'm going to kill you just like I killed your grandfather."

He stepped to the side and ran his hands over a large, wooden desk in the living room. "Don't you want to know how I killed your grandfather? It's really genius, if I do say so myself."

"You're nothing but a rabid animal."

His eyes narrowed. "Careful. You don't want to anger me before the big show."

"What difference does it make, since you're going to kill me anyway?" She had no idea where the gall to stand up to him came from. It was there, and she soaked it up, reinforcing her waning bravado with an infusion of pre-hysteria badass-ness. "If I don't kill you first."

His mocking sneer told her what he thought of that

possibility. "There's many ways to die, and I know each and every one of them. Play nice, and I won't draw it out. Mess with me, and you'll know agony and beg for death."

The flat promise sent a shiver of fear down Taryn's spine. "You don't scare me."

"Oh, really?"

"Really. So, get out."

"You waited all these years for revenge, then you're going to let me walk away? How stupid of you."

"True." She started to pull the trigger.

Suddenly, bright lights exploded in her head, sending violent waves of pain through her entire body. She opened her mouth to scream, but no sound emerged. The gun toppled from her hand and onto the floor as she grabbed for her temples, closed her eyes, and tried her damnedest to block him out. Failing that, she decided for Plan B. If only she could think of one.

"Let her go."

Quint's voice cut through the waves of agony. Taryn forced her eyes open enough to see him stride into the room. He appeared calm and cool, but she knew better. His eyes had taken on a glowing red cast, a sure sign of surging mental power in order to meet Davis's imminent attack.

He was the best thing she'd ever seen. Sure, he'd used her for bait, lied to her, and kept secrets. Yet, at this moment, all of that paled in relation to the fact that he'd come for her, and to complete his mission of taking out one of the men who killed her grandfather.

er, Fate's voice on the other end of thee. If Davis ended up winning, none of it would matter. Besides, she still loved the guy.

Goes to show how blind love can be.

"Ah, young Warren. About time. I've been waiting for you. Didn't think you'd want to miss the big show."

"You mean your death?" Quint strode across the room, making his way toward Taryn.

"Cocky bastard. Just like your father. You can send him my regards once I return to Dalliance and eradicate him, too."

"Gotta get past me first."

"Oh, that's the easy part. I'm stronger than anyone else has ever been. You're like an ant going up against an elephant, Warren. So, say your goodbyes."

Quint narrowed his eyes at Davis. "Get out of here, Taryn." He gritted the words out as if it took all his will to make it happen.

His entire attention had to be on Davis and using his ability to defend himself while finding a way to turn the tables. She understood the severity of the situation and how vital every moment, every breath was. "No. I'm not leaving you."

"I'm not asking." He didn't take his eyes off his enemy in order to answer her. He sucked in air as if punched in the gut. A small shudder ran through his body.

She sensed his pain, his rapid weakening under Davis's attack. She empathized, as she'd just had a brief taste of what Davis could do. Her stomach still churned and head pounded from that little bit. The full brunt Quint received had to be brutal.

Davis grinned as if he were gaining the upper hand and winning. "That's it, Warren. Succumb to your master. Know you're mine to control. Then, I'll make you scream before your mind explodes."

She watched helplessly as Quint stumbled a step. Her pain no longer mattered. Saving Quint did. The realization came along with a crazy idea. "Take my energy. Take it. Now."

"No." The word came out a gravelly bark.

Even in such dire straits, he tried to protect her. *Chivalrous, but not helpful.* "No." She reached for him, only to come up short. *Come on, Taryn, pull yourself together.* "Do it or we both die." She tried for command. It came out pleading instead. No matter, as long as he followed through. "I love you, Quint. I love you and trust you. Take it. Bond with me. If we don't make it, know that I love you, for you, with all that I am."

He spared her a quick glance, one filled with emotion, determination, and great strain, before latching onto her outreached hand.

She pulled up her powers, knew she'd achieved success when her hand he was holding disappeared. The wave sensation she'd felt once before became a ginormous outflow, sapping everything she had.

She felt his power swell as he pressured Davis with a steady, unrelenting mental bombardment.

Too weak to stand, even by holding onto something, she collapsed to the floor.

Quint moved to stand between her and Davis as they continued their psychic battle.

Taryn's head pounded so hard, she feared it would split open. Her ears rang like a sousaphone blasted next to her, and her stomach threatened to upheave at any moment. She tried to keep her eyes open. To stand. To do anything to assist Quint in the struggle for both their lives. But she was drained. Completely, absolutely drained, incapable of the slightest movement no matter the life and death happenings a mere few feet away.

"Taryn, honey. Get up." A woman's voice penetrated the pain and fog.

Taryn opened her eyes to see a shimmering body, a familiar person who resembled her mother from the pictures she'd pored over earlier. The world started to spin. She closed her eyes and held onto her head in an effort to keep it from exploding.

"Taryn. You're strong. Get up."

"I can't." She barely whispered the words.

"You've worked all your life for this moment. It's here. Time to take care of business."

The encouraging voice gave her the willpower to grit her teeth and open her eyes once more.

Quint was on his knees, sweat pouring from his forehead. Pale, he appeared on the verge of fainting. Davis was a little worse for wear as well. His eyes were buggy, hands were clinched, and he grimaced in obvious severe pain. Davis. The man who stole her dear grandfather away, leaving her life in a tailspin. Now, he sought to do it again. This time, taking another man she loved—Quint. Inherently, she knew they were so evenly matched, they'd take one another to the grave.

She rallied. Years ago, she was a helpless child. She'd spent years preparing for this exact moment. More importantly, Quint needed her, and she refused to let him down.

Taryn spied her gun on the floor about four feet away. With extreme effort, she pushed herself along, using every ounce of strength she had left. Depleted, she moved on grit alone, spurred on by the certainty that if she didn't intervene, Quint would die.

"Almost there, honey. You can do it."

The encouragement pushed her that last few inches. Her fingers met the cold steel of the gun. She grasped it, rolled, and lifted. Automatically, she tightened her finger on the trigger, preparing to shoot.

Quint charged Davis, only to be pushed aside.

That was all the opportunity she needed. "Payback, bastard."

Davis turned his gaze on her, just in time for her to pull the trigger. A bright red spot appeared on his chest. His mouth fell open, and his eyes widened.

Before he could utter another word, she pulled the trigger again. He fell backward to the floor and didn't move again.

"I'm so proud of you, Taryn. I always have been."

"Thanks, Mom."

Taryn's vision collapsed down until darkness overtook everything.

Chapter 19

Taryn woke slowly. Remaining still, she struggled to recall the nightmare which plagued her sleep.

Soft, cool sheets comforted her as did a light breeze. The scent of ocean and flowers carried to her, relaxing and soothing. A familiar warmth drew her attention. She opened her eyes to find Quint lying next to her, his fingers on one hand intertwined with hers. He'd curled himself around her as if trying to protect her in his sleep.

Protect her.

The battle came rushing back. Davis. The pain he inflicted on both of them. Quint's misery. And Taryn's last-ditch effort to stop Davis.

Her mother. The voice and apparition of her mother encouraging her, pushing her to complete her vow.

She frowned, trying to decide if she'd imagined the whole thing. She hadn't really believed in ghosts before, but now, she just couldn't say.

Uncomfortable, she shifted her hips a little.

Quint's arm tightened for a second before loosening. "Taryn?" He scooched over and rolled her to her back. His sweat pants and lightweight shirt bore many wrinkles, testament to hours of wear, most likely in sleep.

She stared up into his face, noting the bruising and

darkness under his eyes. His hair was mussed, but she'd never seen him more handsome. Testing out her strength, she lifted her hand to rest against his cheek.

He nuzzled and kissed it. "How are you feeling?"

After taking a quick appraisal, she answered, "Tired. Sore. But I think I'll live."

"You better." He almost growled the command.

She smiled, pleased and thrilled to see him appearing healthy once more. "I was worried about you. So worried."

"I could say the same for you." His face clouded. "When I walked in to find him trying to kill you, I lost my mind."

"Yeah, it was like that, wasn't it? Like a roar you could no longer control." She frowned, then sighed. "But we won."

"Thanks to you." He slid out of the bed, leaned back over, and kissed her forehead. "I knew I was taking too much of your power, weakening you to the brink. I just couldn't control it. Or get control over him. When you went down, I threw everything I had at him, and he countered it. I've never been so afraid in my life."

The memories flashed through her mind. "He was struggling. Big time. I don't think he would have lasted much longer."

Quint grinned ruefully. "Neither could I. Thank God you were able to get hold of the gun."

"My mother got me through it. Told me what to do."

His face furrowed. "Your mother?"

She waved her hand. "I know it sounds crazy, but I saw her. My biological mother. She was a ghost, talking to me, helping me." She prepared for him to either argue with her or tell her she was just seeing things.

To her surprise, he beamed and kissed her temple. "I'm glad you finally got to meet her."

"You don't think I'm nuts?" She blinked.

"Nope. There's a few individuals that can communicate with the deceased. They work for Dalliance."

"Wow." She wrapped her mind around all the recent happenings, or tried to. "Did we both come out okay?"

Quint nodded. "The doctors at Dalliance gave us both a look over. They were more concerned with your extended nap, though."

"Extended nap? How long?"

He glanced up at the wall clock before focusing on her again. "About eighteen hours."

"Wow."

"When you're feeling up to it, they want you to try to go invisible, just to make sure I didn't wind up ripping away your gift when I was borrowing power." He flinched, and his eyes saddened. Guilt appeared on his face.

Her heart tugged. "I wouldn't have changed a thing. You did what you had to do. *We did.* And we're still alive to tell the tale. That's what matters."

"If your ability is gone…"

She shushed him with a finger to his lips. "Then, I'm the same person I was before without the concerns that I'll shock some poor unfortunate person into heart failure if I happen to get zapped by static electricity and disappear before their eyes."

A small smile tugged at his lips.

She loved the sight. Not to mention, those sexy lips of his.

He sobered. "While we're on the subject, I have a couple of confessions to make."

Now he had her total attention.

"I put a listening device in your living room."

She blinked. "Just my living room?"

"Yes. I hated to, but knew if Davis showed up during the night, I needed to have some way of knowing."

She processed that with a slow nod. "Okay. That makes sense and can be forgiven."

His expression relaxed marginally. "I should have told you the truth from the beginning. About who and what I am and about Davis. I…" He ran a hand through his hair. "I was afraid you'd think I was some sort of lunatic and keep a safe distance."

She grinned at his wording. "For your information, I would have thought you insane."

"I ran through all sorts of scenarios, but didn't come up with anything successful. After all, who'd belive 'Excuse me, miss, I'm a hunter tracking a man who kills with brain waves. He's waited eighteen years to find you, and now he's going to make your brain explode as punishment for living through the break-in at your grandfather's house. Oh, by the way, I plan on either shutting down his powers or stealing them for my own while killing him.' " He grinned sheepishly. "You can see why I didn't go with it."

"Oh, yeah." She chuckled. "That had full straitjacket crazy written all over it."

His eyes danced with amusement.

The unfamiliar room drew her curiosity. "Where

am I?"

"My home on the beach."

"You have a house on the beach?"

He chuckled. "Yeah. Seal Rock. Actually, it's a family resort, but this is my home."

"Your family owns a resort? On the beach?" She'd never known anyone with that kind of money to have such a luxury.

"Yes. And when you're up to it, I'll give you a full tour." He brushed the hair out of her eyes. "Hungry?"

"I could eat something." She sat up, relieved to find herself dressed in boxers and one of Quint's shirts. Swinging her legs over the side, she stood. After a second of dizziness and still a bit wobbly, she started toward the end of the bed. "Bathroom?"

"Straight ahead." He escorted her there. "While you're in there, I'll run down to the kitchen and see what they have to eat."

She checked out the extravagant bathroom. It was almost as large as her living room, and the light-colored marble floor shone. The walls were painted in a light blue, with pictures and décor a definite tribute to the sea. All tactfully done. "Wait. My clothes?"

"Your suitcase is right here." He pointed to the corner. "Do you need me to bring it in there?"

"No, thanks. I'll get it." She slowly and a little gingerly made her way over, picked it up, and carried it into the room with her. At least the dizziness had receded. "I'm going to take a shower."

"Make it a bath." His tone conveyed an order.

She rolled her eyes, then regretted it when a pinching pain followed. "Shower."

He shook his head. "Stubborn."

"Yep." She placed the suitcase inside and shut the door behind her.

Several minutes later, she emerged, clean, fresh, and wearing one of her lightweight workout suits. She'd towel-dried her hair, combed it, and fastened it up in a ponytail held by a bright pink scrunchie which matched her outfit. White socks completed the package.

She dropped the suitcase back where she found it. Her hand barely left the handle when she felt a presence.

Slowly, she stood and turned.

The first thing she noticed about the man was his similar features to Quint—the nose, the square chin, and build. But those eyes. They were the kicker. Identical to Quint's. Yet, a few differences existed as well—the gray streaks in his hair, the less-robust package. And the lines in his face. Those spoke of age and worries.

Unable to help herself, she glanced down to his forearm. He made no move to try to hide the black widow tattoo that haunted her nightmares for the past several years.

"Taryn." His voice, soft and deep, conveyed calmness and a hint of something else. Regret, perhaps.

"You must be Quint's father." She managed to keep the hesitation out of her voice. Barely. As many times as she pictured this meeting, it had never been like this.

"Yes. Reginald Warren." He didn't move, just stood barely inside the door, his attention glued to her. "I have many sins and bear them all. My greatest one was against you."

Really? You think? She kept her sarcastic thoughts

to herself.

My father can read minds. Quint's words came back to her.

"Please tell me he only has a mild ability."

"Nope. Strong. Very strong."

She swallowed hard. *Yikes.*

"Please don't make my son pay for my sins. He's a good man and innocent in all this."

She worked to stay composed and not respond vocally or physically.

He waited a beat and sighed. "I know you hate me and have every right to. It was my mission, and I'm responsible for screwing it up." Remorse carried in his tone. "To be fair, I didn't know about you and certainly didn't know about Davis's ability or his loss of control." He took in a breath. "I did the best I could for you, considering the circumstances."

The words were logical. His face matched his statements. If he were lying, she couldn't tell it.

In the scheme of things, she'd given some thought to the happenings. As Davis gave his last breath, her journey of retribution ended. The gut-wrenching fury, hate, and pain flickered out at the same time. While Reginald might not ever be her favorite man in the world, she was finally able to see the situation in a different perspective. And that view opened her eyes in a big way. He was right. He'd saved her life. Others might not have intervened with Davis or whisked her away to a caring family to raise her. He'd taken a risk, for a good cause, and she could no longer blame him for that.

"We do the best we can with what we're given." The strength in her tone mimicked what she felt inside—at peace.

His eyebrows scrunched a little, another subtle reminder of Quint.

"I forgive you."

Relief and wonder monopolized his expression. His jaw eased, and his eyes brightened.

Quint stepped into the doorway, a tray laden with food balanced steadily in his hands. He glanced over at Taryn, then back to his father. "Problem?"

Taryn smiled. "Nope."

Reginald tipped his head in acknowledgement. "Nope, we're good."

Confusion coated Quint's face. "No need to drag out the dueling pistols?"

"No."

"Not today." Taryn echoed the sentiment. "But you'd better hand over that food and soon, just in case."

She saw the twinkle in Reginald's eyes. It matched the happiness on Quint's face.

"In that case, supper is served." Quint kissed her as he placed the tray on the bed. "Need some help?"

"Maybe. I hate to waste, and if I eat all this, I'm going to be round as a pig."

"Never that." He chuckled and nuzzled her cheek.

"Your father?"

"He's gone."

"Oh."

Quint leaned back and smiled brightly at her. "Did I mention he can read minds?"

"Yeah, you did mention that little tidbit."

"Well, I'm pretty sure he was reading mine just now and retreated quick-like to find a large bottle of brain bleach."

Taryn burst out in laughter. "You, sir, are a man after my own mind. It's no wonder I love you."

"I love you, too. I tried to tell you that before and then during the battle. I just couldn't find the right time, then I was too busy trying to survive to speak the words." He leaned a little closer. "When you told me how you felt…you gave me the gift of life. Still do. I was able to beat him down. More than that, you opened up the windows in my soul. You gave me the gift of humanity again—cheer, happiness.

"And love?"

"Definitely love. I love you with my old jaded heart. It's not much, but it's all yours."

She beamed. "You're all I ever wanted and then some. Bad boy and a good man. Who could ask for anything more?" She sealed the compliment with a kiss filled with all the passion and love in her heart.

Chapter 20

Taryn, cell phone in hand, walked to the second-floor balcony of the house and gazed out over the ocean. The view could only be called fantastic. Large rocks stuck up out of the water, each wave bathing them. The pristine sand beach beckoned. Seagulls walked along the shoreline in search of breakfast. A slight breeze carried to her, bringing in the scent of the salty air while keeping the temperature just right.

It was perfect, just like Quint and his home.

For three days she'd done nothing but lounge around enjoying the pampering and spoiling only Quint could provide. He took her for scenic walks, ordered her favorite foods prepared by the resort's chef, and spent many hours pleasing her in bed.

She'd landed in paradise and never wanted to leave.

The down time also allowed her to do some thinking, to rectify some slights in her life, at least within her mind. This morning came time for the real deal—calling her adoptive parents. She'd texted and filled them in with a downsized version of what had happened so they'd know where she was and that everything turned out okay. They'd expressed relief and support, something she wasn't sure she'd receive from them after their last blow up.

She glanced down at her phone and hesitated.

No time like the present.

She dialed their number and waited.

"Hello?"

"Hi, Mom."

"Taryn!"

"Are you busy?"

"Not at all. How are you doing? How's Oregon?"

She stared out over the water. "Beautiful."

"And Quint?"

Taryn smiled. "Wonderful."

"I guess this is the call telling me that you're staying there?"

She pursed her lips. "Yeah, I guess so, if he'll let me stay. We haven't really discussed it, yet."

"He will. I have a feeling if you wander off, he'll be right on your heels."

The comment buoyed Taryn's heart. Her only worry had been that the romance with Quint might fall apart, that he'd tire of her once the excitement and adrenaline of the hunt wore off. "I hope so."

She opted to change topics rather than dwell on the one that made her antsy. "How's Brandon?"

A moment of silence followed. "He's been arrested."

Taryn swallowed. The news wasn't a total shock. "Because he'd been stealing research from his work and selling it to another company?"

"How did you know?" Her mother's tone carried a hint of suspicion.

"That's what he had me helping him with. Those lost keys. Before I went to Texas, he wanted me to retrieve the laptop he'd forgotten. I refused, and he became furious. I figured it out, and he admitted what he'd been doing. The money drove him. He had it good, and it just wasn't enough."

Meredith sighed heavily. "He didn't mention anything about you being involved."

"That's something."

"He shouldn't have done it in the first place, let alone risked you." Her words dripped with regret and aggravation.

"Water under the bridge, Mom. I guess we'll just have to wait to see how it all pans out."

"Yeah. It's hard, but the court system is really slow. We got him the best lawyer we could."

"If you talk to him, tell him…" *Tell him what? That I hope he gets a light sentence? That it all works out? That he gets off the hook?* "Tell him that I love him."

"I will."

"I need to tell you something, too. Dad as well." She bolstered her courage. "I'm sorry about the fight over my adoption information. I know you guys were only trying to protect me. You sacrificed so much for me, took me in, and raised me. That was a burden, and I don't think I've made it any easier for you both."

"Oh, Taryn." Meredith's voice cracked. "You've been a delight. An angel. We couldn't have asked for a better daughter. I'm just sorry that we didn't tell you everything. Maybe it would have saved you some pain, saved you from that trip to Texas."

"No, Mom. I would have gone anyway. The gaps in my adoption just drove me there sooner. I needed to go, needed to see Mary and learn the truth." She still grappled with the childhood memory of her loving grandfather and the hard facts of his ruthlessness.

"We should have pursued your inheritance so you could have had the money sooner. But we were so afraid you'd only track the matter all the more. We thought we were protecting you."

"I know, Mom." And she did.

"You found your heritage, and now you're rich," Meredith pointed out.

"No, I'm not."

"I thought I understood you inherited all of Ruford Dyal's estate and assets." Confusion came through the phone line.

"I do. I did. But I couldn't keep it. At least, not all of it. It's blood money, Mom. Money earned on my parents' thievery and then death." She recalled the momentary meeting with her biological mother—so brief, but so moving. She didn't know if she'd have another occasion to see her or if both her parents had moved on once their daughter was safe. Only time would tell.

Her birthday passed two days ago. She'd celebrated in a lawyer's office drawing up the inheritance. She'd spent much time deciding what to do with everything. Finally, she'd made a hard decision. The house would be sold. The only thing she had Mary box up and send was the box she'd kept all those years and Milo. Everything else would go to auction. None of the material items mattered. That was all in her past, and she was busy living in the present and making plans for a future with Quint.

There was no jewelry left. Otherwise, she'd have to try to get someone who specialized in such things to try to find the original owners. One less trouble for her to deal with, thankfully. She'd signed over a sizeable portion to Mary for all she'd done. Mary had given her the truth. The pictures and clippings were the only link to her heritage. Those were priceless. In return, she made sure Mary never needed to work again.

A check had been mailed to her adoptive parents and should arrive certified tomorrow. Their portion wasn't anything to sneeze at, either. Enough to make their lives comfortable.

Another large chunk went to charity. She spread it amongst her three favorites. That pretty much depleted the liquid assets. She left herself a few thousand dollars to tide her over until she could find another job. Once the house and all the property inside sold, she'd decide where that money should go. Probably to Dalliance. And maybe some to invest in a nest egg for her and Quint's future.

If he'll have me.

"What did you do with it?"

Her mother's question returned her to the conversation at hand. "Mary and charities. Don't argue, but you and Dad are getting a check, too."

"We don't need it."

"Mom, please don't argue. It's a done deal."

"What about you?"

"I kept a little just to support me until I find another job. I have a couple of interviews in the next three days. Dalliance has expressed interest, too." She'd applied for gym positions locally. The community offered up solace and excitement to her. Even if she had to move out of the beach house, she wanted to stay in the area. Thus, there was a job in her near future.

Quint had mentioned Dalliance, assured her that his father would be glad to have her onboard, especially as her gift of invisibility remained strong and unaltered despite the battle for their lives. She hadn't spoken to Reginald about it or put much thought into it. Her thoughts on the company were still a little torn. She'd consider seeking a job with Dalliance, just not right now.

A few seconds of silence followed. "I'm so proud of you, Taryn. Anyone else would have taken the money and sang to the rafters how rich they were. You gave it away." A slight pause followed. "Taryn, are you sure?"

"It's the right thing to do."

Quint entered the balcony, wearing white swim trunks and nothing else. As no water dripped over his body, she decided he hadn't taken a dip in the ocean—yet.

He smiled at her, closed the distance, then wrapped his arms around her from behind.

Leaning back into him, she rested her free hand on top of his clasped at her waist.

"I'm sorry for all this, Taryn."

"Oh, Mom. Nothing to be sorry for. Everything worked out just fine." She giggled when Quint nibbled on her earlobe.

"Sure sounds like it." Meredith laughed. "I can tell you're distracted."

"Yep. Quint's here. I'm going to go. I'll talk to you later, Mom. Love you."

"Love you, too. Bye."

Taryn clicked the off button and tucked the phone in her pocket before turning in Quint's arms. "Hi, handsome."

"Hi, yourself." He stared into her eyes.

"Everything okay with your parents?"

"Yeah. I think so. We both admitted our wrongs."

"And?" He waited for her explanation.

"And Brandon is in jail for industrial espionage."

Quint searched her face. "You expected that."

Taryn nodded. "Yeah. I don't feel bad that he got caught. He knew it was wrong. Greed landed him in this spot. He has to pay the consequences for his actions."

Quint gave her a gentle squeeze. "I'm sorry."

"No reason to be. He's an adult." She wrapped her arms around his neck. "Besides, today is too wonderful to waste worrying. It's beautiful outside, this house is perfect, the beach breathtaking, and the gorgeous, sexy man that I happen to love is right here."

He rested his forehead against hers. "You can have it all and keep it, too."

Her heart stuttered in anticipation. Before she jumped to a conclusion, she needed clarification. "Keep what all?"

"The beach, the house." He met her gaze. "Me."

She smiled softly. "Oh, that sounds delightful. What's the price?"

He chuckled. "Marry me."

She blinked.

He took the opportunity to lower himself down to one knee. Out of his swimsuit pocket, he pulled a little black velvet box. He opened the top and held it out. "Taryn Brisk. Would you do me the honor of becoming my wife?"

Joy filled her heart. She nodded before finding her voice once again. "Yes. Absolutely, yes."

He stood, helped her slide the ring on her finger,

and pulled her in for a soulful kiss filled with the passion they shared.

Taryn cupped his face with her hands. "That made my day just perfect."

He beamed and kissed her again. "Just one rule."

"What's that?"

"Don't shoot my father. He can be annoying and exasperating. But I kinda like him."

She laughed. "I'll let you in on a little secret. I kind of like him, too."

Reginald had visited a couple more times. Always quiet and charming, he seemed to be rolling out the red carpet for her and pulling out all the stops to make sure she was happy. At least, not getting in the way of her relationship with Quint.

In time, she knew he'd grow on her. Right now, her tumultuous life needed a little ironing out before making any lasting declarations.

Quint hugged her tight and peppered kisses along her jawline. "Taryn. You're an angel on earth. One that I don't deserve, but I'm not about to let the best thing in my life go."

"You make me happy, Quint. So very happy." She sighed and smiled as a single tear escaped. "I love you more than life itself."

"And I love you more than that."

"Prove it." She giggled when he swept her up into his arms and carried her inside, not stopping until he laid her on their bed.

"You keep forgetting. I'm good at details."

Boy howdy, was he good at details.

No fairy tale romance could have ended more perfectly for her. She'd found her Prince Charming and decided to hang onto him for another lifetime or two. That's what love meant—giving, sharing, supporting one another. He'd risked his life for her and claimed she'd showed him the joys of living once more. She had his back, and knew he'd always be her rock. Love made that happen—a special, unbreakable bond. That's what they had. True love. She understood that now.

In wrapping up her past, she'd found her future. With Quint. The man who'd stolen her heart and promised to keep it safe and secure. Just like she had with him.

Quint. Her love. Her soon-to-be husband. Her bad boy who just happened to be the man of her dreams. He promised a lifetime of cherishing her. She couldn't wait.

A word about the author...

CHEYENNE MEADOWS, while growing up in the Midwest, began reading romance novels in high school, immediately falling in love with the genre, to the point where she decided to write professionally for a career. However, that dream splattered against a brick wall, resulting in a quick death, in her first writing class in college when the professor told her bluntly that she wasn't any good at it. She shifted gears quickly and left her writing dreams behind, eventually settling on becoming a nurse. A few years back, she stumbled across a fan-fiction writing site on a favorite author's webpage. She began to read stories others wrote, not only making some wonderful close friends from the experience, but also really learning to write for the very first time. Here she was able to share short stories, practice her writing skills, and truly develop into a writer. More than that, the experience allowed her to revitalize her dream, as she rediscovered joy in writing. Now, she spends her days off with her alpha-male characters, quick-witted heroines, and seeing how much trouble everyone can get into. When she's not working or writing, she enjoys playing in the garden, hanging out with her diva kitty, and using her backyard as a living canvas for her whimsical landscaping, and, of course, reading romance novels.

Facebook:
https://www.facebook.com/cheyenne.meadows.10
Blog:
http://cheyennemeadows.blogspot.com/
E-mail:
Cheyenne1.meadows@yahoo.com